Mishaps
at the little sh

OCTOBER HOUSE BOOKS

Illustration © John Gillo
'Brixham Harbour'
www.johngillo.co.uk

ISBN: 9798735904656

Mishaps and Mayhem

at the little shop on Beach Street

This book is set in the fictional town of Torringham, which is loosely based on Brixham – chosen because I adore its gorgeous coastal scenery and beautiful harbour.

All the characters and storylines portrayed are fictitious. The Brixham traders work together to create a welcoming place and to provide a wonderful service for both tourists and the inhabitants.

I hope you enjoy *Mishaps and Mayhem at the Little Shop on Beach Street* and find it a fun and entertaining read.

To my wonderful friend,

Iulia Stancu

*Thank you for your tireless rescue work
and for saving so many cats and dogs.*

Chapter 1

A tongue lapped at my toes. I tucked my foot back under the duvet and wrapped myself tighter in the covers. Claws tapped the wooden floor and a wet nose nudged my cheek. Groaning, I opened one eye. Eight o'clock? Not so bad. Then the digital numbers on the alarm clock sharpened. Nope, six o'clock.

"For goodness sake, Roo, it's Sunday!" I shoved my head under the pillow, pinning down the sides so she couldn't tunnel her way beneath, but she thwarted me by finding a weak spot, burrowing her head into the centre.

I twisted around, swaddling myself in the covers, and squealed, "Go away!" But it was pointless. I was awake. Huffing, I threw the covers back and staggered out of bed as Roo bounced around me, her tail whipping against my legs, her blue eyes sparkling with delight. I stumbled into my cosy lounge, rubbing my eyes. My abandoned calculator and bills were strewn over the coffee table. On the settee lay my pad, a frightening minus figure underscored by gouged red lines, below which I'd doodled a sad face. Mine. I stashed them into a drawer. Out of sight, out of mind. Sunday was a day of rest – and that included from worries about my precarious finances, which the previous evening's festivities had made even worse.

An hour later – I needed three coffees to recover – Roo and I headed down the cobbled alley. My bunting flapped above us. As we made our way down Beach Street, a door opened and Amber rushed out, jerking to a stop at the end of her lead. Meg hissed at her to wait while she locked her shop. She took one look at me and grimaced.

"You look like death warmed up."

"Thanks." I scowled. "I feel it too. Next time Becki brings out her sloe gin, remind me to say no."

"I did! But you wouldn't listen." She grinned. "It was worth it, though. I've got a fab video of you two singing along to 'Bohemian Rhapsody'. I might stick it on Facebook later."

"Don't you dare!" I growled. "Or I'll post the pic of you looking like a beached whale."

She stuck out her tongue. "I wouldn't bother, Jenn. We both know you'll lose when it comes to dodgy pics." As Amber tugged her towards a lamp post, she said, "Let's go to Pixie Cove. I fancy a change."

I was about to point out that it involved a climb there and another back, but I decided against it. Yesterday, one of my customers had told me she'd seen a family of seals basking on the rocks. It would be lovely if they were still there.

We turned up Ansley Steps, Roo taking half a dozen at a gallop until the lead yanked taut, then she paused to let me catch up before dashing away again. Kirstie, the dog trainer I'd called for advice, wouldn't be impressed but, given my hangover from hell, it felt better to risk having my arm pulled off than having to shout "Heel!" every few minutes. Breathless, we reached the top in silence, passing

5

the closed doors of the Fisherman's Rest, where we'd begun Becki's fortieth celebrations – or commiserations, as she'd put it – the previous evening. She had no one to wake her, and would still be tucked beneath her duvet, competing with her teenage son for the longest lie-in. She often moaned about trying to drag him out of bed, but on some days it had distinct advantages.

I stifled a yawn and hugged my coat around me as we walked along the street. The front doors of the colourful cottages opened onto the pavement. Many had decorative pots outside, some with notices begging people not to let their dogs use them as a toilet. Roo dived over to one, sniffing, ignoring my attempts to drag her away.

"Let's go up Daisy Steps," I said.

Meg eyed the steep flight. "Really? That's seventy-one steps. I've counted them."

When Roo strained at the lead, desperate to make her mark on a pot of tulips, I hauled her over to the steps, staking my claim on them by clutching the metal railing. "It's a shortcut."

"I'd rather go around the Wrekin." Sighing loudly, Meg shrugged. "Okay, fill your boots."

She wasn't a Midlander, but she'd claimed an honorary status last night after being taught a few expressions by Andy, who owned the bakery. He came from Dudley, settling here after marrying a local woman, and liked to pull my leg when I asked him for bread rolls, insisting that I called them cobs before he'd serve me. He also called Meg 'yampy', which I guessed meant a bit loud and mad, because she could be. She'd been on fine form when we'd been singing karaoke in the pub. It was her fault we'd ended up around Becki's house, knocking back her sloe gin. She'd got up on the table to sing, then had knocked a drink over a man. Worse, she'd then attempted to wipe his crotch with a bar mat in front of his glowering wife. After apologising and buying him another drink, we'd scarpered.

Another memory popped to mind. Becki returning after chatting to a friend. She'd started to tell me what she'd learned about the empty shop unit beside mine when we were called up to sing 'I Will Survive'.

"Do you remember what Becki was saying last night? You know, about the shop next door?"

"Give me a mo." Meg panted and patted her chest. "I'm done in. Next time…" She paused for breath. "Remind me to buy a place in Norfolk."

We had reached the large park that gave the Parkside Green area its name. To one side sat a bowling club, playground and football pitches. To the other lay a beautiful rose garden crossed by tarmac paths. Terraced houses clustered around three sides, but the section by the cliff edge remained undeveloped, except for a small stone wall, which afforded us beautiful views of the glittering sea and the headlands on either side. Two ships sheltered in the bay, taking refuge from the promised storm. I glanced up at the milling grey clouds. Maybe it was a good thing that Roo had woken me early. We might have got drenched later.

When Meg released her extension lead to its full length, I did the same, and the dogs sprinted off, chasing each other in circles around us, forcing us to turn with them unless we wanted to become a ribbon-entwined maypole. We retracted the leads by the road, heading past large houses that had balconies overlooking the bay and into a wooded area where we started the downhill trek. Later, when our thighs burned when we headed back, we'd wonder whose idea this was but, for now, it was a relief. The path narrowed as we moved on, the red soil becoming rutted with limestone, until we descended a flight of uneven steps and strolled beneath a brick and stone archway to the pebbled cove. Shells crunched beneath our feet and waves shushed against a shoreline littered with seaweed and rocks. But those were the only sounds. We had the cove to ourselves.

Meg unclipped Amber's lead to let her go off for a sniff, but I couldn't do that with Roo. Auntie Peg would have my guts for garters if I lost her pooch. Having said that, I had no idea if my aunt would ever go back home. The hospital social worker was making noises about a care home, and I didn't know any that took pets. Much as I'd enjoyed spending the past fortnight with Roo, I preferred meeting other people's dogs to having a full-time mutt of my own. Especially one with a built-in alarm clock.

I perched on a boulder. Once Meg had unscrewed her flask of coffee and poured us each a cup, I returned to my earlier conversation.

"So, what did Becki say about the shop next door to

me?"

Meg gulped her coffee and winced. "Ouch! That's hot." Blinking away the tears, she turned to me. "The new pet shop?"

"The new *what?*" I leapt to my feet, scaring Roo, who bolted to the other side of the rock. "Seriously?"

"You didn't seem that fussed about it when Becki mentioned it."

"I didn't hear." In truth, I'd been too sozzled to notice. "Of course it bothers me. How would you like it if someone opened up a sewing shop next to yours?"

"It's a craft shop," she said.

"Whatever." I shrugged in irritation. "I'm struggling to keep afloat as it is. I'll sink if I lose half my customers." I dropped onto the rock and put my head in my hands.

"Aw, Jenn! Don't worry. Torringham is a tight-knit community. They won't let a local stalwart like you go to the dogs." She gave me a hug, her hot, alcohol-infused breath making me grimace.

"But I'm not local. I haven't got one family member in the graveyard, let alone ten generations or whatever's needed."

"We'll put our heads together and come up with a plan," she said, as if it were that simple. "We're not called the three witches for nothing."

"*What?*" I'd never heard anyone call us that.

She slapped my leg. "It was a joke! No one says that. Well…" She shrugged. "Except for that awful Peter Drew. He'd be glad to see the back of us."

9

Chapter 2

After waiting an age on her doorstep to the odd muffled cry of, "Hold on, won't be a mo," Becki greeted us with a yawn, showing a tongue stained red by the previous night's red wine and sloe gin. Wearing her tatty dressing gown, she waved us inside as her yowling cat shot past, his hackles raised. I kept a tight grip on Roo's lead in case she decided to follow. Cowardly Custard – or CC for short – could have stayed hidden in Becki's lounge, but he preferred to conceal himself in the front garden's cherry tree when visitors arrived – with or without pets in tow. Becki rolled her eyes and shut the door on him, telling us to put the kettle on while she freshened up.

The kitchen was in the same state we'd left it. Our empty glasses littered a table strewn with crumbs and ash from the incense sticks she liked to burn. A sickly-sweet smell hung in the air. Along the back wall sat a huge dresser, filled with knick-knacks and books rather than crockery. Unlike Meg and me, Becki didn't live in the flat above her shop. She rented it to a young couple, as she liked to keep home and work separate. But some bits overlapped, like the crystals dotted around the rooms and a pack of angel cards on the table. Sometimes she'd ask us to pick a card so she could offer us a few words of wisdom. She'd done that last night, but I had no idea which card I'd chosen. Probably something about love, as usual.

Ten minutes later she reappeared, taking the now-cooling coffee I'd left for her on the kitchen worktop. She joined us at the table, curling one leg beneath her on the chair as she swept a few errant crumbs onto the floor.

"I'll sort the mess later," she said, brushing her hands together.

She'd tied her pink and blue hair in a crimson and gold headscarf, toned down by a plain T-shirt and jeans, but she hadn't washed her face: mascara speckled her skin and a hint of blue eyeshadow shimmered in the corner of her eyes. She liked to match her make-up to her hair.

The dogs ignored her, slumbering at our feet – or, in Roo's case, on mine.

Meg leapt right in. "Do you remember being told about the new pet shop opening?"

Her hands cupped around her coffee, Becki looked across to the window, frowning. Then she clicked her ring-laden fingers. "Yes! I'd all but forgotten about that. Whatsisname, from the Torringham Traders, was telling me how exciting it would be."

Meg grimaced. "Peter Drew's bestie, Grant Brown-tongue?"

Becki mirrored her expression. "The one and the same."

"Where does that leave me?" I asked.

Becki put her cup on the table. "Between a rock and a hard place, although Grant said Peter Drew reckoned competition is good as it'll keep prices down."

"But I'm barely scraping a living now!" I gasped.

"How would old Brown-tongue like it if I opened up a florist's next to his. Or perhaps I should wage clothing wars with Peter Drew? His prices are ridiculous. They're both rich enough to have shops in the High Street with plenty of trade. Us Beach Street traders need to support each other to stay afloat."

But most of the traders in the High Street paid higher rates than us – their shops were on the main thoroughfare into town, the prime destination for day-trippers. Tourists staying more than a day often chanced upon our street – with many of the ones holidaying in self-catering accommodation bringing their pets, who left decked out in my seaside-themed wares. But the only reason I'd been able to afford my little shop was because it fronted a cobbled alleyway rather than Beach Street, so the leasehold wasn't exorbitant. Still, it was a huge sum for me. It had a Beach Street address because it had once been part of the larger building that housed my future neighbour. This created another complication. The flats above both shops shared the little courtyard at the rear.

I clutched my head. The past eleven months – after Tim had left – had been bad enough. Now this! It was all too much. "If that pet shop goes ahead, it'll wipe me out."

Meg turned to me. "You know we'll support you. What can we do to help?"

Unable to think, I gave her a blank look.

"Perhaps we should convene a committee meeting?" she said. "Get some ideas."

Becki groaned and slumped into her chair. "That's all

I need! I'm still scarred by the last one."

◆

The problem was Hilda. At a sprightly ninety-two, she gave fifty-year-olds a run for their money. Or so she told everyone. She owned the antiques shop (a junk shop, really) at the bottom of Beach Street – sadly, the end that tourists viewed first, so their impression of the street was marred by her shop frontage. It had a mildewed awning, a peeling door and paraphernalia piled in the dusty window, while old prams, lawnmowers and other rubbish sat on the wide pavement.

I envied her the outside space. When I'd put an advertising board on the street to show visitors where they could find my shop, the council had told me to move it. The path was too narrow at that point, apparently. The sign now sat outside Becki's spiritual shop, which sold tarot cards and crystals. Unfortunately, the arrow with the words 'Find your pet supplies here!' no longer had the desired effect. Unless dogs wanted to have their fortunes told.

Things not going to plan was the story of my life. That was how I'd ended up with a pet shop rather than my dream bookshop. My ex, Tim, loved animals and had always wanted a pet shop. I wasn't quite so keen, but his wistful expression and puppy-dog eyes made me long to make his wish come true. He'd also wanted to live beside the sea. After my mum died and left me a few thousand in her will, we'd come down here on a scouting expedition. I'd fallen in love with the quaint building with its bowed bay window and low beams. I'm five foot nothing, so it suited me, but Tim got fed up with banging his head on the beams. After having the sense knocked into him – as he put it – once too often, he packed his bags, leaving me holding the lease – and the leash.

To be honest, it wasn't just the building. Living in such a confined space meant we'd discovered things about each other, with the bad outweighing the good. Tim might have been the expert in pet care, but he didn't realise that starting a business meant working long hours. He kept telling me that I needed to take it easier, and annoyed me by saying stupid things like 'if you build it, the dogs will come'. But stacked shelves didn't bring in the customers, or pay the bills. Flyers, advertising and accosting owners out walking their dogs had done that. Maybe I should try more publicity again – although perhaps not. Whoever had bought the large shop unit might have pockets deep enough for bigger adverts and glossier business cards.

I'd ask everyone what they thought when they arrived. That's if they ever did. The committee meeting should be starting in two minutes, yet I sat alone in the Fisherman's Rest, nursing a black coffee, Roo lying across my feet. Puzzled, I opened my phone to type a brief message to Meg, only to find four missed calls. I'd forgotten I'd put my phone on silent when I'd been chatting to a customer earlier and a particularly annoying sales rep kept ringing me.

Someone tapped my shoulder and I spun around to find Meg standing behind me, panting.

"Ignoring me, are you?" She pointed outside. "You're missing Hilda."

Roo got to her feet, her tail banging against the table.

"Hilda? Is she okay?" I asked.

"She's barricading the street. Come on! You can't miss this."

"She's what?" I followed her out. "Why?"

"Someone's made a complaint to the council about the state of the path outside."

I shrugged. "They've got a point."

"I know! But try telling her that."

As we headed down Ansley Steps, shouts rang out above the blare of car horns and what sounded like a tinny drumbeat. Below us, a van attempted a three-point turn, while a large man in the car behind leaned out of the window, bellowing abuse.

Roo's ears shot back and her tail slid between her legs.

"I'll have to take Roo home first."

"Hurry or you'll miss the fun," Meg said. She rushed off towards the commotion, while I took a detour via the flat. Inside the noise was muffled but I switched on the radio to make sure that Roo wouldn't get upset. I should have stayed with her but, I had to confess, I wanted to see what was going on. Back outside, fumes filled the air, mingling with angry voices and calls of amusement. A man walked past, shaking his head and laughing to himself. He gave me a wink.

"They've taken on the wrong person."

I smiled and hurried down the street, more intrigued than ever. People milled around as I passed Becki's spiritual shop and hurried down the slope. The distant sea glinted. Soon it would be the tourist season. Thank goodness it wasn't yet. This was hardly a welcome to Torringham.

Becki's pink and blue hair stood out among the bystanders, so I went over, pushing through a group to reach her. She grinned at me and jerked her thumb towards Hilda. "Meg's threatening to join them, but I think Hilda's got enough back-up there."

She made room to allow me to squeeze beside her, where I saw a policeman failing in his efforts to move the onlookers away. In the middle of the road was a barricade heaped with lawnmowers, prams, old railings and other items, behind which Hilda directed operations. An old tin army hat perched on her head, and her wrists were cuffed to a chain that ran between two lamp posts on either sides of the street.

Half a dozen friends and her children stood with her, holding scribbled biro messages on sheets of paper, made even more intelligible by the wind curling them over. None of the protestors were spring chickens. Hilda had invited me to her daughter Agatha's seventieth birthday celebrations the year before.

Amid all this, her grandchildren (my age) and great-grandchildren continued to haul piles of junk out of the shop, circumventing the policeman, to add to the defences. On the other side stood Tanya, Hilda's granddaughter, her body language suggested she was pleading with her grandmother to see sense. Of course Tanya would. She was high up in the council and this might not go down well with her bosses.

One of the great-grandchildren came out with a megaphone. Soon it was being passed around the group, each person setting out their demands for Hilda's right to put her prized possessions outside her own shop.

Tanya snatched the microphone. "Have some sense! This could easil—"

Another grabbed it back. "She pays rates to give you a cushy job. You'd rather put your ninety-two-year-old nan on the street, would you?"

I rolled my eyes as the crowd booed and hissed at Tanya. Why let truth get in the way of a good story? We all moaned about the mess in the street. I couldn't be the only one secretly hoping that Hilda wouldn't win this battle. Her external display seemed to take half the morning to heft outside, and the best part of the late afternoon to bring back in. Unlike my poor advertising board. But I kept my thoughts to myself.

A siren's scream split the air. I turned to find blue flashing lights behind us. A bit OTT; it was hardly an emergency. The crowd surged apart like Moses' wave, drawing me with it. Pushed backwards, I bumped into someone. When I turned to apologise, my words drained away. Peter Drew, of all people. He glared at me and wiped the sleeve of his jacket as if I'd defiled him in some way.

"I suppose you think this is funny," he snarled. He waved his hand towards Hilda and her crew. "It makes Torringham nothing but a laughing stock."

I could see his point, but I wasn't going to tell him that. "I don't know. It's a bit of entertainment."

"Entertainment?" His face reddened. "You and I have very different ideas on that. What will the tourists think?" He jabbed his thumb towards the queue of cars behind us. "It's hardly a welcome. At least everyone is now seeing you for what you lot are. Hilda might have had friends in high places, but not for long." He looked at Tanya with grim satisfaction. "It looks like the scales have finally fallen from the council's eyes. The day can't come too soon when you all shut up shop and leave us professional traders to get on with our jobs."

"I think you'll find..." But he didn't give me the chance to tell him, as he stormed across the path of the police car to his friends on the other side. Shaking my head, I wandered away muttering, "I am a professional."

Keith, the fishmonger, had moved beside Becki. He no longer wore his white coat – he usually closed the shop at four o'clock after starting at the fish market at six – but he couldn't have yet gone home to change as the scent of fish drifted in the air.

"Sorry for missing your meeting, but..." He gave me an embarrassed shrug.

"I know, you don't get this happening every day." I smiled at him before speaking to Becki. "I couldn't see

Meg."

Andy, the baker, chuckled. "Last I saw, she was clarting around inside the shop with the kids."

Behind us, the mishmash of chants from the demonstrators had become a unison song of 'We Shall Not Be Moved'. Now we'd lost our prime position, Andy left us to get a better view.

Keith adjusted the collar of his shirt and cleared his throat. "Are you going to the Fisherman's when this is all over? I mean, for the meeting."

"It'll be midnight before that happens." Becki rubbed her arms. "Brr. If the council doesn't send someone to sort this out, Hilda'll be suing them for giving her hypothermia."

"Did your crystal ball tell you that?" Keith said.

She pulled a face and shook her head. "Common sense. Talking about that, I need to fetch my coat."

She headed away, leaving me with Keith. I didn't mind him but, since I'd found out that he had a soft spot for me (which came to light after a fumbled attempt to kiss me one evening), I preferred to keep a sociable distance. He was such a kind man that I didn't want to do anything to lead him on – not when there was no chance of anything between us. He must be in his mid-fifties at least while, at thirty-seven, I was one of the youngest Beach Street traders. Our ages alone wouldn't be an issue, but we had nothing in common. Once he'd told me about his favourite Bucks Fizz winning in 1981. I'd assumed he'd been talking about the drink. Even when he'd told me that

Ireland had the most wins and listed the countries not far behind, I didn't click. I mean, who would? It was only later when he dropped the necessary 'Eurovision' into the conversation – or possibly I'd zoned out when he'd first mentioned it – that I clicked. Later I'd looked up Bucks Fizz and I couldn't believe anyone would admit to saying they were their favourite.

Keith flushed. "Just us two, then."

"And a hundred others." I smiled as a man jostled me.

"No, I mean going to the pub."

"Oh," I said, because I couldn't think of anything else. "Er ... let's see what Becki wants to do when she gets back."

Chapter 3

The committee meeting reconvened at eight thirty after a local councillor arrived at the protest and promised to review the order preventing Hilda from using the pavement as additional shop space. Maybe I should chain myself to my advertising board, to see if I got the same result? Perhaps not. I could see the council's point. Buggies and wheelchairs struggled along the narrow pavement outside my shop, even without it being blocked by a board. At least the pavement outside Hilda's shop was wider.

Another positive was that, after we'd helped Hilda's family move everything back inside, she'd been too tired to join us at the pub. Thankful for small mercies, we'd sneaked home to grab a quick bite – and to collect our dogs – but when Roo led the way into the pub, I gazed in dismay at the crowded space. It seemed that half the town had decamped to the Fisherman's Rest.

Becki touched my shoulder. "How about we go back to mine?"

"Are you sure?" I nodded towards Keith and Andy, who'd gone straight to the pub and were sipping their pints in the corner. "They'll be here for the meeting."

She shrugged. "The more the merrier."

The men said they'd join us when they finished, so Becki rounded up a few others and we set off up Daisy Steps to her house at the edge of Parkside Green. Roo strained at the lead, dragging me up. I let her. We made it to the top first, where Roo sat on the pavement beneath a streetlamp, her tongue lolling, her breath misting the air. Behind us, Meg squealed at Amber to slow down. She reached us, red-faced and clutching her chest.

"You have got to train that dog not to rush everywhere."

"It's not my fault your Amber wants to be in front all the time." Then I gave her a sly chuckle. "Maybe you need to get fitter."

Minutes later we arrived at Becki's house, to be greeted by a yowling CC who sprinted outside and up the cherry tree. While Becki fetched a few put-up chairs from her shed, Meg raided her drinks cabinet for sloe gin, wine and brandy.

"A warming tot." She held up an expensive-looking bottle.

Becki returned, chairs under each arm, wafting cold air into the cosy kitchen. With a look of alarm, she dropped the chairs and snatched the bottle from Meg.

"Not that one, if you don't mind."

"Only the cheap plonk for us?" Meg grinned and put the sloe gin and bottles of red and white wine on the table.

This would cost Becki a fortune – and it was all for my benefit. But when I offered to pop to the convenience store and buy more drinks, she turned me down. A rap at the door interrupted us. Meg rushed off to answer it, returning with Keith and Andy, who clutched their beer in plastic cups. Andy tossed a few bags of crisps on the table, his smile widening when he eyed Becki's bottle of brandy.

"Before you say anything, I'm hiding this." She whisked it away to the lounge.

The men set up their chairs and sat down. Keith rubbed his hands and beamed at me.

"I've got tonnes of ideas for you. We'll see this usurper off."

Andy frowned. "How do you know the shop's definitely going to be a pet shop? I heard something else."

Becki came back in and caught the thread of the conversation. "Grant told me. He'd spoken to Peter, who'd spoken to the owner. He's a nice bloke, apparently."

"Must have a few bob to buy that huge lump," Andy said.

If the buyer had deep pockets and could weather a price war, I'd be in trouble. My bank balance hovered between black and red. So far this year my statements had been printed in blood.

Meg snorted. "If he was that nice, he'd have thought about the existing traders. How long have we got before he moves in?"

Becki shrugged. "I don't know if he's a cash buyer or if he's got to get a loan. I guess a month or two."

"A lot can happen between now and then," Keith said. "I've got some great ideas to get rid of him—"

"No!" I blurted. "I don't want to put him out of business or anything like that. I just want to think of ways to make my shop more competitive. More innovative, I guess. You know, offering a service he wouldn't or couldn't. There must be something I can do."

"Special services, eh?" Andy's eyes glinted.

I shook my head and sighed. That man had a one-track mind.

Keith pulled a crumpled sheet of paper from his jacket pocket and placed it on the table. He'd titled it 'Pet Shop Wars', underlining it twice. Meg's eyes sparkled with mischief. I sighed.

"Tell me your ideas, Keith, and then we'll try to work on some positive ones too."

♦

We had decided on a list. I'd managed to knock all but one item from Keith's sheet. I'd vetoed his ideas to graffiti the new shop owner's window, to start up rumours that he bought all his stock from a country with animal welfare issues, and to organise a petition against him. I didn't want to ruin his livelihood – not when I knew how much had to be sunk into a business when starting up.

One idea I liked was to name my alleyway – give it a proper sign. When Andy had pointed out that I'd need the council's permission or they'd remove the sign, Meg had countered by saying that we could ask Hilda to organise another protest if needed. We moved on to ideas on the name. I'd refused all the better ones: Dog-gone-it Alley, Paws This Way – and settled for boring Dog Alley, as I thought the council was less likely to notice the new name.

I'd also put a sign beneath it with my shop name and an arrow pointing to my shop.

The other items were a mix – some sensible, some plain daft – but beggars couldn't be choosers. I needed to do everything I could to save my business. I had to get a head start, to build a bigger customer base, and to offer a service that – I hoped – my neighbour would find hard to replicate.

Not all the suggestions would just benefit me. Some, like a stall at the May Fair, would help all the traders. Decorating the lamp posts and adding a few more hanging baskets, in addition to the council ones, would make Beach Street a prettier place for everyone. We all agreed that it would be good if the council could tame Hilda's external junk display. Andy knew the councillor who'd attended the demo, so he said he'd have a quiet word with her about a compromise – half a dozen items to sit outside, at the most. While it had been fun watching Hilda's shenanigans, the council was right about the jumble outside being dangerous and an eyesore.

First thing the next morning, I ticked number one off my list and phoned Roo's trainer, Kirstie. I hoped she'd accept my proposal. She answered after three rings. I set about explaining the background to my call and ended with, "So, you see, it could be a win for you and for me. That's if you're up for trying it out."

Silence greeted me.

"Hello. Are you still there?"

"Er, yes…"

"Is that a yes to still being there, or are you up for the challenge? This might be a way of building your business. You said you wanted to do that."

She swallowed. "I guess we could try it. Do you think anyone would know what it's about? I mean, they might think that I'll be talking to the dogs about their issues, rather than to the owner."

I chuckled. "Knowing some of my customers, you might get more sense from their dogs."

Chapter 4

A few days later, Meg rushed into the shop carting a huge box. With a grin, she dumped it on my counter. Then she stepped back, dusting her hands and ignoring Roo, who sniffed at her legs.

"Well?"

I gave her a puzzled look. "Should I open it?"

When she rolled her eyes, I picked up a pair of scissors and started to cut through the tape. On opening the flaps, I found a strange furry thing. Confused, I gazed at her. But she gave me a smug smile, like a parent does when they buy their child a dream gift for Christmas. I hefted out the heavy folds of material, becoming more puzzled, until I came across an eye hole.

I groaned. "I thought you were joking."

"You've ordered the leaflets like I said?"

"They won't be ready yet. Kirstie, my dog trainer, had to check her schedule."

"What about the signage?"

"That'll be here next week."

I turned my attention back to her costume. It must have set her back a fortune, although it did seem a bit dog-eared in places, with a few matted tufts of fur. Maybe it was meant to look realistic?

"How much do I owe you?"

"Nothing. I've always wanted to have a reason to dress up as a dog."

I'd learned that it was safer not to investigate the inner workings of Meg's mind, so I let her comment drop.

"Anyhow," she continued, "my mate gave me it for nothing. He worked for a company that toured schools, talking about road safety and suchlike. He had a lollipop stick too. I'll bring that around later."

I guessed she meant the ones carried by school crossing patrollers. "Aren't they really big? Where would I put it?"

I gazed around my little shop. Shelves lined both sides, filled with bags of food and bedding. In the centre was a section devoted to pet toys, leads, bowls and grooming equipment. I'd already cleared out part of the stock room to make space for Kirstie's consulting room. Thanks to my efforts, my cosy lounge now featured an ornamental display of tinned food, while the space beneath my bed was packed with bags of dry pet food and hay for rabbits. A fire safety officer would have kittens.

She shrugged. "Put it on the road. You could change it to read dog crossing point or something." Then she gave me a mischievous grin. "Or use it to barricade his pet shop."

The doorbell jangled and Edna Sully waddled inside, as usual carrying her Flossie.

Meg hissed. "I forgot what day it was."

As the elderly pug turned its bulbous gaze in my direction, Roo slunk away, tail between her legs, and clipped up the wooden stairs to the flat. I had no idea why she was scared of Flossie. The little dog rarely moved of her own accord. But I understood Meg's desire to get away. She skirted around them, eyes on the door, making her apologies: she'd love to stay but she simply had to get back to Sarah, who she'd left holding the fort. Meg knew my pain only too well: Edna was also a regular visitor to her craft shop. But Meg had a staff member to take up the reins, which meant she could escape Edna by running an urgent errand – which usually involved coming to mine or Becki's for a cup of tea.

I often wished I had an excuse to leave when Edna arrived. It might sound mean, but she was one customer I'd happily hand over to my future competitor.

Then I realised Meg had left the dog costume. "You've—"

But she had gone. She shot past the window, head down, not daring to look back.

"Always in a rush, that one," Edna said. "She needs to take a break or she'll do herself a mischief."

She waddled over and plonked Flossie on top of the dog costume on the counter. Her gnarled fingers nipped at the material. "What's this, then?"

"It's Meg's," I said.

"A rug, is it? I thought it were a dog bed. She must have been in a right old rush, forgetting this." Then she rubbed more salt into my festering wounds. "Poor girl, she works so hard. It's always busy when I go past. Wednesday morning is their only quiet time."

She gazed around the empty shop, letting her words sink in. Unlike you. But she was the reason for my sales slump. Unless a customer had a masochistic streak or an hour to listen to Edna chirping away, they'd leave their shopping until the afternoon when Edna toddled home. I could do as Becki suggested, and actively discourage her visits, but she was lonely. Her tales were rarely her own, but ones she passed on from others. Wheezing, she slumped onto the chair I'd set to one side of the counter for quieter periods. Many of my customers liked to sit while I sorted out their items.

"What a morning I've had. Don't s'pose you fancy putting on the kettle, dear? I could do with a brew."

"I ... er ... of course not."

I picked up Flossie from the counter and placed her in Edna's arms, before heading off to make a cup of tea.

It had been a mistake to offer her one a few weeks before, but she'd had a bit of a fright when a dog had jumped up, trying to reach Flossie. She'd staggered into the shop, shaking and clutching her chest. Since that morning, she'd arrived on the dot of ten each Tuesday and Thursday, begging for a brew. Meg and I had worked out her rota: she spent Monday in the High Street, at the post office then the neighbouring café; Wednesday was Meg's craft shop; Fridays in the library, while Saturdays were her day of rest, as she couldn't abide the queues and, any road (her expression, not mine), she had a busy Sunday ahead at church. Why I got two visits, I had no idea. Disloyally, I'd tried encouraging her to spend one of the days she allocated to me in Becki's cosy spiritual shop – after all, Becki had said that I should send her away – but Edna didn't care for what she called mumbo-jumbo.

Edna wasn't a bad person. It's just that no one had told her that God gave us two ears and one mouth. In Edna's world, her ears were only there to hear gossip or the click of the boiling kettle. She was halfway through a story she'd heard about Hilda's protest – ignoring my pointed comment that I'd been there – when a face appeared through the glass panes in the door. As the woman did an about-turn and scurried away, I shot out, leaving Edna mid-sentence.

"Can I help?" I called. The woman turned back, shoulders slumping.

"I was looking for a dog brush," she said. "But I'll come back later."

"I could fetch you one now, if you'd like. I'll bring it out to you."

Her face brightened. "Would you? I'd like a handled one. I'd come in but…" She prodded her watch. "My bus is coming in twenty minutes."

"I understand." I rushed back into the shop and took the brush out to the customer. "Is this the one?"

She smiled and rifled through her purse. Her face fell when she realised she only had her debit card, which would mean a trip into the shop to use the machine.

"Pay me back another day," I said. "Any time other than Tuesday and Thursday mornings." I glanced back towards where Edna sat inside. "If you get my drift."

As the woman dashed away, I sighed. I had a business to run, bills to pay. But what could I do? Technically – on the few occasions she bought something – Edna was a customer. Even though she annoyed half the population of Torringham, she was classed as one of their own, although, like Hilda, she hadn't been born here but had married into one of the long-standing families. She might not be like Hilda, with relatives in every street, but she was cherished by the locals – from a distance. Which left me with a dilemma. So far this morning, I'd made minus five pounds and forty pence.

Then I had an idea. Not the kindest one, but ... needs must. "Did you hear about the new pet shop opening next door?"

"No. I heard—"

I cut Edna off. "You could be really helpful in that respect. Grant says all competition is good, but..." I gazed around the empty shop. "I can't afford to lose any more customers. When it opens, could you spend a few days each week checking him out?"

She pursed her lips. "Well, I could cut back my visits to Maria at the café, and Meg too."

"Or coming here?" I gave the back of Flossie's ears a rub. "Much as I love seeing you, my competitor might guess that you're a double agent if you go from his place to mine."

She chuckled. "A double agent, eh? Talking about that, did you see James Bond on TV last night. *Goldfinger*. When I were a lass, I tried to cover myself in yellow paint after watching that. Gave my mum a right fright. She..."

Edna set off on another story, while the time ticked slowly on the clock above. At this rate, it would be going backwards. Breathless, she gabbled, "That reminds me…" She galloped on to gossiping about one of her friend's grandchildren before swerving on to the subject of baking, then coming to a halt with a, "Must be off. Can't stay here all day. I've got things to do, people to see."

I glanced at the time. Twelve thirty. Two hours had passed, but it felt like I'd put in a full day's work.

Groaning, Edna got to her feet, clutching Flossie. Why didn't she put the pug down? I'd never seen it walk. She reached the doorway, where she turned to me. "That Grant's such a liar. He told me a right story. His friend, Peter, was also spouting nonsense about you and Meg. But I put him right. You're not witches. You're the nicest people I know."

With that, she waddled away. I felt awful about trying to get rid of her, but I had a more pressing matter to worry about. That was the second time I'd heard that Peter and Grant had been calling us witches. What was going on?

Chapter 5

I didn't bother to close the shop for lunch. There seemed no point when I'd done so little work during the morning. Instead, I munched a roll while Roo sandwiched herself between myself and the shelf I was attempting to stack one-handed. I soon recouped my morning's five pounds and forty pence loss and, by the time I swung the open sign to closed, I had a bundle of notes and card machine receipts in the till.

I WhatsApped Becki and Meg to see if they fancied meeting at seven thirty for a drink. Just the one; I couldn't afford more. Both replied within minutes with a thumbs-up. First, I finished the leftover lasagne from Saturday and took Roo for a brisk walk, stepping over the threshold of the Fisherman's Rest ten minutes before the others were due to arrive.

The pub buzzed with chatter, although just half the tables were full. A noisy bunch sat in the corner, their voices echoing as Roo pitter-patted over the flagstone floor to the bar. I stole a glance in their direction. Most of them were High Street traders. Grant nudged Peter, jerking his head as I passed and muttering something. Peals of laughter filled the air and one of them slapped his thigh. Were they talking about me? Puzzled, I perched on a bar stool and ordered a medium rosé from Heidi, who gave Roo a treat, asked how my auntie was doing in hospital, and told me about her mum's illness.

When Becki and Meg appeared, with Amber in tow, the men in the corner did the same to them, causing Meg to shake her head.

"Idiots," she hissed. "They're like a bunch of schoolboys."

While I admired Becki's new dangly earrings, Meg ordered their drinks.

"Tourmaline." Becki fingered the black stones. She flashed her wrist, showing similar stones threaded into a bracelet, then darted a look towards the huddle in the corner. "You might want to consider it. It blocks out negative energy."

"I'd need a ten-foot wall to do that. Shall we sit there?" I pointed to a table nearby, away from the men's view.

We soon forgot them when we started to talk about our plans to thwart the new pet shop owner's planned enterprise – until one of the group came to order a round at the bar. We fell silent. I'd never seen him before. He was around forty, with brown hair, more salt than pepper at the sides. He gave Heidi a friendly smile as he placed his order. Still smiling, he glanced over at us. He seemed about to say something genial, until Meg scowled. Her scowl deepened into a snarl when Grant appeared, taking two of the poured pints. As Grant turned, his gaze locked with Meg's.

"What are you looking at?" he sneered.

"Not you," she said, but continued to stare at him.

I sighed. They were behaving like children. As Grant walked away with the pints, Meg glared at the man at the bar.

I mouthed to her, "Don't be mean." Just because he sat with Peter and Grant, it didn't make him like them. Also, while the occasional spat with some of Peter's crowd might seem harmless, we didn't need a full-scale war.

Heidi's voice filtered over as she chatted to the man. "Oh, don't worry about them. They're actually really nice."

She caught my eye and smiled, then turned her attention to the stranger. He passed her a twenty-pound note, telling her to keep the change before heading back to his gaggle. Chuckling, Heidi waited until he'd turned away before holding up a 2p coin to show us her tip, which she slotted into an RNLI lifeboat-shaped box.

"You were saying about Edna?" Becki brought the conversation back to where we'd left it.

Feeling pins and needles in my foot, I shifted it out from under Roo's heavy body and took a sip of my wine. "Yes. I've asked her to spend her mornings in the new pet shop when it opens. I said she could be a double agent."

Meg and Becki snorted. "You mean a spy!" Meg said.

"Do I?" Then it dawned on me. "Of course! I don't think Edna realised either. She sounded excited to be offered the chance to be a female James Bond."

"So, you are trying to get rid of her. What was all that nonsense about feeling sorry for her because she's lonely?" Becki said.

Since when did she get to take the high ground? Although she chatted to Edna in the street, and took time to check on her welfare, Edna didn't seem keen on going into Becki's shop.

"I do feel for her, but I don't get a single customer when she's there." I told them about the woman who'd come in that morning for a dog brush. "So you see why she'd be doing me a favour if she went to his place."

Becki frowned. "The other night you were adamant that you didn't want to do anything detrimental to his business."

During our committee meeting, Becki had made her feelings clear, supporting me when I'd vetoed any suggestions I didn't feel comfortable about. Do no harm, she'd said. She was a firm believer in the expression 'what goes around comes around'.

"I know. I don't … but…" Flushing, I floundered for words. She was right. I'd vowed to act honourably. Not only was I being mean to Edna, but sending her around to the new competitor might cause real damage to his business. But I couldn't help feeling that it might solve two problems in one go.

Becki wore a strange smile as she twiddled the stem of her wine glass and gazed into the plummy depths, her eyes widening. Then in a slow husky voice, she said, "I see…"

As she gave the glass another slow swirl, Meg and I looked at her, confused.

Keeping her voice low, Becki continued, "A person on this table has been also telling Edna that she should spend a morning or two in my shop."

Guilt etched Meg's face, just as it must have shown on

mine. Becki glanced at each of us and grinned. "I knew it must be one of you, but not both. You devious pair!"

"How did you know?" Meg scrutinised the wine glass, as if Becki could see our misdeeds in the liquid.

Chuckling, Becki took a swig of wine. "My crystal ball." Then she cackled, loudly enough for Grant and Peter to hear on the other side of the room and reinforce their view of us being witches. "Edna told Maria at the café that she'd been told about the amazing hot chocolate I gave my customers. But, apparently, Edna's having none of my mumbo-jumbo. She'd rather have Maria's second-rate coffee, even if she has to pay for it." She took another victorious glug of wine. "I wondered which of you it was. I mean, why would someone tell Edna about the hot chocolate if they didn't want her to pay mc a visit?"

I could imagine Edna telling Maria that. Not in those exact words, but with a pointed underlying message about her coffee. Maria used the cheapest stuff she could find, which left a bitter aftertaste. But I hadn't mentioned hot drinks when selling Becki's place as a potential venue to Edna.

Becki pointed at us. "You messed up there. A customer bought me a fancy tin as a thank you, but I can't stand the stuff, so that's why I had it in the shop. I can count the number of people I've offered it to on one hand."

"I'm innocent," I said, as Meg reddened. "I wouldn't dare mention hot chocolate to Edna, in case she asks me to make it instead of her usual tea."

Meg gasped. "No wonder she's around yours twice a

week. If I were you, I'd stop making her so comfortable."

"Too late." I shrugged. "It's expected now."

If Edna paused for breath when she came in, I might enjoy her company more. I'd been amazed to have a two-way conversation with her that morning, even if it lasted just a few sentences. Usually, she didn't give me a chance. An image of Edna sitting alone in her house, stroking Flossie and staring at the TV, popped into my mind. Perhaps she spent too much time on her own and, like a child, needed to get rid of her excess energy? Her mornings in the shop were like a verbal keep-fit class, after which we both needed to recuperate.

Meg wiggled her glass in front of me. "Do you want another?"

I'd promised myself that I'd just have the one. But my empty glass called to me. I got to my feet, surprising Roo, who banged against the table leg. I bent to give her an apologetic pat. "It's my round. I owe you from last time."

Heidi greeted me at the bar. "Same again?"

When I nodded, she fetched three bottles of wine – white, rosé and red – and set about pouring our drinks.

"Your new neighbour is a bit worried about you," she said.

Puzzled, I frowned. "Neighbour?"

She jerked her head towards the table where Peter and his crowd were getting ready to leave. The man who'd been at the bar earlier gave her a wave and called, "Thank you."

Waving back, she gave him a pleasant smile. "Isn't he

sweet?" Then she pulled a face. "If a bit tight."

"And double your age. Anyhow, who is he?"

She gave me a 'duh' look. "I told you. Your neighbour. You know, the one who's buying the place next to yours."

"The pet shop?"

"Yeah, neighbours tend to live next door." She shook her head. "Catch up!"

"Did he say anything?"

If I'd hoped for gossip on his plans for the shop, I was mistaken. She shrugged. "If you three hadn't scared him, he would have introduced himself. I told him you were nice, that he should ignore Peter and Grant."

Back at the table I told Becki and Meg what Heidi had said. Meg grimaced. "He's friends with the High Street mafia? He can't be on the Beach Street traders committee if he's on their side. Well..." She slurped her drink. "At least I won't feel so bad about our plans now. That'll teach him to be a double agent."

Chapter 6

Sunday dawned with a sunrise the colour of blood oranges. When I stepped out of my shop, my breath misting the air, the silence unnerved me. What I was about to do would probably wake my neighbours. While my friends were in the know about my shenanigans, Bert, one of the town councillors, lived two doors up. His eyesight wasn't great – he'd been known to walk past me in the street without doffing his cap – but if he heard me speaking to someone, he always stopped to say hello. Much as I liked him, I couldn't trust him not to tell his fellow councillors.

I unreeled the extension lead, brought out Andy's hammer drill – mine would be no good for this task – and set about putting up the signs. The sound reverberated, causing the gulls to screech in alarm. Panicking, I stopped. After a few minutes, I decided that stopping and starting would be worse than getting it over and done with quickly, so I set to work. The old stone made my task harder than I'd anticipated.

A man hurried past in fishing overalls, giving me an odd look. I grimaced. "It fell off."

It wasn't a lie. The small nameplate had clattered to the ground when I'd first tried to attach it. He gave me a thumbs-up, as if mending a sign was a normal thing to do at six o'clock in the morning, and rushed on.

Job done, I stepped back to admire my work. The top

nameplate looked just like the one at the bottom of the street signposting Beach Way (in reality, another alley, no wider than mine). The sign beneath was a different matter. It glinted in the morning sun, pointing a finger (I'd chosen a pointing hand rather than an arrow) of blame towards my door. 'For all your pet shop needs' – and if you want to find out who put this sign up – 'go to Happy Paws & Shiny Claws'. Grimacing, I scratched my chin. The sign was pristine. Too pristine. I picked up a few clumps of moss that had fallen from the rooftop onto the cobbles and wiped the sparkle from the sign. Then I picked a few smaller bits from the wall and pushed them into the sign's corners, hoping they made it look like the sign had been there for years.

After taking Roo for a long walk to Pixie Cove, I dropped her back at the flat before heading off to the harbour. Originally, the Torringham market had showcased arts and crafts, but it had since widened to include a successful food area, where Andy sold his bakery products. The enticing smell of pastries wafted into the craft section. Meg had a regular stall here, and she'd badgered the market organisers to allow us to put a table next to hers to showcase the various wares sold by some of the shops on Beach Street. With Meg busy entertaining the crowds, Becki had taken over Meg's craft sales, leaving me with Keith – who'd come along to help even though he wasn't selling his fish – and Sheila, who owned a small art gallery. I thanked my lucky stars that Hilda had turned down the opportunity, saying it would do her 'rheumatics' no good.

Dressed in her strange costume, Meg looked more like Bungle than Fido. I wasn't sure how dressing up like a dog would improve my pet shop sales, but she seemed in her element prowling the aisle with puppy-like spurts of excitement that scared and thrilled little children in equal measure. When she pounced behind an elderly man, growling and barking, he spun around in shock, clutching his chest. After pressing one of my flyers into his hand, she bounded away leaving him muttering and using the sheet to fan his face.

"I don't think you'll win many admirers with her help," Sheila hissed.

I grimaced. "Do you think I should see how he is?" But another woman beat me to it, placing her hand on his shoulder. The man shrugged her off, glared at Meg and left.

"I think she looks rather fetching in that outfit." Keith winked at Meg, who shook her head and moved on to harass another cluster of passers-by.

Sheila rolled her eyes. "You're into dogs, are you?"

"You've met my ex, then?" Keith guffawed, then turned to me. "Sorry. That was a bit out of order."

It took me a moment to work out what he'd said. "No need to apologise to me."

A couple came over with a King Charles spaniel that shied away from Meg. One picked up my flyer, while the other checked out the display stand behind us, which showed a selection of Sheila's artwork.

"A dog agony aunt," the woman said. She nudged her neighbour. "Dave could do with one of those."

Was Dave a friend or her dog? I couldn't imagine she'd called her cute little pooch Dave – or that he needed much help. He looked adorable with his bright eyes, lolling tongue and hair curling at the tips of his ears, as if it had been crimped.

"Can I stroke him?" I asked, then wished I hadn't when the dog hoovered what looked like a piece of slime from the pavement.

"Mind Dave doesn't take your arm off." She gave me a mischievous chuckle. "You're welcome to try, though. We never know when he'll like someone … or not."

How could I refuse? Seriously, though. She held a card promoting my dog agony aunt service – which Ella would be running for dogs with behaviour issues – and, while I might not be the actual agony aunt, I was the shop owner. I slid my hand into my coat pocket – the hiding place for Roo's snacks – and, keeping one tucked from sight, I knelt beside Dave, holding out a tentative hand. He sniffed, then nosed between my fingers (after what he'd just eaten, I'd have to wash them), his tail wagging furiously.

"Oh, he likes you." When the woman turned away to answer her companion's question about one of the paintings, I let her pooch snaffle the treat. Naughty, I know, but if he could eat slime, what harm could this do?

As I did, Meg backed next to us to make room for a large group to get past. Dave spun around to find a furry leg beside him. He let out a low growl, baring his teeth. I rifled in my jacket pocket, hoping to placate him with more food, but he launched himself at Meg, yapping and snarling. Pinned by the people milling in front of her, she had nowhere to go, other than to one side, not spotting me kneeling there.

"Watch—"

Too late. In slow motion, she fell, her arms flailing, the dog's teeth fastened to her leg. Oof! Meg landed on me. My back jolted, my head smacked the ground. Around us, cries of alarm filled the air. Then there was silence, except for a low growl beside my ear. As my vision swam, I met one of Meg's eyes. I say one, as her costume head had been knocked askew, the second eye hole now covering her cheek. Too winded to speak, I tried to push Meg off me.

When she struggled to get up, something pulled her down. "What the—"

The woman screeched. "Dave! *Dave!*"

I shuddered. Had we injured her dog? The woman bent down and snatched the King Charles spaniel from the ground. He appeared to be attached to something. A flash of brown crossed my eye line – not the dog, as I could see him in the woman's arms, but something furry.

"Get off!" Meg shouted. She wriggled away, releasing me.

"Dog fight!" an idiot shouted to the delight of onlookers.

Pain shot through my back and hips. Panting, I staggered to my feet, helped by Keith. I could finally see what was going on. Dave's muzzle was embedded in the fur hem of Meg's dog suit, and he was resisting all efforts to prise his teeth apart. Unable to do much more than twist around in a fruitless attempt to free herself, Meg had resorted to expletives.

"There's no need for that!" a man said.

I pulled out a dog snack from my pocket and tried enticing Dave, but he wasn't having any of it. There was more fun to be had wrenching Meg's costume from side to side, as if it were a rag. A ripping sound tore the air and the woman shot backwards, still clutching Dave. A strip of fur dangled from his mouth as, tail flapping, he gave us a victorious grin. Meg sat up, planting her arms behind her on the pavement, and shook her wonky head.

"I'm sorry," the woman said. "He's not usually quite this bad."

After hauling herself to her feet, Meg snatched one of my agony aunt leaflets from the stand, keeping clear of Dave's fangs as she handed it to the woman.

"I think you and Dave could definitely do with this."

Chapter 7

It must have been a quiet news day for the Herald as Dave's incident made the bottom of the front page, with the headline: *For fur's sake. Free me!* The video had also made it onto local Facebook groups, with several people showing surprise that one person could use the full alphabet of swear words in minutes. To give Meg her due, she took it well, even posting a newspaper cutting by the till in her shop, along with her quote telling the woman to use my dog agony aunt service – although some wit on Facebook suggested that Dave's bite brought new meaning to the term. I was delighted. The publicity had brought dozens of new enquiries.

As a thank you, I invited Meg to Beachers on the Thursday night, promising to buy her a slap-up meal. I didn't have the money for it but, hopefully, the new enquiries would turn into actual sales and would pay towards our night. If not, it would be another month of value baked beans on toast.

When we walked in, Meg spotted Peter Drew and his wife, Barbara, in the corner. She huffed. "Great. Of all the people."

The waiter showed us to the neighbouring table – a prime position with views across the harbour. As I sidled past the couple, I gave them a polite greeting. Barbara looked up, her mouth too full to speak, and waved her fork at me. Peter refused to meet my eye.

I picked the chair furthest from them and sat down. "What is his problem? He was really shirty with me the other day."

Meg shrugged and said in a too-loud voice, "The male menopause?" Then she leaned closer to whisper, "He's been funny ever since we put those posters up in the High Street last month to publicise Beach Street. But there's more to it…"

I had to stop her. She had her back to him, so she couldn't see Peter's head stretch in our direction – he was trying hard to eavesdrop. I put my finger to my lips and mouthed that he was listening. Her eyes widened and she grinned.

Grabbing my hand, she said, "Thank you so much, darling. I'll treasure this dinner for ever."

I snatched my hand away, but she put on a hurt voice. "There's no need to hide our love. People have to find out sometime."

I tried to twist my hand from hers, hissing, "What are you playing at?"

She grinned and leaned across to me, keeping her voice low. "Just having a little fun with the rumour mill."

Barbara forked more food into her mouth, her attention on the waiter heading our way. She couldn't have heard us. Thank goodness! While Peter wasn't known for his discretion, Barbara would have the beacon gossip fires lit within minutes, puffing out messages to all and sundry.

Meg picked up her menu. "Darling, I fancy the John Dory. What about you?"

I gave her a quick kick, banging the crossbar instead of her leg. "Will you stop it!"

She patted my hand. "There, there."

"I'm going to thump you," I growled.

"Darling, it's the twenty-first century, not the nineteenth. No one cares."

I ignored her, turning to the menu. "What about a starter?"

"A sharing platter?" she said in a suggestive voice and blew me a kiss.

What had got into her? She might think it funny if people thought we were a couple. It shouldn't be a big deal if they did, except – I'd never confided this to anyone – I missed having a boyfriend. Since my ex had left, finding a new one had proved an impossible task. Most of the men who came into my shop were attached, while the rest were too old, young, not my type. I didn't need her to put up another hurdle on my journey to find my dream man.

Not that I had an unhappy life – if you discounted my precarious finances. I had lovely friends. And Roo was making herself comfortable in what had been my too-quiet flat. I didn't feel so alone at night when I heard her soft snores. But, unless my aunt couldn't have her back when she left hospital, she'd be gone soon. Still, even though I enjoyed having a doggie companion more than I had thought possible, it would be nice to snuggle into a man on the settee or in bed.

Sighing, I gazed through the leaded window. Opposite, cottages rose in colourful tiers, their reflections shimmering on the darkening sea. A boat covered in orange buoys, like party balloons, motored into the harbour, trailing a wake that glinted beneath the apricot sky. It reminded me of the gorgeous sunrise on Sunday morning and my new signage – which had, so far, escaped the attention of the council.

I kept my voice low in case Peter overheard and grassed on me. "What did you think of my signs?"

Meg frowned then seemed to guess what I meant, but she was still playing her stupid game. "If you call gazing at me like that 'giving me signs', you're playing hard to get."

Groaning, I said, "Seriously. Did you see them?"

She nodded and lowered her voice. "You could do with them on both sides, though. Anyone heading into town wouldn't spot them."

I shrugged. "I can't see how I'd get away with that."

"Use my lollipop – just like I said. Anyhow, I wouldn't worry…" She stole a glance towards Peter and Barbara. "If the council agrees to our decorations, that should help."

Andy had put forward a proposal to decorate the lamp posts to promote our wares. The one opposite his shop would feature an ornamental cake, Keith's a fish, Becki's a crystal ball and mine a dog.

"Except tourists will think my one is for the new pet shop."

"Make it clear that it's your place." She tapped the side of her head. "You'll think of something. Anyhow, it's the

May Fair coming up. We've got that to contend with first."

♦

It was official. Or, I should say 'we' were, as I discovered when Edna congratulated me the following Monday.

"It couldn't have happened to a nicer couple," she said, not giving me time to refute the gossip before launching into a reminiscence of all her family's weddings, starting with Vera and Stan in 1958, where she'd met her dear husband, moving without stopping for breath through the decades to Chelsea and Steve last year. Even when I left to make the tea, she didn't stop, raising her voice so I could hear her hollering up the stairs. Every so often, she'd call, "Can you still hear me?", pausing for my answer before rabbiting on.

When she got up to leave, I decided not to bother explaining that Meg and I weren't an item. To be honest, I didn't care if she thought I was sleeping with half of Torringham if it meant I could have a few moments' peace. But I hadn't considered – or guessed – the wider repercussions.

Later that evening, when I was walking with Roo, I spotted Keith through the open door of the Fisherman's Rest, hunched over his pint. He looked so forlorn that I came to a stop and backtracked, confusing Roo, who strained at the lead, desperate to sniff at a flowerpot. We stepped into the pub. It hummed with chatter, although the tables around Keith were empty. The answer lay in the crackling log fire. Who'd want to bake on a warm spring evening?

Heidi stood at the bar wiping the counter and pump handles, wearing a vest top. She pulled a face and jerked her head towards Keith, who – focused on his finger which circled the rim of his pint glass – hadn't noticed me. I went over to speak to her. She might know what was up with him.

When I asked about Keith, she wiped away the perspiration on her forehead. "He was a bit quiet when he came in, but…" She glanced over to the huddled figure. "Maybe he's ill. He's got up twice to throw more logs on the fire. The second time I told him there was no need, it was warm enough, but it was too late. I've taken the rest away."

I ordered an orange juice and, after a brief chat, headed over to Keith. "Do you mind if I join you?" Not waiting for an answer, I chose the chair farthest from the fire. It juddered over the flagstone floor, waking him from his reverie. He gave me a weak smile.

"I'm in my own world. I can't say I'd be much company."

Roo shuffled towards the crackling fire. Within moments she started panting, her tongue lolling, but she didn't move. The breeze wafting through the door cooled one side of me, while the other prickled in the heat.

I took a sip of my orange juice, glad that Heidi had been generous with the ice cubes. "It's a bit hot in here."

"Is it?" He gazed at the fire. "I'm a bit chilly myself."

As I twisted in my seat to hang my jacket over the back of the chair, I gazed in surprise at his thick cable knit jumper. Perhaps Heidi was right – he was coming down with something.

"It looks like everyone's getting paired up. I saw Becki in the pub with a new man and I hear that congratulations are in order for you," he said in a morose tone.

Becki and a man? That was interesting – but more to the point – what did he mean by congratulating me? I frowned. "Are they?"

His red-rimmed eyes met mine. "First Becki. Now you and Meg."

"Ah, that." I chuckled. "You're the second person today. Let me guess, Peter told you that Meg and I are an item."

His voice flat, he said, "Aren't you?"

"No!" I laughed. "She's not my type. For a start, I'm not into women." Then I shuddered. I could be opening myself up to another offer here. After all, it wasn't long ago that he'd attempted to kiss me one drunken night. Much as I liked Keith as a friend, I didn't want him to get ideas. "And … I'm not interested in a relationship at the moment." I nodded towards Roo. "I've got enough on my plate with the shop and her."

He gave me a thin smile. "So, you and Meg aren't an item?"

I blinked in shock. All this time I'd thought he fancied me, when it had been Meg he liked. I blushed at my assumption. How big-headed! Saying that, he'd done nothing to suggest he had a thing for her. Maybe shyness made him reluctant to approach Meg. I couldn't imagine them together though. He had a gentle demeanour, unlike Meg's bolshiness. Both were lovely, kind people – although, at our committee meeting, they'd both come up with devious plans for my future competitor.

"It'd be a brave man to take her on."

He chuckled. "That's true." Then he frowned. "Why would Hilda lie about it, though? She likes her gossip, but she's not one for making stuff up."

"Hilda!" I choked on my drink, coughing so hard that my eyes watered. Crikey! If she'd told her family, we'd have no chance of putting a stop to the rumour before it reached every household in Torringham. Keith slapped my back until I held up my hand, begging him to stop.

"It's Meg's fault," I said. "She was trying to wind Peter up, but it's backfired. But do me a favour – don't tell anyone that part. Meg was adamant that her plan – whatever it is – would only work if no one knew it was her idea."

Chapter 8

The next day, I put up my 'back by two' sign and headed to Meg's craft shop, still thinking about how upset Keith had been, and why Meg had started her stupid rumour. It wasn't the first time I'd asked her. Within minutes of Peter and Barbara finishing their meal and leaving us in peace, I'd demanded she tell me, but she'd tapped her nose, saying there was method to her madness. Maybe she'd guessed that Keith liked her and this was her way of getting him to back off. But that didn't make sense. She'd never had a problem exercising her vocal cords, although she took care not to turn her whip-like words on her friends.

I dashed past Becki's spiritual shop, feeling guilty as I hadn't seen her since the market day, and darted into Meg's, where I found her surrounded by piles of boxes and a counter heaped with reels of ribbon.

"I made a typo on the order." She scratched her head. "I have no idea what I'm meant to do with this lot."

"Send them back?" I said.

She shrugged. "Maybe. Some of them might come in handy to decorate our May Fair stand. Anyhow, are you here for a cuppa or something else?"

"Both," I said. "But I'll talk once you've put the kettle on."

She disappeared, leaving me holding the fort at the till as her assistant, Sarah, was on her lunch break. Moments later Sarah returned, so I shot upstairs to Meg's tiny kitchen. Dirty plates were stacked beside the sink, pots drowned in a scum-laden sink, while cups were upended on the draining board. Two watery circles showed where our mugs had been. Meg had found a space in front of the toaster on which to perch the mugs but, when she passed me my coffee, I got a handful of crumbs.

"Sorry. It's been a bit chaotic lately," she said when I wiped my hand down the leg of my jeans.

She ushered me through to her cosy lounge, sweeping Amber and a stack of magazines off her two-seater sofa. Grunting, Amber flopped down on the rug, her dejected gaze making me feel guilty. While Meg took the seat she'd warmed, I sat primly against the other arm rest. Meg curled her legs, her bare toes resting against my thigh. A slight smell wafted. Not the dog.

Catching my sour expression, she grinned. "They could do with a massage."

"No offence, but I'm not touching them." I grimaced. "Talking about us touching…" That sounded odd, so I amended it. "Being together… You haven't explained what the other night was all about. You do know that the whole of Torringham thinks we're lovers. I had Keith crying over his pint last night after Hilda told him. Even Edna offered her congratulations."

Her eyes glinted. "Hilda knows. That's perfect."

She placed her cup on one of the many coasters scattered around the coffee table – although, going by the coffee rings on the utility bills, she didn't often use them.

"If you must know…" She leaned back into the sofa. "I wanted to pay Peter back."

"How? I mean, it doesn't make sense. It's you and I they're gossiping about. Not him."

"Hear me out. Do you remember when he kicked up a fuss when we asked the council to put up an information board in the harbour, pointing the tourists to Beach Street? Then he told the Torringham Traders that Beach Street is bringing down Torringham, and said that a change of use on Nancy's old place – to holiday accommodation – would be better. It'd keep all the retail in one place – in other words, the High Street."

I frowned. I vaguely recalled being told something along those lines but, to be honest, I'd lost interest in the Torringham Traders since Peter had become its chairman. He only cared about the High Street traders and the ones around the harbour. The ones in less prestigious locations, such as the shop owners in Beach Street, didn't bother attending the monthly meetings. Not because we had an issue with the other businesses, but we no longer felt part of the group. Also, Peter liked the sound of his own voice too much. Thankfully, many of the sensible business owners had refused to support Peter's idea for Nancy's old hardware store in Beach Street to become a holiday let, saying that we should be looking out for each other. Peter had backed down, especially after rumours started to swirl that the person who wanted to change the property into seaside holiday apartments happened to be a good friend of his.

Thanks to the opposition from the Beach Street traders and the lack of support from other quarters, the council had refused the change of use application. The hardware store had become a deli instead, selling posh conserves and an amazing range of local produce. A win for the Beach Street traders and a bloody nose for Peter Drew. But that still didn't explain why Meg had been so keen for Peter to think we were a couple.

"What's this got to do with us being an item?"

Meg shrugged. "I can't lie." Although she had. "It wasn't planned. If I'd had a bit more time to think about it, I would have come up with something miles better, but…" She chuckled to herself. "It's gone down a treat. Hilda will be furious when she finds out that Peter's told her a load of rubbish. You know what she's like about being fibbed to. Who knows what she'll do to pay him back?"

I shook my head. All this palaver for nothing. "But Barbara was there. She heard you. She'll stick up for her husband."

"Hilda and Barbara don't get on. Look, there's method to my madness. Too many people still trust Peter. They've either forgotten or they don't know what he's really like. He's become the voice of reason. What he says, goes. But he's using the Torringham Traders for his own ends. It used to be for everyone until he joined. We all let him get away with it by not attending – and now he's leading it. Us Beach Street traders might have our own committee, but no one listens to us. This is one more step on the road to showing him for what he is. A no-good liar."

I didn't agree. But it seemed pointless to argue further. It was done now. Except someone had been hurt. Keith.

"I told Keith the truth, as he was in bits about us being together."

She raised her eyebrows. "Keith was upset? He must really have a thing about you."

I smiled at her. "Actually, it's you he likes. He told me."

She gasped. "*Me?* Seriously?"

I'd thought she might laugh, but instead she stared into space with a strange expression on her face. Then she whispered, "Well, I never."

♦

On Thursday Edna stormed into my shop, carrying Flossie. She hefted her onto the counter with a grunt and pointed her finger at me.

"You're not with Meg."

Confused, I tried to work out what she meant. Then it clicked. "I never said I was."

"I told you on Monday and you never said a word."

I kept my voice light. It was pointless saying that she hadn't given me a chance to speak.

"To be honest, I had no idea what you meant. It was only later that I realised."

"Hilda's on the warpath. She doesn't like spreading lies. Nor do I."

I shrugged. "Don't blame me. It's not like I'd want that rumour going around."

She pursed her lips. "It's that awful man, Peter Drew, up to mischief. Hilda'll sort him out. Mark my words, he won't pick on you two again."

She slumped into the chair beside the counter, giving me a warm smile as I lifted Flossie into her arms. "I could do with a brew if you're making one, dear."

My morning cup of tea sat cooling by the till, but dutifully I obliged. When I returned, I found her fingering a pink tutu.

"What on earth is this?" She held up the tiny garment.

"It's for Carla Jones' shih tzu."

She frowned. "Dog ballet? That's a new one. That reminds me…"

Her granddaughter, who lived in Doncaster, had just got a Labrador. Weeks later she'd discovered she was pregnant – the woman, not the dog. I'd have offered Edna my congratulations if she'd given me the chance to speak. Instead, I sipped my fresh cup of tea and listened to her tale of woe.

"They've gone all biblical on boys' names. Why they can't go for Matthew, Mark, Luke or John is beyond me. But *Balthazar?*" She grimaced. "That's their top choice, above Jeremiah. They're even thinking of Ezekiel, although I don't mind Zeke. The girls' names aren't much better. Lavender, Honey or Mildred. *Mildred!* Imagine that! Do you remember that TV show with Yootha Joyce?"

"Lavender?" I chuckled, amazed that Edna had given me a moment to answer. "I'm not sure about Mildred or Joyce for a baby nowadays. Saying that, look at Violet and Amy. They've come back into fashion again."

She darted me an odd look. "Yootha Joyce. That's the name of the actress. From *Man About the House* and *George and Mildred*. Those were the days. TV gold. You young 'uns don't know what you're missing…"

By the time she got up to leave at noon, I'd learned more about sixties and seventies sitcoms than I'd thought possible. My mind reeled. A couple of times, I'd recognised the names, but only when she'd strayed from comedies to shows that had made it into my era: Dr Who, *Coronation Street* and *Emmerdale*. At least she'd called me young, although I didn't feel it.

While I held Flossie, she heaved herself to her feet. "It's been a lovely morning, dear, but I best get on." As I bundled Flossie back into her arms, she looked at me. "You're such a kind girl. I'm sorry that Peter told those stories about you and Meg."

"I don't mind. It's not like it's something terrible."

"That's one of the few good things about these modern days. Morecambe and Wise might have shared a bed…"

I frowned. I mean, I'd vaguely heard of them, but what had they got to do with us?

She added, "In their pyjamas, of course. But woe betide anyone else doing the same. A slip of the tongue and a person's reputation could be ruined." She pursed her lips. "Hilda and I think along the same lines. We're wise monkeys. Speak no evil. Although…" She winced. "I have to confess that I've promised Meg that I'll do her dirty work for her. But only because that Peter deserves his comeuppance."

"What has she asked you to do?"

Edna tapped her nose. "I've promised not to say. Anyhow, I must be going before Flossie pulls my arms from their sockets."

Wheezing, she turned and waddled away, choosing to be burdened by a pooch who had more legs than she.

Chapter 9

The May Fair was the one Saturday where I could shut up shop early without my customers moaning. By lunchtime, the street would empty as the townsfolk went home to prepare for an afternoon and evening of festivities in Parkside Green. I'd put up a sign saying that the shop would close at one o'clock, but I could have done so an hour earlier as, from noon, Roo and I sat alone, watching the clock tick. Usually, I'd use the spare time to restock the shelves or make a sandwich, but today I didn't feel up to doing much.

On the dot of one, we left the shop and joined the throng heading up Ansley Steps, then past the Fisherman's Rest to Daisy Steps. Most of the crowd kept going – taking the longer, but easier, route – but Roo strained at the lead, eager to bound up the steep flight. I debated whether to give them a miss today but, after doing so little that morning, I decided to join the few energetic people tackling the climb. Halfway up, I regretted my decision. Why did I find these steps easy one day and tough the next? Breathless, I paused on a landing to let a group go past. My chest thudded, making me feel woozy. Below lay the moss-covered rooftops and crooked chimneys of Beach Street. Further back, car windscreens glinted in the half-empty car park, which was usually full. The distant sea dazzled the colour of mercury in the bright sunshine. While I waited for an energetic bunch to pass, I rifled through my bag to check I'd remembered my sunscreen, then hitched the strap back over my shoulder before setting off. Impatient, Roo nosed at the heels of their trainers, but soon they were a dozen steps ahead, then another dozen, before they disappeared over the brow.

By the time we reached the top, my chest heaved and my thighs burned, forcing me to rest on a low ivy-covered wall. Across the park, the luckier crowds streamed in. Unlike those from central Torringham, the ones who lived in the Parkside Green area had a level walk to the fair. I envied not only their easy walk, but also the stunning sea views many would have from their houses. Those who didn't had just a short stroll to catch a breath-taking picture of the wide bay. I hoped the Beach Street traders' stand would be in the same place as last year, as I'd spent the day admiring the view from it.

It was. Becki and Meg had set up the stall earlier that morning, using Andy's bakery van to take boxes of stock from each shop. Becki hadn't opened her shop – many of her clients were appointment only and she'd said that being closed for a morning would be fine – while Meg had handed over the reins to her assistant. They'd done a wonderful job of making the stall look cheerful. Meg had decorated the table with ribbons, which flapped brightly in the breeze. She had reels of them on the table too, beside a huge sale sign. A selection of my pet shop wares sat next to Becki's crystal jewellery. An incongruous pairing, but it meant we'd be able to sit together for most of the day. Even better, they had put three tables together in a horseshoe, so we could all chat during a lull in customers. When I arrived, I sank into a chair.

Putting her hands on her hips, Meg sighed. "I see how it is."

"I'm knackered," I said. "Give me a minute, then I'll help."

Becki frowned. "You look a bit peaky."

I grimaced. "It's the steps."

"I keep telling you to go around the Wrekin, but you won't have it," Meg said. "You're getting on a bit now. How long before you're Becki's age?"

Becki gave her a friendly shove. "Get over. Forty's the new thirty."

"Going by the state of her, I'd say it was the new eighty."

Too exhausted to join in their banter, I watched Roo lap at the plastic tub of water that Meg had brought. Roo flopped down beside Amber in the shade beneath one of the tables. The sun scorched my scalp, so I pulled out my hat and tugged down the brim to cover my face.

"Hangover?" Meg pursed her lips.

"I didn't touch a drop last night. Maybe I'm dehydrated."

I pulled out my bottle of orangeade, twisting the cap. It gave a welcome hiss – the jolting up the stairs hadn't made it go flat. After a few glugs I felt a bit better, although Meg didn't seem impressed by my burps. I slapped my thigh and heaved myself to my feet.

"Okay. What shall I do?"

Our attention was taken by Keith's arrival. He looked dapper in a tweed jacket – which he'd need to take off soon if he didn't want to boil – white shirt and jeans. Meg glanced up, flickered him a smile and set about rearranging her collection of Torringham tea towels and other knick-knacks. He stepped beside me, smelling of a fancy cologne.

"Are you okay?" He frowned. "You look a bit pale."

I shrugged. "Nothing a bit of sun won't mend."

Squinting, he shielded his eyes to gaze at the sky. "We've got that all day, by the look of it. I'm judging the children's fancy dress competition. I saw a red-faced bunny hopping past earlier. I don't envy them that costume." He turned to Meg. "Not dressing as a dog today?"

She pulled a face. "Not yet. I'll wait until it cools down."

"You don't have to do that on my account," I said.

"I do," she said. "I'm going to win a prize for it too."

Becki rolled her eyes and whispered in my ear. "I'm not sure it's going to help your business."

"How come?" I hissed back, but she grinned. "You'll see."

The tannoy blared, telling fairgoers about the displays in the exhibition area. I wasn't needed until four o'clock, so I looked after the stands when the traders took turns to go for a wander, telling them they could repay the favour later. The afternoon rolled by. My earlier peakiness subsided as I chatted with customers old and new, did a roaring trade with my range of seaside-themed dog neckerchiefs, and watched Keith who talked to Becki and the other traders, as Meg studiously avoided him. Strange. When I'd told Meg that he was keen on her, I thought I'd detected a spark of interest on her part. But maybe I'd been wrong.

Andy headed over with a tray of cupcakes. "Not mine," he said. "My lass's started a new venture: Wesley's Bakes. You're welcome to a couple or three."

"Wesley?"

He grinned. "It's her intended's name. She's planning ahead."

My mouth watered as my hand hovered over the scrumptious rainbow collection of glittery iced cakes. An hour or so before, I would have waved him away, saying I couldn't face food, but my stomach rumbled, reminding me I'd missed breakfast. I took two but soon wished I'd taken him up on his offer of more. Buzzing on a sugar high, which I needed to work off, I happily handed my stall over to Sheila when the tannoy announced that the dog show would be starting soon. I looked around for Meg. Wasn't she coming back for Amber? Neither dog was participating, but they needed a stroll after spending a few hours panting under the table, sneaking surreptitious treats from Keith.

By the parade ground, Becki wore a wide grin as she took Amber's lead from me. When I asked where Meg had disappeared to, she smiled secretively and told me that we'd see her soon. Groups of people stood with their dogs, waiting for the start. The tannoy introduced the best-dressed pooch competition and a line of silky dogs trooped out, decked in ribbons and other strange items, which would look better in the children's fancy dress competition. I spotted Arabella wearing her tutu along with frilly bands around her ankles – very eighties – while her proud owner matched her in a luminous pink tracksuit.

Becki sniggered. "Where on earth did she get that?"

"From me. She asked me to order a few tutus and other frilly stuff in for Arabella. It's not my usual line."

"I'm talking about the tracksuit."

I turned my attention back to the competition. When a dog in a denim jacket and a cowboy-style neckerchief was proclaimed the winner, Arabella's owner looked most put out. She trailed out behind the others, head down, her runner-up rosette dangling from her hand.

"This is what I've been waiting for." Becki chuckled.

"The friendliest mutt class? I've sponsored that, and the rescue dog one."

Becki nudged me as the entrants came out, the dogs springing about and wagging their tails. Then I groaned. "Surely not?"

At the rear gambolled Meg, wearing the dog costume, wiggling her bum and holding out her arms as if begging for a snack. She cocked her leg, pretending to pee on another competitor. When the crowd roared with laughter, it inspired her to drop to the ground and sniff a Great Dane's rear.

"She can't win, can she? I've promised to put the

winner's photo in my shop."

"Just wait." Becki gave me a devious grin. "The best is yet to come."

Her hand shot to her mouth and she gasped. "Oh dear! I didn't mean that."

Looking indignant, the Great Dane had yanked himself free from his owner's grasp and leapt onto Meg's back. As she floundered, trying to get to her feet, the huge dog humped her while his owner stood behind, desperately tugging him by the collar. From our angle, it looked like an awkward threesome. It hadn't gone unnoticed by a gang of young people nearby, who jeered and filmed it all on their mobiles. The judge rushed over to help.

Meg ripped the head off her costume. "I'm a woman!" she yelled.

"Sure you're not a bitch?" a nearby wit quipped.

"Brings new meaning to the friendliest dog!" another called.

Becki watched the mayhem through her fingers. "Trust Meg."

Even Amber seemed embarrassed. She circled around beside us and flopped onto the grass, her back to the goings-on, while Roo hoovered the ground for crumbs.

Finally Meg was rescued, the Great Dane was reunited with his owner, and a tannoy announcement told us that Meg had been disqualified for not being friendly enough. I hoped that meant she wouldn't be participating in the next event. While I wouldn't get to see what she'd planned to do, I viewed that as a bonus. As the owners tried to calm their dogs, she picked up her rucksack and stomped away, brushing herself down and shaking her head. Soon she appeared at our side, red-faced, her hair all over the place, smiling broadly.

"That's a first," she said. "I've never been shagged by a Great Dane before. Usually it's terriers."

When I gave her an odd look, she shrugged. "They have a thing about my legs."

I nodded to Keith, who was ambling towards us from the direction of the stall. "I think he does too. I saw him checking you out earlier when you were in your shorts."

She slapped my arm. "Give over!"

"What's this?" Becki asked.

"Keith likes—"

Meg cut me off. "Keith has a thing about you," she said. "About you."

"Really?" Becki eyed Keith with a new interest.

"N—" I went to tell the truth, but Meg trod on my foot, making me wince.

"Yes," she said, with determination. Out of Becki's sight she glared at me, mouthing 'shut up'. "He does." She gripped my arm, leaving Becki to talk to Keith. Once out of their earshot, she said, "You got it wrong, as usual."

Chapter 10

As Meg dragged me away, with our dogs in tow, I twisted around, struggling to get back to the show.

"I'm the sponsor," I told her. "I'm meant to be awarding the prize for the friendliest dog."

"Oh!" She released me. "I thought you were trying to wreck things for Becki and Keith."

"But he likes you!" I said.

"No!" Meg let out a loud sigh. "You got the wrong end of the stick. Keith was upset at the pub because he'd seen Becki with another man. He didn't know it was her cousin."

"But…" I scratched my head. "At the pub he said—"

"He'd just heard the gossip about us. He was curious. Nothing more."

"How do you know?"

She put her hands on her hips. "I asked him. There's no point beating around the bush. He told me the whole story. The good thing is Becki likes him too, so leave our love birds to it."

"Does she?" I frowned. How come she hadn't mentioned it to me? Before I could ask, my name was called over the tannoy.

"Are you coming?" I said. "You're in the next competition too."

But she shook her head. "They've barred me. Apparently, I need an actual dog and it's too late to register Amber. It's a shame, as…" She hefted her rucksack from her shoulder and pulled out a small barrel attached to a collar, followed by a tabard emblazoned with a red cross on the front and the words 'Happy Paws & Shiny Claws for all your rescue needs' on the back. "I was going to do this."

"That's lovely of you, but you don't look like a St Bernard."

She shrugged and shook the barrel. "Well, this is the real thing. Brandy. I think I need it right now too."

Chuckling, I handed over Roo's lead. When I reached the judge, I was surprised to find he'd chosen the Great Dane as the winner.

The judge shrugged and, with a twinkle in his eye, laughed. "He was very friendly."

To prove the point, the dog jumped up, planting his feet on my shoulders. I staggered backwards, desperate to keep my footing. No way would I end up on all fours like Meg.

Thankfully, the best rescue dog competition was a more sedate affair. I would have loved to enter Roo, but I couldn't win my own prize, a basket of dog treats. After awarding the rosette to a shaggy mutt with stumpy legs, a huge body and a tiny head – but the most loving eyes I'd ever seen – I went off in search of Roo and Meg. Behind me the arena was being set up for the evening's festivities. A man stood on the stage, looking every inch the moody pop star as he twanged his guitar. Delicious smells drifted from the barbecue stall, and tables were filled with an array of beers, lagers and wines. Guessing I'd find Meg hovering nearby, I headed over.

I was right. Meg stood beside Andy, both clutching a plastic cup – hers with red wine, his with beer. Andy spotted me first, grinning as he pretended to mask his beer with his hand.

"It's ginger beer."

"Of course," I said. "What else would it be at not yet five o'clock?"

"We're celebrating his success," Meg said, raising her cup to me. "He's sold everything."

"Well done! Your daughter's cakes were delicious." I checked the time on my mobile phone. "I'd better get back and start packing my stuff away. I've got to take Roo for a walk and get her home before the night starts."

"I don't s'pose you fancy taking Amber with you?" Meg fluttered her eyes at me, making Andy burst into laughter. Were these their first drinks? I had a sneaking suspicion I'd find the barrel of brandy empty if I checked.

Sighing, I took the lead from her. "Will I find you on your back when I return?"

"You should be so lucky!" Andy grinned. "I won't be getting any of that tonight. My missus has got a right cob on after I forgot to buy her a drink. I told her to stop blarting about it and I'd sort it, but she buggered off while I was in the queue."

Meg wiggled her cup. "Thanks to her, I won something today. This."

♦

After feeding the dogs and making sure they were curled in their beds in their own homes, I returned two hours later to find Becki laughing with Keith, while Meg held a cup of white wine in the air as she did a solo jig around her handbag. The fairground was in full swing. Shrieks mingled with the smell of diesel. On the stage a band tinkered with their instruments, the chords vibrating through the speakers. Nearby, Andy stood with his wife and another couple I didn't recognise. They all had wide smiles and rosy cheeks. In comparison, I felt like the boring parent, especially when Meg tugged my arm, begging me to join her. I pointed out that I was too sober to dance, especially when no music was playing.

"Spoilschport," she slurred. She pointed an unsteady finger at me and jerked her head towards Becki and Keith. "Don't bother our lovely couple over there."

I surveyed them. They were standing closer, so their arms brushed. A strange pairing. Becki's pink and blue hair had been muted by the deepening dusk but, decked in a selection of her crystal jewellery and a colourful shawl, she could have slipped through a time warp from the era of peace and love. In contrast, Keith seemed to have stepped from a stint in the forces with his short back and sides, upright posture and tweed jacket. Even his jeans looked formal next to her pyjama-style trousers.

"How did you know that she liked him?"

"I've got eyes." She stuck two fingers up and pointed

to her eyes in case I couldn't work it out for myself.

"But, when I told you, you seemed interested in him too."

"Come on, it's Keith. He's lovely, but it would never work. I might get a lifetime of free fish, but I'd get sick of him agreeing with me all the time. There'd be no fireworks. Our relationship would be like a damp squid."

"You mean a damp squib."

"He's a fishmonger, so it's a squid." She cackled.

Sighing, I muttered, "I think I need a drink."

She clutched my arm to steady herself. "Get me a water. I need to sober up."

Leaving her to continue her solitary dance, I meandered through the clusters of people seated on the ground. When one of the singers on the stage introduced themselves, cheers rose and people leapt to their feet, some dancing before the first chords were struck. I chuckled. At least Meg wouldn't look so out of place now.

I brought Meg her pint of water and a large cup of wine for myself, which Meg tried to take. She pulled a face when I pushed the water into her hands, but she sipped it while watching the band. Soon we were joined by another trader, Sheila, and her friend. Not long afterwards, Keith and Becki headed over.

Sheila pulled a bottle of wine from her bag and winked at me. "Cheaper than buying it over there. Especially with the rubbish they're serving." Without asking, she tipped the bottle into my cup, filling it to the brim. Meg held out her now empty cup and gave Sheila puppy-dog eyes.

"Please!"

Sheila chuckled. "Lucky I brought three bottles."

As the music slowed, people around us started settling back on the ground, leaving our group standing. Even when a new band came onto the stage and played livelier music, the crowd didn't get to their feet. Meg grabbed my arm.

"You have *got* to dance to this."

I tried to shake her off. Everyone would be watching us, and I was far too sober for that. But she kept begging until I gave in. When I put our drinks down by Becki's feet, I couldn't help grinning when I spotted her fingers entwined with Keith's. Meg linked her arms through mine, swaying from side to side. As the tempo picked up on stage, her hips banged my legs.

"I love country music," she drawled.

I frowned, certain it was a sea shanty.

She began to drag me around in an involuntary – on my part – circle. Laughing, Sheila and her friend pointed at us and knocked back their wine, dumping their cups into a carrier bag along with the empty bottle.

"Doh-see-doh!" Meg cried, even though she was more like a very merry go-round.

As we turned, Sheila joined us, linking her arm with mine, while her friend coupled up with her. At first we went slowly, until Meg changed direction, whizzing backwards, spinning us faster and faster. Grinning, Becki stood watching us, holding up her mobile phone.

"Put that down!" I shouted, but she ignored me.

The music sped up. So did Meg. She hurtled around, drink making her both brave and stupid, a grin plastered to her face. When I stumbled on the uneven grass, I tried to slow down but, stuck between her and Sheila, I had no choice but to keep up. Again, I tripped but managed to stay upright. Next time I might not be so lucky. Without thinking, I yanked my arm from Meg's. She shot backwards, a blur of blue, her arms flailing, her mouth open. Someone screeched. Another yelped. Unable to watch, I hid behind Becki and Keith, peeking out to see Meg lying on top of Peter Drew, her legs in the air. I'd been right about her ending up on her back. I just hadn't expected this.

"You stupid cow!" He shoved her to one side and jumped to his feet, holding out his sodden shirt. "You've spilled my drink!"

Meg lay on the ground, her hand covering her mouth, unable to mask her smile.

"Do you think it's funny?" Peter yelled.

Sense took over. I couldn't leave her to face Peter alone. Not when her fall had been my fault. But someone else beat me to it. A man hefted Meg to her feet. I recognised him from the pub. My competitor!

"I'm sorry," I told Peter. After briefly thanking the man, I went to lead a wobbly Meg away, but Peter grabbed my shoulder.

"She owes me for dry cleaning this." He grasped the lapel of his jacket.

"Don't be daft," Meg said. "It's just one of your cheap

knock-offs. The beer probably cost more than that." She rifled in her pocket and pulled out a tenner, which she shoved into his hand. "Here, if you're so desperate for money."

Peter's eyes narrowed and he jabbed his finger at her. "So it was you that started that rumour." He pointed at me. "Along with your bed mate."

"Eh?" Confused, I looked at him. What was he talking about? "I said I'm sorry. Anyhow, I'm not the one who's been spreading false rumours."

"Really?" he growled. "You're just about to find out the meaning of the word 'sorry'."

My future competitor drew him away, throwing me an apologetic grimace. He seemed lovely, so I had no idea why he was friends with Peter.

Becki arrived beside us. She wrapped her arm around Meg's shoulder. "What was all that about?"

"War, that's what." Meg clutched her head. "I think I could do with a black coffee."

Chapter 11

The following day, my sickness returned with a vengeance. I had a pounding headache and dodgy stomach. If I hadn't felt so unwell yesterday morning, I'd have assumed it was alcohol-related. But it must be a bug. Rosemary Boddy had mentioned there was one going around. After a sleep interrupted by trips to the bathroom, I finally staggered into the kitchen at nine o'clock, where I upended the medicine box onto the worktop, thankful to find both paracetamol and Rennie.

I poured myself a peppermint tea – something I kept in the cupboard for Becki's visits – and tottered back to the bedroom. But Roo hovered at the top of the stairs, whining. Sighing, I stumbled downstairs to let her into the courtyard. I left the door ajar and went upstairs to slump onto the settee. Roo didn't reappear. Maybe she was enjoying the morning sunshine, although it wasn't her usual routine. Once she'd had a sniff and a wee, she'd follow me around until I made her breakfast. Then she'd expect a walk. But I couldn't ignore my thumping head and cramping stomach. I curled into the cushions, wrapping my dressing gown tightly around me. When I woke at eleven o'clock I was disappointed to find I didn't feel much better, so I snuggled back into the settee. The buzz of my phone broke into my doze. I opened one eye and gazed at the screen.

Meg.

I'm coming round. Got some gossip for you.

I'm not feeling great, I typed back, hoping it would put her off.

I didn't want to face her. Partly because I felt so lousy, but also because I didn't want to confess that last night's contretemps with Peter had been my fault. After we'd decamped to a different part of the park, away from Peter and his chums, Becki had replayed her phone footage time and time again. To the innocent eye, it looked as if Meg had strained too forcefully against my arm, breaking our chain. Only I knew that I'd let her go.

Spilling Peter's drink had been an accident. I understood his anger – I wouldn't have been happy if someone had landed on my head – and Meg should have had the grace to apologise. But his accusation about a rumour unsettled me. Edna had mentioned that she didn't like lying, but she'd do so for Meg. Neither had elaborated. Now, thanks to Meg, I was also in Peter's sight line. Yet I had no idea why. I'd make Meg tell me … another day. I didn't feel up to it today.

I looked around the room, ignoring the pile of bills on the coffee table. Although business had been doing better recently, my account was still in the red by the end of the month. At least I could hide the paperwork in a drawer, but the rest of the room needed a good clean. Dog snot smeared the dusty TV screen and hair matted the rug and settee – no doubt covering me too. While it was no worse than Meg's place, I prided myself on being a little tidier than she was. I simply didn't feel up to entertaining anyone, even Meg. Her voice would be like a drill in my head. I collapsed back onto the sofa and lay staring at the ceiling. Then I realised that Roo hadn't come begging for her breakfast. After checking the bedroom and the kitchen, I headed down the stairs, unable to believe she could still be outside. But where else would she be? Sunlight pierced through the open back door and into the gloomy passage. Blinking, I stepped into the courtyard to find Roo lying on her back, her feet in the air, beside a man who was stroking her belly.

Smiling, he lifted his head. I stepped back, startled. Had the purchase gone through already? I thought house sales took weeks, maybe months. Sometimes commercial sales could be even more painful. That's unless he had wads of cash and didn't need a loan.

"She's lovely," he said, giving traitorous Roo another rub.

I forced a smile. "Yes, she is."

"Bit of a to-do last night, wasn't it? I hope your friend's okay. Ignore Pete. He was a bit shocked, but give him time and he'll get over it. He's been really helpful to me." He tickled the back of Roo's ear and was rewarded by a tongue-lolling grin. "We all need to be more dog-like, don't we? They're such lovely creatures."

Something about his tone rankled. While Meg's recent behaviour hadn't helped matters, it was Peter who had started all this off by trying to prevent the Beach Street traders from promoting the street. Of course he'd be helpful to my neighbour. Peter would be laughing his socks off about putting my business in jeopardy.

Incensed, I blurted, "It's a shame you don't think much of people, though, or you wouldn't be buying the place next to mine."

The man frowned and opened his mouth to speak, but I stomped off. Roo clearly thought better of staying with him and dashed after me. I slammed the back door and shot the bolt across. I'd been rude, I know, but what sort of person would start a pet shop next door to an existing one? At least if he'd bought a shop in another street – even the High Street would have been better – it could be argued that customers might come from different parts of town. While large clothing chains grouped together, they were different to my tiny shop, with its long lease, small client base and far too many bills.

Upstairs, I peered out of the kitchen window. Someone had joined the man. Both gazed up at the roof, frowning. By the time Roo had wolfed down her food and I looked again, my future competitor stood at the foot of a ladder, holding it steady, while the other man stood at the top inspecting the roof and guttering.

The doorbell rang. Meg! In my annoyance, I'd forgotten that she'd threatened to come around. I could have pretended to be out, but Roo's bark reverberated loud and clear. I let them in. Amber nosed her way inside, followed by Meg, who beamed at me.

"Guess what?"

I shrugged. "What?"

"No, *guess!*" She jittered on the spot.

Sounding bored, I said, "You're pregnant?"

She slapped my arm. "Don't be silly. Have another go."

Yawning, I shut the door behind her and walked off, feigning disinterest. No doubt I'd find out soon enough. She looked like she was about to burst if she held it in much longer. We followed Amber up the stairs and into the kitchen, where she licked Roo's empty bowl.

"I hate having a shared courtyard." I tiptoed over to the sink to see if my future competitor was still outside, but I couldn't see him. "It was okay until he came."

"Who?" Meg asked.

"The bloke who's buying the shop next door."

"Is he out there?" She moved beside me to gaze through the window.

"He was earlier. He saw me out like this." I gestured to my tatty dressing gown and shapeless pyjama bottoms. Strangely, since my outburst, I felt a bit better. Maybe it was the adrenaline, which still buzzed angrily inside me.

She grinned. "Lend me your spare jimjams and we can go outside and really stir the gossip pot."

I shook my head. "Give over. Like Peter needs more ammo. That reminds me, what was all that business with him last night, when you said about his knock-off clothing and he said we'd been spreading rumours about him?"

"Oh, that. It's nothing." She bent down to pat Roo, ensuring that I couldn't see her face. When she glanced up, her eyes sparkled. "I didn't tell you my gossip. It's Becki. I saw a man leaving her house when I took Amber for a walk this morning. He'd definitely slept over."

I know I shouldn't have allowed her to divert me, but seriously? I couldn't help myself. Becki with a man? This was gold dust, especially if it was who I thought.

"Really? Was it you know who?"

"Put the kettle on first." She leaned against the worktop, arms folded, but before I'd even poured the tea, she'd told me everything. I was right. It had been Keith. He'd left Becki's house wearing the same clothes he'd worn the previous night.

"His face was a picture when he saw me. He hitched up his collar and scurried away."

She followed me through to the lounge, where our dogs snuggled side by side on the rug. It was too late to hide my paperwork, which littered the coffee table, or the tufts of dog hair that sprouted from the settee. Either Meg hadn't noticed, or she was being polite. Behind us, my bedroom door was ajar. My duvet was a tangled heap on the bed, my clothes scattered across the carpet. I shut the door and joined her on the sofa, where I cupped my hands around my too-hot mug before putting it down on the coffee table.

"I was right about the pair of them." Meg looked pleased with herself.

"You must be psychic, because I would never have guessed."

Meg chuckled. "You're not far off the mark there. While we were waiting for you to arrive yesterday, Becki read our tarot cards. They foretold her finding a man linked to fish, while my future love was an adversary."

"I thought you said that tarot cards were nonsense." I laughed. "She said that about herself? You're right – it shows she was already angling for Keith. But your adversary? Do you reckon it's Peter Drew?"

"Even if he was my type – which he most definitely isn't – I don't go for married men."

"Maybe you bump off Barbara? Or…" I couldn't help grinning. "Grant Brown-tongue! That's it."

"No way. Anyhow, with him being a florist, I'd have permanent hay fever." As if to prove her point, she wiped her hand across her nose. But I hadn't heard her sniffle once recently, let alone sneeze.

"But you'd never be short of—"

A loud drilling noise vibrated through the wall, cutting me off. When the dogs started barking, Meg joined in, yelling, "Amber! Be quiet!"

I clutched my pounding head as my neighbour, the dogs and Meg fought to outdo each other.

"I don't suppose you've got anything stronger than paracetamol?" I asked Meg.

"No!" she yelled over the din. "But I can find something."

♦

The next morning Kirstie, my dog trainer, arrived at the shop at eight thirty to prepare for her first agony aunt session. I'd just got back from a hurried dog walk, after sleeping through my alarm, so she caught me with hedgehog hair and breath that would make a skunk faint. She breezed inside, giving me a smile, which transformed into a worried look.

"Are you okay?" She rested her hand on my arm.

I brushed her concern aside. "Meg led me astray. She insisted that I needed a hair of the dog to make me better."

"It didn't help?"

I gave her a wan smile. "Worse than that. We thought it might be funny to decorate your agony aunt room. I haven't had time to, er, undo some of our work."

We went through to the storeroom, where I'd made space for a table, two chairs and a dog bed. That looked fine. Unlike the purple silk backdrop, which featured a huge poster announcing 'Auntie Kirstie's agony room', surrounded by all the pictures we could find from the pet magazines stashed under my coffee table. After we'd used up all my staples, we'd got creative by sewing on the cut-outs. Then there were the crystals. They were supposed to drip like coloured rain from the ceiling. We'd borrowed them from Becki's shop, telling ourselves they might lend a calming vibe, but we'd spoiled the effect by sellotaping them to Meg's ribbons, which we'd strung across the doorway to give an aura of privacy. In the fug of alcohol, we'd forgotten that simply closing the door would do the trick.

Kirstie gave one a tug. It fluttered down and a drawing pin rolled across the floor. "These will have to come off." Looking horrified, she pointed to the crystal ball on the table. "What on earth is that? I'm a dog trainer, not a fortune teller."

I blushed. "We stole it from Becki's shop. She said we could take some crystals from her storeroom." I didn't want to admit that Meg and I had spent ten minutes planning ways to persuade Kirstie to gaze into the crystal ball and foretell a sweet doggy outlook if the owners did as she said. I took the ball from her, vowing that my future would be one of sobriety.

Kirstie chuckled. "It was lovely of you to do all this, but I think most of it will have to go." Then she grimaced. "If I'm honest, all of it will."

"I'll get a box," I said.

At nine o'clock the doorbell jangled, and Jasper dragged Muriel Connibeare into the shop. She gripped the lead for dear life, while he bounded towards us, tail wagging, his jowls flapping, speckling the air with saliva. When he leapt up at me, I patted his head, taking care to avoid his mouth.

"Down!" Kirstie pointed to the floor.

Jasper sat, looking expectantly at us. Muriel clutched her chest. "Well, I never! I tell him that all the time, but he won't listen to me."

Kirstie took the lead from her and smiled. "Let's have a chat about what he gets up to and then maybe we can go for a stroll. Come through here."

Frowning, Muriel gazed around the bare space. "Oh, I don't know why, but I was expecting something with an agony aunt feel. You know, like Becki's fortune-telling room – it says what it does on the tin." She turned to me. "You could have made more of an effort, Jenn."

Chapter 12

Kirstie gave me an apologetic smile but didn't mention that I had indeed decorated the room. Neither did I. Muriel was one of Becki's customers, and her choice of décor might not be to everyone else's taste. Instead, I went off to make drinks and to replenish the bowl of water that Jasper had lapped dry.

Twenty minutes later, they left the shop, returning with a docile Jasper and a beaming Muriel.

"Well, I never," she said for the umpteenth time. "Kirstie is an absolute marvel."

Kirstie pulled out her diary. "Let's get another date sorted and then you can order that harness from Jenn I told you about."

"I'll have a few bags of those training treats too," Muriel said.

As Muriel left, another woman came in, with a King Charles spaniel. I recognised them from the craft fair. Dave had attacked Meg when she'd dressed as a dog to promote my shop. But now his gorgeous eyes turned on me, begging me to stroke him. I kept my hand clear, preferring to keep my fingers.

The woman looked around the shelves and shook her head. "In all my years in Torringham, I never knew this was here."

As Kirstie ushered her through to the back room, I heard her say, "I'm glad I've brought my purse. Dave needs a few new toys."

I smiled to myself. This was working out better than I could have hoped. Kirstie had three new customers today and more lined up over the next few weeks. With the small cut she was giving me and the extra sales, my till would be ringing a healthy balance.

When I returned after making the drinks, I found Meg in the shop, her eyes gleaming. "What did Kirstie think of our makeover?"

"She made me take it all down."

"No! What a meanie. We spent ages on it."

I shrugged. "It did look tacky. At least Becki can have her stuff back."

"Tacky?" she gasped. "It looked amazing."

I didn't say anything. We'd been drunk the night before, but once my beer goggles had worn off, I could see the room as it really was. Tasteless, vulgar, cheap. Take your pick.

"Why are you here? Aren't you meant to be working?" I asked.

She pulled a face. "I needed to warn you. Peter Drew's on the warpath. When he came into the shop looking for me, I slipped out the other door, leaving Sarah to deal with him."

"Why would you need to warn me?"

Without explanation, she dropped to all fours and scurried behind the counter.

"What are…"

I trailed to a stop as Peter Drew's angry face loomed

through the door pane. As he stomped inside, the doorbell jangled and Dave gave a gruff bark from the back room. Confused, I glanced down at Meg. She put her finger to her mouth.

I greeted Peter as if he was a customer. "Hello—"

He jabbed his finger at me. "Don't you dare hello me. Not after what you've done."

I kept my tone civil, aware that behind the door sat Kirstie, her client and Dave, who gave another bark. Thank goodness I'd kept Roo upstairs, worried that dogs needing an agony aunt might not welcome his presence.

"Please keep your voice down. I have customers here."

He looked around the empty shop, sneering, "Yes, of course, you must feel overwhelmed. No wonder another pet shop is coming to town."

I gritted my teeth. I wouldn't rise to his bait.

He took a deep breath, as if readying himself to launch again, but he was distracted by a squeal of "*No!* Dave!", followed by another growl from the other side of the door.

Then Kirstie's more measured tone. "Sit."

Peter came closer. Forgetting that Meg was crouching behind the counter, I stepped back, treading on something. A muffled groan told me it was her fingers.

How dare he come here, accusing me of goodness knows what. After all, he'd been the one calling me a witch and spreading rumours about my relationship with Meg. Okay, she'd been the instigator of the gossip and no doubt she was behind his appearance now, but I decided that attack was the best form of defence. "I heard what you've been saying about me." I kept my voice low, but I couldn't mask my fury. "But I have absolutely no interest in your boring little life."

"But you do in my business." As he leaned forward to snarl at me, the strip light reflected on his bald head, accentuating his strange, pointed scalp. Along with his beanpole body, it gave him an alien appearance. If I had to place him on any planet, it would be Mars. His hue was the same reddish colour. It deepened when I joined him in finger-pointing.

"I have no interest in your shop. In fact, I have no idea what you're blathering on about." I'd never used that word before, but it seemed appropriate.

From the storeroom came the sound of chairs scraping on the tiled floor. I gave Peter my most condescending smile. "I'd advise you to leave now, before you get to meet Dave. Believe me, his bite is definitely worse than his bark."

Peter didn't move. Surely he wouldn't cause a fuss in front of Kirstie's customer? The storeroom door clicked open. Still he hesitated, his gaze darting from me to Kirstie, the woman and Dave. His lips parted, as if he was going to say something, then he whirled around and marched off, pausing by the door.

"I don't want to hear you spouting any more of your wretched nonsense." With that he left, slamming the door behind him. The building seemed to shudder, then fall silent. As Kirstie walked over with her customer and Dave, Meg popped her head above the counter. She got to her feet, rubbing her hand and wincing.

"Thanks for that—"

A sudden ferocious barking brought her to a halt. She shot back. Behind her a large spider scuttled across the wall. I liked spiders, whereas she didn't, so I was grateful she faced Dave. But I doubted she'd see it that way. Especially when he strained against his lead and bared his teeth, showing impressive fangs for such a small dog.

"Dave! Dave!" the woman screeched.

Kirstie quietened Dave with a sharp command, then turned to me. "We heard shouting, so we decided to take Dave outside as he was getting a bit upset."

Wide-eyed, Meg pointed towards the dog. "Is that…"

Dave snarled again, tugging at his lead to get to Meg. When Kirstie frowned, I said, "She and Dave have met before."

"Dave really doesn't like you, does he?" A thoughtful glint lit Kirstie's eyes as she turned to Meg. "I wonder … are you busy right now? Could you give us a hand with Dave? I have an idea."

Meg gave Kirstie an apologetic shrug. "Sor—"

"Yes, she can," I said, awarding Meg a beatific smile. "Meg owes me a favour. Don't you, Meg? She'd be only too happy to help. I'll let Sarah know that she's going to be a bit longer."

Chapter 13

Although Meg had tried to change the subject when I'd asked about the rumour she'd started about Peter Drew's business, it wasn't long before I discovered the truth. Rosemary Boddy came into the pet shop while I was serving Anita Davies.

She tapped Anita on the shoulder. "You didn't buy your top from Peter Drew, did you?"

Anita shot around, glaring at her. "What do you mean?"

Rosemary looked affronted. "You advised me to try Peter Drew, as his clothes were top quality. But I've heard different. Have you spoken to Hilda? She's furious – she bought her granddaughter an expensive party dress from his shop and it's fraying already. Edna told her that's what comes from buying clothes off the back of a lorry."

Anita's face paled and she delved into her handbag to draw out her purse. "It seems I've been duped."

Rosemary mirrored her tight expression. "It seems we've all been. Edna was telling Hilda that his clothes don't meet current fire regulations, so the material could burst into flames at any minute. I've read about those poor mites and their nightclothes catching fire."

Puzzled, I asked, "For no reason? Like spontaneous combustion?"

She harrumphed. "Don't be daft! But they don't need more than a whiff of a flame and poof!" Her hands shot in the air. "Frazzled to a crisp."

At this rate, the gossip would change, like Chinese whispers, into accusations of Peter Drew murdering someone. While I wouldn't defend him, neither would I join in. But as I rang up Anita's cat food, Rosemary folded her arms and gave me a hard stare.

"So, what do you think of this business? I heard what he said about you and Meg. My Jim says we need a better man in charge of the Torringham Traders, not a self-serving liar like him."

When Anita nodded, Rosemary ploughed on. "Meg was telling me how he stopped the council from telling the grockles about this street." I winced at the term the locals used for holidaymakers, but Rosemary didn't notice. "He wanted to keep their custom all to himself. Hilda told me that was true."

Their gazes fell on me. I swallowed. "That part is right. I'm not sure about the rest." Then I swore to myself. Knowing my luck, they'd rush out to tell everyone that I'd confirmed all the gossip about Peter Drew. "Look, please don't involve me in this. I don't need Peter Drew coming back here and shooting his mouth off again."

They gaped at me. "He did that? What a bully!" Anita gasped.

"You wait until I tell Hilda that. She won't be happy with him picking on a woman," Rosemary muttered.

I rolled my eyes. Now I'd gone and done it. I had a feeling that, thanks to my ill-considered comment, things were about to get a lot worse.

♦

A few days later Meg banged on my shop window, interrupting a phone order. I stuck up a finger to show that I'd be a minute, but she pointed towards the road and mouthed at me to come out. I guessed what she wanted me to do. The previous day she'd told me that she and Andy would be measuring the posts in the street, to get the dimensions for the new decorative signage. They'd also check the distance between lamp posts, so the traders could create bunting. The committee had taken that idea from the bunting in my alleyway, so I was pleased to know that it had a thumbs-up from them.

Outside a builder's van sat on the double yellow lines, blocking my view of Meg and Andy. On its roof perched a herring gull, its beak cavernous as it cried to the other gulls circling above. The banging and clattering from my new competitor's shop clearly didn't bother them, unlike Roo and my customers. While Roo kept up an incessant barking at some of the louder hammer blows, my customers soon dashed out.

As I stepped out of the shadowy alley, the warm spring air made me long to spend a few hours lazing beneath the azure sky. But I couldn't leave my shop unattended too long, so I hurried across the road. Meg stood at the top of a ladder that Andy was holding. He gave me a broad smile.

"We're going to make this the biggest one. That'll show them," he said. "That Peter Drew is in for a right lamping when I see him."

I wasn't sure what he meant but, from the way he brandished his fist, I imagined that it involved a fight.

"Meg was telling me what he said to you. Now the fool's started on me."

Meg shouted down, "Some idiot called the council on Andy."

"Said they'd seen mice in my place. Bunch of lies! Environmental Health found nothing." Again, Andy held up his fist. "Next time I see him, I'm going to shove this down his cake hole."

Meg laughed. "That's about right coming from a baker." She stretched the tape measure along the post, which had a T-bar on which to hook hanging baskets. "This'll be the size. Will it be fine here, Jenn? The council said we have to ensure there's a good clearance below."

"That's perfect, thanks." I gazed back towards my shop, but the van hid the alley from view. "I'd better get back."

A splatting sound stopped me in my tracks. Meg stood there, frozen, gooey stuff dripping from her shoulder, speckles daubing her hair.

"I don't believe it!" she groaned.

Andy laughed. "They don't call them shitehawks for nothing."

"It's meant to be lucky," I said, although I'd never understood why anyone would believe that.

She scowled at me. "Says who?" Grimacing, she used her sleeve to wipe her shoulder, smearing the gloop into a bigger mess.

"Oh, look who that is," she growled.

A car pulled up behind the van and my soon-to-be competitor got out. He gave us a brief smile, which faded when Andy folded his arms and glared at him. Even though I knew he could put me out of business, I felt a twinge of sympathy for him, especially after I'd been so mean the other morning.

I touched Andy's arm. "It's not his fault."

"I can't believe you're sticking up for him," Andy said. "He didn't have to pick the place next to yours to open a pet shop. Strange that Peter Drew was all for pushing for the retail units in Beach Street to get residential planning – until his mate moves here. Maybe he's got a bigger plan. Why else would he be trying to shut me down with all that nonsense about mice?"

I didn't answer. Although Peter had misused his power as chairman of the Torringham Traders to convince the council to support the High Street at the expense of Beach Street, I couldn't help wishing that we could get back to how we'd been. No 'them and us'. No 'this street' and 'that street'. But, as I'd feared, Meg's war with Peter had already escalated. We had to put a stop to it before it impacted on our livelihoods. But there would be no speaking to Peter. Or Meg. They were as pig-headed as each other.

Back inside, I found Rachel Arscott standing inside the door.

"Sorry, I was just across the road," I said.

She smiled. "I saw you all. Andy didn't look happy. I heard about his mouse issue."

"But that was someone playing dirty. The council didn't find anything. He's got five stars for hygiene."

She picked up a pack of canned food and put it on the counter. "I thought there might be something more to it. Keith had a visit too."

I shook my head. "Did they think that mice have a taste for fish?"

She shrugged. "Maybe the council thought they'd kill two birds with one stone and check them both at the same time." Then she chuckled. "Talking about that, I heard Keith and Becki are a right pair of lovebirds. I didn't believe it at first, but I saw Keith leaving her house the other morning."

I hadn't seen much of Becki since she'd got together with Keith at the May Fair. While we'd messaged a few times, she'd answered my questions about their relationship with a standard 'It's going well'. Maybe I'd suggest a Sunday outing to the beach. It had been ages since we'd gone there – and the weather forecast promised a wonderful day. As soon as Rachel left the shop, I WhatsApped Meg and Becki on our shared group, first offering condolences to Meg on the state of her top, then suggesting a picnic at Pixie Cove. Moments later my phone dinged. Keith responded, saying it was a grand idea. I frowned. Had Becki invited Keith into our group? Another message popped up: Andy with a picture of a poop-covered Meg, that he must have taken when she wasn't looking.

I'll bring cakes, he said.

Then Hilda – how on earth would she make it down the steps? – messaged, saying she'd be delighted to come.

The penny dropped. I'd sent the message to the Beach Street WhatsApp group. For a moment I felt annoyed with myself, but then I shrugged. What harm could it do? They were a nice bunch.

Then another message popped up. Meg this time, with an 'angry face' emoji. *Delete that photo now, Andy, or there will be murder on the beach.*

And his response? Three 'crying with laughter' emojis and the ominous words *Bring Peter and I'll make sure of it.*

Chapter 14

Meg and I arrived at Pixie Cove to find that Becki and Keith had already set up their chairs, picnic basket and a blanket by the base of the cliff. After assessing the overhanging rocks, the ridges of grass and weeds, and the tumble of debris from a recent rock fall, I suggested they move. When they brushed aside my concerns, I placed my chair opposite them – well clear of potential danger. Meg dropped into her seat, leaving me to put up her large garden umbrella, holding it fast with stones, and to decant the dog's water into a bowl. Before I'd finished, Amber and Roo had moved into the shade.

The cove was filling with people, but I'd never seen it packed. Like Beach Street, it wasn't easily discoverable by day-trippers, who tended to congregate around the harbour or the larger pebbled beach. But we preferred the quieter cove. Enclosed by tall, red cliffs and the woodland above, its main entrance was down uneven steps and through an old stone archway. The beach offered a wonderful view across the bay. Ahead a ferry crossed to Berrinton, gliding past a fishing boat and yachts with billowing sails.

While the others chatted, I settled back to watch the waves whispering over the pebbles and lapping at the seaweed-strewn rocks, which were dotted with limpets. If we lifted them, we'd find crabs. I'd rescued a few from Roo – or, to be more accurate, I'd saved Roo's nose from being pincered.

The arrival of Andy and his wife interrupted my reverie. He stuck his tongue out at Meg, who picked up a pebble and threw it at him. Laughing, he ducked, and tossed a shell at her, which hit her on the nose. When she threatened him with another one, Becki stepped in.

"Where's Hilda and the others?" I asked.

Becki shielded her eyes with her hands and pointed out to sea. "They should be arriving soon."

"By boat?"

I couldn't imagine Hilda wading through the water. But my query was answered when a small boat chugged into view. Minutes later, a woman and man jumped into the shallows to drag it ashore. Once a few other traders had clambered out, they helped Hilda onto the pebble beach without a toe getting wet, but she batted them away when they tried to help her into a deckchair.

"Call me when you're ready to go back," her great-granddaughter said, putting the finishing touches to Hilda's parasol.

"Her's a lovely maid, her is." Hilda beamed and waved her away. Unlike her children and grandchildren, she spoke in what sounded to my uninformed ears like a typical Devon dialect, even though she'd moved just thirty miles from mid-Devon to be with her husband and had lived in Torringham for most of her life. Maybe hers was mixed with the original Torringham accent, which rarely heard since us incomers had moved in. "Now, what's this nonsense I've been hearing about mice and whatnot?"

"My visit wasn't about mice," Keith said, surprising us all. "I've been accused of selling black-market fish, among other things."

Meg frowned. "How's that possible? Don't all fish come from the sea?"

Keith grinned. "Yes, but fishermen have quotas, so they can't land certain fish. Like bass, for instance. Someone said my bass had been bought on the black market and I was doing other dodgy stuff with mislabelling and so on. But I could prove I got it from the fish market and a boat with the right licence, and my labelling was all above board. I don't know what whoever it was hoped to achieve – they must have known I'd have legit. papers."

"And I didn't have a single mouse or dropping in sight," said Andy. "Not only that, but my paperwork and hygiene is top-drawer. Whoever's doing this is a right barmpot."

"Well, we're definitely being targeted," Meg said. "And we know who's doing it too. So what are we going to do about it?"

"Nothing," I said.

They gawped at me – even Becki, who wasn't one to join in a spat. The shade of her floppy straw hat – which hid her blue and pink hair – couldn't mask her flaming cheeks. She touched Keith's knee and whispered, "Should I say something?"

When he nodded, she cleared her throat. Her gaze

flickered towards me and Meg. "I haven't told you yet."
She shrugged. "To be honest, I'm embarrassed about it, as
it's a difficult accusation to defend. But you know me. I
don't lie—"

"Honest as the day comes," Keith broke in.

She gave him a wan smile. "Apparently, I'm a
charlatan. In my readings, I tell people what I've found
out by stalking them on Facebook and the like. It doesn't
help that I do know many of my customers, but someone
has just put a horrible post on the Facebook Spotted
Torringham page – anonymous, of course – saying that
I'm an out-and-out liar."

To gasps, Sheila nodded. "I saw that. I put them right."

"Thank you," Becki said. "But there were enough
people bundling in to say that what I do is a load of bull,
although none of those people had been to my shop.
Whoever it was said they'd booked a reading and they'd
been making up fake posts beforehand to test me.
Apparently, I spouted their lies in the reading, which
proves I'm a fake." She shrugged. "The thing is, I know
that I don't stalk people, but I can't prove that they haven't
visited my shop. It's difficult when you don't know who
they are."

Andy grimaced. "Can't you look into your crystal ball
or something and find out?"

She gave a forced chuckle. "It doesn't work that way.
All I know is that I'd never stoop to researching people
before I do a reading, but who will believe me now?"

We fell silent. So far, three of the Beach Street traders

had been targeted. But only one had been harmed immeasurably. How could we help to salvage Becki's reputation? She was one of the kindest, most gentle souls I knew. I went over to give her a hug.

"So what are you going to do about it?" Hilda's beady eyes turned on Becki.

"You have to do something. We *all* have to. It's only a matter of time before it happens to the rest of us," Meg said.

Sheila pursed her lips. "I think it already has. Are you selling out-of-date dog food, by any chance, Jenn, and covering the dates with price stickers?"

My mouth fell open. *What?* But I didn't get the chance to ask. She looked at Meg. "And did some of your wool contain moth eggs that hatched and destroyed a customer's clothing? It wrecked her whole wardrobe, leaving her cardis full of holes, by all accounts."

"That's ridiculous!" Meg leapt to her feet. "Who said that? For a start, none of my customers has mentioned a thing. If it was true – which it isn't – I'd have whacking great big holes in the goods in my shop."

Hilda surveyed each of us. "Folk would have to be daft as a brush to believe that nonsense. But, what I want to know is, where's this all leading to?"

I sat, dumbfounded. Unlike the rest of them, the gossip about me could be plausible. I mean, maybe a tin had slipped through – and possibly I'd put the price tag at the top, accidentally covering the date – but pet food had long sell-by dates, so it seemed unlikely.

Hilda raised a bony fist. "If they said a word about me, I'd bleddy give them what for!"

"Well, they've given us a bloody nose all right." Meg's eyes glimmered with anger, but a devious smile lit her lips. "Now it's our turn."

"Meg…" I said. "Should we be stirring things even more? I mean, this wouldn't have got so bad if we'd left well alone."

She glared at me. "You know full well that Peter started this with his attempt to turn Nancy's hardware shop into holiday lets. And he reckons competition is a good thing. So why don't we take it from them?"

But Peter must have changed his mind about Beach Street being a good location for more holiday apartments. After all, he was friends with the man who'd bought the shop next to mine. And this latest spat was Peter's revenge after Meg had spread the rumour about his poor-quality clothing. We could keep going forever in a constant battle of tit-for-tat. Even if we won this war, it would be a hollow victory if we ended up with damaged businesses and reputations.

I didn't say anything, though. None of my friends were in the mood to listen.

"How?" Becki frowned. The others leaned forward eagerly.

Meg grinned. "Well, we could do with Hilda and her gang of helpers."

Chapter 15

It took a week for our plans to fall into place. I say 'our' plans, as I agreed to join in with part of the scheme when I realised that some of Meg's ideas were positive. Thankfully, the gossip didn't seem to have harmed my business, although I did catch the odd customer checking the sell-by dates on my products. I knew they wouldn't find anything wrong, as I'd already gone through the shop, and the stock in my lounge and bedroom, and discovered nothing amiss.

Another blessing was that the soon-to-be pet shop next door was quiet, with not a hammer blow or a scrape to be heard. The windows had been whitewashed to hide whatever was being undertaken inside. No vans pulled up outside either, which made me wonder if the builders had disappeared, telling the owner they'd be back 'dreckly' – the West Country version of 'mañana'. When Tim and I had bought the pet shop, we'd hired a builder who'd moved from Cornwall. He'd used that expression all the time – but, as we soon came to learn, tomorrow never comes.

I couldn't help being pleased about this. It gave me more time to win extra customers, for Kirstie to build her agony aunt business, and to progress Meg's plan. Also, the street decorations would arrive soon and we had another craft market to attend at the weekend. That would be the start of the Beach Street traders fighting back.

In the meantime, I invited Becki and Meg out for a dog walk, followed by a few drinks in the pub. I felt bad for not contacting Becki recently, even though it had been difficult to see her as she and Keith seemed glued together. She agreed to come after tea but, as I was eating mine, she phoned to say she had to help her cousin with an urgent issue and would I mind leaving it until eight.

"We can make it another night," I said.

"That's all right. I could do with some fresh air. I've been cooped up in that shop all day. I won't be long."

Famous last words. When Meg arrived with Amber in tow, she looked aghast at the thought of waiting an hour to go for a walk. Unfortunately, the hour stretched to two, with Becki pleading by text for us to wait for her.

"She's bringing her cousin's dog. Her cousin's hurt her foot and she can't walk her."

Meg's face fell. "Not Mandy!"

"Mandy? Is that a dog's name?"

Meg took a glug of wine. "What is it with people getting Great Danes? That sodding thing humping me in the fancy dress comp wrecked my chances."

Finally, Becki texted to say she was on her way and she'd meet us outside her house. We arrived there, panting, after taking the steps rather than the longer route. When Becki appeared at her front door, a huge black dog dragged her halfway down the path before she shouted, "Heel!" and yanked her back so she could close the door.

"She's a bit lively," Becki said, as Amber and Roo cowered behind my legs.

I studied her sandals. "Haven't you got something more sensible to wear?"

But she waved me away. "They're comfy."

The dusk deepened as we headed towards Parkside Green, scene of the May Fair debacle with Meg and Peter Drew. The moon shimmered on the horizon and the lighthouse beamed out over an inky sea. Across the bay, Berrinton's lights twinkled from houses and streetlamps, and the flashing blue lights of an emergency vehicle rushed along the coast road. Becki and Meg had become silhouettes, Amber and Roo hues of grey, while Mandy had become invisible, her whereabouts signalled only by the thump of her paws and her heavy panting. One of the lovely things about mid-May was being able to walk the dogs in the lighter evenings but, since Becki was so late, we had no choice but to put on our mobile phone torches so we could see what the dogs were doing.

Meg pulled out a poop bag and traipsed off to clean up after Amber, while Amber bounded away to join the other dogs, becoming shapes hurtling around the park in a game of chase – too close to the road. We called them back and moved to the other side of the park, beside fenced gardens.

Becki's phone rang. "It's my cousin," she said, and headed a few paces away to take the call in private.

"Are you going to fetch those leaflets about our promotion day from the printer?" Meg asked me. "If you're too busy, I can do it."

"It's fine," I said. "I'm happy to go during my lunch break. Do you think it will work?"

She shrugged. "Like all best-laid plans ... who knows? It's worth a try, though."

The dogs' paws pounded the grass, closing in on us. Meg and I spun around as Roo and Amber swerved past. But I couldn't see Mandy. A shriek cut the air. Becki! Then there was a loud thud. Light pierced the night before disappearing. Meg and I directed our torches in Becki's direction: the beams picked her out, lying on her back, groaning.

"Blasted dog!" she gasped. We held out our hands to pull her up, but she waved us away. "Don't move me yet. I think I've done myself a serious injury."

Mandy appeared and slurped at her face, ignoring Becki, who covered her head with her hands, screeching, "Get off, you daft mutt!" But Mandy wagged her tail and nosed between them.

"Watch out!" Meg said. "She'll be humping you in a minute."

The two other dogs raced over, joining Mandy's game.

"Ouch!" Becki cried as one of them trod on her stomach, while Mandy pawed her head. "Get me up!"

But we couldn't. Meg was bent double snorting with laughter, which made me crease up too. Finally, we composed ourselves and hauled Becki to her feet. She brushed herself down and tried twisting around to inspect any damage, while Mandy bounded around her.

"My phone!" she said.

I trained my torch on the ground, relieved to spot Becki's mobile glinting in the grass. As I handed it to her, she wailed, "My shoe!" and lifted a bare foot.

Unlike the park, the patch between the path and the gardens was unkempt. As Meg and I stumbled over the uneven ground in search of her missing sandal, we couldn't help sniggering at Becki, who hopped along the path.

Finally, Meg shone her torch at a wooden fence. "Are you sure it didn't go into this garden? I saw something flying through the air."

"I hope not," Becki said. "That's Grant's place."

Meg frowned and assessed the house. "So it is."

"I don't suppose—"

"No!" Meg said. "Do your own dirty work. You wanted to wear those flimsy things."

"I can't." Becki wriggled her toes. "I'd get splinters."

They gazed at me. "Oh no!" I said. "I'm not knocking on Grant's door."

Two minutes later, they were hefting me over the fence. This way, they reasoned, I didn't have to ask if I could search his garden. Straddling the fence, I could see the back of Grant's head. He was watching TV. Hurriedly, I slipped down the other side, wincing as a splinter cut into my palm. It was only when I landed in a flowerbed that I realised I'd have little hope of finding the shoe without being able to use my torch. If I did, Grant would spot me in his garden. Moaning about my stupidity, I gnawed at the splinter, surveying my surroundings. But the only way I'd find it was by touch, so I knelt on the grass and skimmed the flowerbed and surrounding area with my hands. Nothing. If Becki's shoe was here, it was doing a fine job of staying hidden.

"I can't see it," I hissed.

Then I gazed at the fence. How would I get back over it unaided? The cross-boards were on the other side. The vertical planks were like a cliff face. I could touch the top, but I wasn't fit enough to pull myself over.

Grant got up and headed towards the patio door. My heart thudded. Had he seen me? Hurriedly, I crawled across the flowerbed, earth squidging into the knees of my jeans. The stem of a plant snapped, and I cursed. It was bad enough being here, never mind damaging his garden.

As I tried to hide at the foot of his fence, the patio door scraped open and Grant called, "Ruby, come on in now."

At that moment, Meg chose to pop her head over the parapet. "Are you still…"

She dived back down. Too late. Grant had spotted her. "Who's that?" he called. "Ruby!" He slapped his legs. "Come here, girl, and get them."

Was the dog inside or out? It was hard to tell – except, if it was in the garden, I'd have expected it to have found me by now. I hoped it wasn't a guard dog. I knew Grant lived alone, but I hadn't seen him walking a dog and he'd never been in my pet shop. Having said that, he was Peter Drew's best friend, which meant he was unlikely to do so. Meg didn't call him Grant Brown-tongue for nothing. But any dog would soon sniff me out. Hurriedly, I scrambled along the fence line until I could pick out next door's fence.

"Ruby!" he shouted. He went back inside, leaving the patio door ajar. His irate voice echoed from the house. Then he stepped onto the patio, clutching something. A treat? His voice turned concerned. "Ruby! Where are you, girl?"

Spurred on by adrenaline, I hoisted myself up the neighbour's fence, using the horizontal beams for support. Once on the other side, I felt safe – which was daft, as I was in another garden. Which might also have a dog.

The back fence to this house was easier to climb, so I pulled myself over and dropped to the ground. The three dogs pounced on me.

"Ruby! Ruby!" Grant's voice moved closer, sounding despairing.

"He's lost his dog," I kept my voice low as I brushed myself down.

"A good thing too, or else you might not have a leg," Meg hissed, then she grinned. "Don't worry, it's only a small thing – although it still has teeth."

I glared at her. "And you let me go over there knowing that?"

Becki's face fell. "You didn't get my shoe."

"Ruuubbbyyyyyyy?" Grant's plaintive cry rose in the air.

"We should go and help him," I said.

Meg shook her head. "Are you daft? The dog's probably hiding somewhere. I'm forever searching for Amber."

I gave her a doubtful look. Amber was too big to hide

for long in Meg's small flat.

"So I've got to walk home with just one shoe?" Becki said.

"'Fraid so." I plucked a twig from my hair. "Because I'm not going back in there. I feel bad enough that I crushed half his plants – and I've wrecked my clothes."

Meg shushed us, putting a warning arm on my shoulder. A beam of light scorched the night sky. It came from the direction of Grant's garden.

"He's got one of those million-watt torch thingies," she whispered. "Let's get going before he sees us."

Chapter 16

Leaflets in hand, I made my way down to the market. After being walked and fed, Roo was safely tucked in the lounge – no doubt now on the settee. The sun dazzled in a sky littered with white puffs of cloud, making the street feel a cheerful place, especially with the new bunting fluttering above.

As I passed a lamp post I pulled to a stop. A 'missing dog' poster had been attached to the pole. It showed a gorgeous Pomeranian pup, while the text below said her name was Ruby and she'd been taken from her owner's garden in Parkside Green. I grimaced. My foot – and knee – prints would be on the crime scene. Would they lead the police to my door? Worse, this gorgeous little puppy had been taken and neither she nor poor Grant – it didn't matter if I liked him or not – deserved that. My mood dampened, I walked on. We should do something to help Grant and Ruby. But what? I didn't get the chance to ask Meg, as she greeted me with a snarl and a screwed-up sheet of paper.

"You won't believe what Peter sodding Drew has been doing." Without waiting for a response, she said, "Tearing down our posters, that's what. How can we advertise our promotion day if he's going around taking them down and putting up this?" She flattened the sheet and thumped it. "The High Street … the only place in town for a quality-guaranteed buy. What rubbish!"

I sighed. "He's just playing us at our own game."

"Well, he won't win," she snarled and stomped off to our stall.

"Not wearing your dog costume today, Meg?" Keith called.

"No!" she growled. Then she gave him a radiant smile. "Well, not yet. I've got something else I need to sort out first."

Keith raised his eyebrows and hissed to me, "That sounds ominous."

I had no idea what she was planning, until I saw Kirstie. Looking horrified, she pointed towards Meg. "Have you seen what she wants me to wear?"

I shook my head. "A dog costume?"

"Worse. She wants me to dress up like Mrs Brown."

When I gave her a puzzled look, she dragged me over to where Meg sat. "Show her that awful dress."

"What, this?" Meg held up a flowery garment she must have found in the back of Hilda's wardrobe. "It's the perfect agony aunt garb."

Kirstie sighed. "Have you ever seen Dear Deidre wearing something like that? And what about that awful wig?"

Becki peered over my shoulder. "Very, er..." She trailed off.

"Why don't you wear it if you think it's so great?" Kirstie asked Meg.

"I'm your dog," Meg said. "You're going to teach me a few tricks."

Kirstie rolled her eyes. "Look, I know you mean well, but I'm a professional. If you want to do this, fine, but please don't involve me."

"I'll do it. I need something to hide my hair." Becki flattened her blue and pink fringe, showing a strip of dark roots. "Anyhow, I owe Jenn a favour, even if she didn't find my shoe."

I wished I could tell Kirstie that none of this had anything to do with me. But it felt disloyal to do so when my friends were just trying to help. Although I suspected that it gave Meg an outlet for her unrealised childhood dream of stardom, or something like that. She'd once mentioned joining the local am dram society until she'd discovered that Grant was a member.

Shaking her head, Kirstie walked away. Meg passed Becki the flowery dress and a grey wig. "Hold on," she said. "Don't forget the Nora Batty tights."

♦

An hour later, Becki and Meg were providing an entertaining side show, with Becki giving commands to Meg, who dutifully rolled over, sat down or pretended to lap up a treat. Becki's outfit fitted her well, even if her tights – or, more accurately, pop socks – wrinkled around her ankles. Thankfully, with no Dave the dog in sight, both were safe in their costumes – until Mrs Hollacombe headed their way in her mobility scooter. Grim-faced, she ploughed through the fleeing crowds, tooting as parents dragged children away from her and people hoiked dogs to safety. Even the gulls knew better than to stand their ground. Posters advertising her nephew's mackerel fishing tours and her son Gary's café had been sellotaped to the scooter's bars, basket and the rear of her seat. I wondered what her family thought about her mowing down potential customers. It wouldn't win much trade. As she closed in on Meg and Becki, she seemed to speed up. Would they move? Trapped behind the table, I had no chance of getting to them before she did. But Becki grabbed Meg's furry arm and hauled her to the protection of our stand.

Meg rounded on Becki. "What did you do that for? I wasn't going to let her win." She shook her fist at Mrs Hollacombe and shouted, "You'll kill somebody one day!"

But the woman drove on, people scurrying like ants to either side. Finally she disappeared, and the laughter and chatter resumed, drowning out the faint sound of tooting.

Among all this, Kirstie stood calmly with real dog owners and explained the benefits of her services, while I looked after the stall with Keith.

A familiar man came into view, wearing a checked jacket and beige trousers: my soon-to-be neighbour. Groaning, I occupied myself tidying up the leaflets and sale items on the stall. Even so, I couldn't help peeking at him. He stood grinning at Becki and Meg's antics. Neither seemed to have noticed him. He turned to me and a warm flush rose to my cheeks. I glanced away. How daft. But something about his smile made me want to look again.

He wandered over to Kirstie, who chatted to a woman. Was he thinking of poaching her for his own business? The thought annoyed me so much that I headed over. He seemed surprised to find me standing beside them, his gorgeous brown eyes widening. No wonder – the last time we'd met in our shared courtyard, I'd hardly been polite.

"Hello," he said.

I returned his greeting.

"I'm Dan." He held out his hand.

Behind me, Meg stood up, putting her furry hands on her hips. Even with her dog costume hiding her face, I could guess her expression.

"Jenn," I said.

His smile widened, showing white teeth and a dimple cutting into his cheek. If he wasn't in competition with me, I'd be simpering. The sun shone through his hair, giving it a warm, chestnut colour. He was trim and, by the quality of his clothes, he cared about himself. Unlike me. I wore an old pair of jeans, which sagged around my bum, and my comfy trainers, since I knew I'd be on my feet for most of the day.

"I'm just off for a walk along the coast path," he said.

Someone tapped my back. I groaned, knowing who it would be.

"I need you over here," Meg said.

After giving him my apologies, I followed her. Becki shook her head, but her eyes twinkled. "Fraternising with the competition?"

"I'm not rolling around on the ground for your benefit if you're going to sleep with the enemy." Meg handed me a pile of leaflets offering 10% off at all Beach Street shops on our promotion day. "Here, give these out. But don't let him have one. He'll tell Peter sodding Drew, who'll probably go one better and offer a 20% discount."

I left them to restart their training charade, while Dan continued to talk to Kirstie. What were they discussing? If only Meg hadn't hauled me away. Keeping an eye on them, I distributed the leaflets to passers-by, frustrated by my inability to lip-read. Finally, he left and I dived over to Kirstie, beating an elderly man with a doddering Jack Russell.

Before I could ask, she pre-empted my question. "He seems nice. He's opening up next door to you."

"I know."

"He's calling his shop The Rover's Return."

"At least he's picked a proper dog's name for it," I said. "Better than Mandy's Bone Palace or Dave's Doggy Delights."

She frowned, then shook her head. "No offence, but I think your barking mad friends have rubbed off on you."

The elderly man tapped her on the shoulder. He jerked his head towards Becki and Meg. "They said you could help me with my Jack—"

"Of course," Kirstie said. "What can I do for little Jack?"

He looked confused. "That's not his name. He's a Jack Russell." He scratched his head. "I thought that was obvious. Are you in training?"

"Yes, I am," Kirstie said.

"Well, that's no good. My Patch needs someone with experience."

Now it was Kirstie's turn to look perplexed. "I've been doing this for five years. I've got references and an excellent track record of working with dogs."

The man looked put out. "Only a moment ago, you told me you were in training."

"That's right," Kirstie said, missing his point.

Interrupting, I touched her arm and addressed the man. "Kirstie means training is what she does. She's not still learning the ropes."

He glared at her. "Well, why didn't she make that clear? I hope she speaks to dogs better than she does to humans."

Chapter 17

The Beach Street traders' promotion day had arrived – but we'd given it the jazzier name of 'fun day'. The street decorations had only been put up the previous day. Ornamental features such as a fish, needle and thread, and scones had been fixed in between the hanging baskets. I had to admit that my dog looked great, a bit like Scooby Doo. I'd heard that Peter Drew had called the decorations tacky, but they made the street look cheerful.

As agreed, we all got up early and made it to Becki's shop for six thirty, where helium gas had been delivered for the balloons. Once we'd blown up the balloons, tied to Meg's excess ribbons, and distributed them around the shops in the street, we started to put out tables and chairs on the wider sections of pavement, making sure to leave room for passing prams and wheelchairs.

Hilda had left one of her grandchildren to run her shop, so she and her team were free to organise the car park. This was the part that made me squirm and cover my ears whenever they mentioned their plans. But I didn't succeed in blocking out their excited chatter. When the holidaymakers – or locals – drove into the car park, they'd find the High Street closed, and would be 'encouraged' to take the longer route via the top of Beach Street, forcing them to walk the length of the street to the harbour. I'd tried pointing out that many visitors would want to go straight to the beach but Hilda wasn't having it. She'd lived in Torringham for all but seventeen of her ninety-two years, and no one knew the grockles better than she. Or so she said.

Each of us had agreed to dress up in clothing featuring our shops, which meant I'd reluctantly agreed to wear Meg's hot, stuffy dog costume. The smell reminded me of my old school's mildewed changing rooms. I popped a bottle of perfume in my pocket, ready to spray liberally when the need arose.

Becki had baulked at the idea of a costume, saying the coins strung around her silk headscarf were stereotypical claptrap. At least she looked fabulously mysterious – in contrast to Keith, who wore his usual white overcoat with a string of plastic fish around his neck. Andy's costume was just odd – it looked like an American hot dog to me – but he assured everyone it was a good old British sausage bap (even though he didn't sell sausages). His wife made up for it in her doughnut costume. But the outright winner was Meg, who'd fashioned an incredible mini dress from her stock of Torringham tea towels. With the sun blazing in the morning sky, we all gazed at her with envious eyes.

Rather than hide inside my pet shop, I'd agreed to pay one of Hilda's brood to man the till while I roamed the street outside. I wouldn't entertain Meg's idea of doing dog antics. I was far too boring for that. Unable to fit a table on the pavement, I put out a couple of coat stands to show off my range of dog neckerchiefs, collars and raincoats. But just as I'd finished setting everything out, a transit van pulled up. I groaned.

The builders had returned. As they put up ladders outside the shop next door, I went over to plead with them to move the van so my goods could be seen, but Meg beat me to it.

"Do you have to do that today, of all days? You can see it's meant to be a fun day."

The young lad shrugged and turned to his companion, who grimaced. "He didn't tell us about it. Give us a mo to get this done, then we'll go."

True to their word, before the church clock chimed nine, they'd installed a sign saying 'The Rover's Return' at the front and driven off, leaving us in a fug of diesel fumes.

Frowning, Meg gazed at the logo beside the wording. "Is that a bird?" She squinted as the sunlight dazzled the plastic. "Or a book?"

I shielded my eyes. It reminded me of a child's simple line drawing to illustrate a bird in the sky, but a little more artistic. Then again, it could be a book. Well, sort of … with a liberal dash of imagination. I frowned.

"Maybe he's going to specialise in…" I was about to say bird books – after all, what else would fit the bill in a pet shop? – then my hand flew to my mouth and I gasped. "I know why he wanted to speak to Kirstie, but he couldn't say anything in front of me. He's going for that angle. Books about dogs and training."

Groups of people moved towards us, shepherded by a teenage boy who pointed in our direction then shot off. Most of them continued down the street, their eyes masked by dark sunglasses, but one or two stopped. Those with dogs had the most time – they wouldn't be allowed onto the beach – so their owners had come to meander around Torringham and its harbour. For them, Beach Street was as good a place as any to start.

As time passed, more visitors appeared – and many locals too. Nearby one of my customers, Rosemary, stood talking to another woman. The word 'gas' filtered over and I cringed. Blasted Hilda! Why had I let them go ahead with this daft idea? But I kept my promise, and when a holidaymaker mentioned gas to me, I kept my expression blank. "A gas leak? I hope it gets sorted soon." Then I pointed towards the shop, telling her she could pay for her dog's neckerchief inside.

By one o' clock things were quietening down. Most of the day trippers had arrived and were at the beach or ambling around the harbour. Hopefully, many would come back this way. We'd done a roaring trade and my profits were better than they were most weeks, even with the 10% discount we'd all agreed to offer. As we congratulated each other on our successful morning, news reached us about a commotion in the High Street. Apparently, the police were in attendance.

Puzzled, I headed over to Meg. "I thought Hilda and her crew were going to stay there until noon, then come back?"

She frowned. "So did I."

A downcast figure hurried towards us. Grant Brown, of all people. Meg couldn't help trying to force a flyer into his hand. "Ribbons, tea towels – all 10% off."

He ignored her, but a few steps later he paused and turned back. "I-I … have you heard about my Ruby? I mean, you must have talked to loads of people today. Have they seen anything?" His eyes welled with tears. "The police think she's been stolen."

I'd seen reports of pet thefts in the area. But if I'd had such difficulty getting out of his garden, how would a thief have got in and taken Ruby? There had been no one around when we'd been there. I couldn't tell him that, though.

"There were footprints in my flowerbeds," he continued. "They must have come in from the rear, although goodness knows why. My garden only has a small side gate."

"I'm so sorry." I felt awful. I'd seen the poster about Ruby, but I hadn't done anything. When it came to something as important as this, I should have laid our old animosities aside. "What can we do to help?"

Meg put her arm around him to lead him towards her shop. He pulled out a wad of leaflets from his jacket pocket. Identical to the poster, but smaller.

"I can't stop. I have to distribute these."

"Have a cup of tea and we'll see what we can do to help." She turned to me. "I'll get Sarah to come out. Bring your stuff with you and she can direct buyers to your shop."

Embarrassed to be dressed as a dog in front of poor Grant – talk about rubbing salt into his wounds – I tossed my costume behind the counter in the pet shop and gave my helper instructions about where to find me. Outside, a welcome breeze rippled through my creased T-shirt, wafting away the claustrophobic smell of sweat that repeated sprays of perfume hadn't masked. After hefting my two coat racks laden with goods over to Meg's table I went into her shop, where I found Grant sitting on a chair. Gone was the proud, sneering man we'd often seen behind Peter, egging him on.

"Ruby is my life," he said. "I don't have anyone else."

Meg came out, clutching three mugs which she laid on the counter. "When did you last see her?"

"It was most odd. Usually Ruby goes out several times a night, but she's scratching at the patio door within a few minutes. This time, she didn't come back. I couldn't see her in the dark, so I left it a while before calling her again, thinking that she must be doing her business or something. But when I called again, I saw something by the back fence. Did I tell you they found a woman's sandal there? Why would you wear something like that to steal a dog?"

Meg glanced at me and swallowed. "I ... er ... I…"

We had to tell him the truth. The police might be looking for a person with size four footprints and another who wore size three sandals (Becki had tiny feet).

"That wasn't your dog nappers."

He gasped. "How do you know?"

"Because…" Meg trailed to a halt.

"It was us," I said.

"You?" His face flushed and his blue eyes glinted.

"Why?"

Meg laid her hand on his shoulder. "It was a complete accident. Becki was walking her cousin's dog – a huge thing – when it ran into her in the dark. She ended up injured on her back and with a missing shoe and phone. We searched everywhere. We found the phone, but not her shoe. We thought it had gone into your garden."

"So you thought you'd trample my plants?"

Meg winced. "That was my fault."

"No, it was mine," I said. "It was dark. I didn't want to go over the fence, but we couldn't leave Becki shoeless."

Except we had. Becki had hobbled home, cursing each time she stepped on a stone chip – I had no idea how many there were until we did that walk – or squidged in something she hoped wasn't what she thought it was.

"I heard you calling for Ruby."

Grant's startled expression told me I shouldn't have admitted that. Meg pulled up another chair and sat beside him. "Look, I'm sorry we went in your garden. But we were trying to help a friend. Like we're going to do for you. Tell us everything you can and we'll get the traders together. Hilda knows everyone – I reckon she could have the whole of Devon searching for Ruby by tomorrow."

Grant gave her a wry smile. "Talking about Hilda, have you seen the chaos in the High Street?"

Just then, Sarah popped her head through the door. "Becki's looking for both of you. There's big trouble."

"You go," Meg said to me. "I'll stay with Grant."

Chapter 18

Like me, Becki had taken the first opportunity to rid herself of her costume, whereas Keith seemed to have forgotten that he wore a plastic fish necklace that rattled as we sprinted across the car park to the High Street. We arrived to find Hilda, her arms folded, refusing to move, as she told the police that she'd been saving people from getting themselves killed if the gas main exploded. Keith whispered to us that, while stealing emergency roadwork signs and cones was illegal, no one could prove that they hadn't been put there by real road workers and opportunistically 'borrowed' by Hilda's team. The police didn't question Hilda's outfit – she looked like an air raid warden with her tin hat and felt jacket – but I suspected that they didn't want a repeat of their last stand-off with her.

"But," Peter Drew burst in, "there isn't any gas leak. You and your swindling family are just trying to put us out of business."

Hilda's grandson stepped into the fray, shrugging off a policeman who tried to hold him back. "Who are you calling swindlers? You're the one trying to put the Beach Street traders out of business with your lies."

"Lies?" Peter glared and jabbed a finger at the burly man. "You should hear what rubbish your grandmother has been spouting about me."

"I'll have you know that my word is my honour," Hilda

shouted.

The policeman stepped between them, trying to usher Peter away, but he dodged past to launch himself at her grandson, who pushed him off. Peter staggered backwards into another policeman, who grabbed him.

"It's not me you should be attacking!" Peter squealed as he squirmed to free himself from the policeman's grip.

"You need to arrest him!" Hilda shouted. "We're trying to be good citizens here. The likes of him give Torringham a bad name."

The policeman beside Hilda rolled his eyes. "I think you all need to calm down."

A crowd had formed, some videoing the scene on their mobile phones, others smirking. This didn't put any of us in a good light. And Peter was right. We had blocked off each end of the High Street, stopping his fellow shopkeepers from getting much-needed footfall on a busy Saturday. Whether we liked it or not, us Beach Street traders needed to leave and let the shops here make some money today.

I went over to Hilda to say we should go, but Peter wrenched himself free and flew at me.

"You started all of this!" he screeched. "I'm going to sort you lot out once and for all."

Strange how he had been the one to instigate this stupid battle between the traders, with Meg eagerly seizing his baton, yet he was blaming me. I'd tried to be the voice of reason, although I'd been drowned out by the rest of the Beach Street committee.

Keith moved beside me. "Leave her out of this. She's done nothing wrong."

"Shut up, fish face." Peter glowered at him. "Go back and sell your black-market bass or whatever it is you do."

"So it was you!" Keith growled. He tore off his fish necklace and bundled it into Becki's arms. For a moment, I thought he was about to go for Peter, but the policeman stopped him.

Peter smirked. "I didn't need to say a word when everyone knows the truth." He surveyed the crowd as if everyone could vouch for it, and pointed a trembling finger inches from Keith's chin. "You Beach Street traders give us all a bad name. Just because you've got failing businesses, there's no need to wreck ours."

Keith swatted his hand aside. "Failing business?" he growled. "It was doing really well before you started your shenanigans. And bringing Becki into it with your lies about her place is just not on."

Again, the policeman stepped beside Peter. "You need to move on now," he said to us all. "Go home." He pointed to Hilda's grandson, then the emergency signs. "Move those away. I want them back where they belong. And I never want to see this nonsense again."

Hilda burst in. "I told you—"

The policeman put his hand out to quieten her. "And I told you, I don't want to hear it."

"Is that all you're doing?" A furious Peter rounded on the policeman. "You and your cronies must be in cahoots with her."

His eyes bulged in his puce face. Spittle bubbled in the corners of his mouth. I'd never seen him so angry, even though he seemed to spend half his life in a world of hatred. His arm shot out, but the policeman's colleague caught it. "Don't!" he warned.

Furious, Peter shoved him. When the crowd gasped, Peter paled, perhaps realising he'd gone too far.

Grim-faced, the policeman seized Peter. "You can come with us."

As he was hauled off to the police car parked nearby, the crowd muttered and shook their heads. Even Hilda looked worried – even though, not five minutes earlier, she'd been telling them to arrest him.

"Where're you taking the boy to?" she called. "It were just a bit of fun."

Her grandson patted her shoulder. "Come on, Gran. You look done in and I best be getting this lot back to Stan's yard."

♦

We met up in the Fisherman's Rest that night to congratulate ourselves, although I felt awful about Peter. He'd behaved appallingly, but who wouldn't when we'd closed the High Street? I was surprised that Hilda's scheme had worked for so long, but Heidi – who poured our drinks at the bar – assured us that it was all very convincing.

"She had men in hi-vis with logos and everything.

They weren't locals, though, or we'd have recognised them."

"They scarpered when the police arrived," a customer said. "Never seen workmen run like that before."

I took my drink over to where we'd commandeered several tables, choosing a seat beside Becki. Meg had hung her cotton jacket on the chair to the other side, although she wasn't sitting there.

"It's for Grant," she said. "If he feels up to it, he's popping down later."

"Grant?" Andy's eyebrows shot up. "What, old Brown-tongue?"

"Don't call him that. It's mean," Meg said.

"You coined the name," Andy retorted.

"He's lost his dog and we're going to help find it." Meg took a sip of her drink. "The police reckon it was stolen."

"It's a scrawny mutt," Andy said. "Who'd want to steal it?"

Keith's chair scraped the tiled floor. He sat down on the other side of Becki. "Hilda's not joining us. She's upset about Peter being carted off by the police."

"Are you all getting saft or something?" Andy tapped the side of his head.

"We could just do positive stuff in future," I said. "Like the market stall and today's fun day."

"But we wouldn't have had so many people coming if Hilda's team hadn't sent them our way." Becki grimaced, then added, "Not that I think closing down the High Street was the best of ideas."

Keith scratched his head. "Positive stuff only, you say? What about music? If we made it loud enough, it might attract people from the harbour."

Meg banged the table. "Great idea. We are in Beach Street, after all. Let's have a beach-themed party – a beach day. It'll go down well with the holidaymakers." She took a pad and a biro from her bag, pulling the pen lid off with her teeth. "Right, who's doing what?"

Grant came in an hour later, looking a tad apprehensive, but Meg made him feel welcome, pulling out the chair she'd saved and insisting that he sat down.

"Becki'll buy you a drink," she said. "After all, it was her fault your plants got damaged."

Becki rolled her eyes, but got to her feet.

"While you're there, mine's a beer." Andy waggled his empty glass.

"And make mine a vodka and lime," Meg said.

Becki sighed. "Write everyone's down."

I noticed that Meg had turned her pad around so Grant couldn't see it. She tore off the sheet with our ideas and folded it into her bag before jotting down our drinks order. So, she didn't trust Grant – but that was to be expected. After all, he'd only been friends with us for a few hours, and wouldn't be with us now if he hadn't lost his dog.

When Becki came back with the expensive round of drinks, we moved on to the subject of Ruby, pooling ideas on how to find her. A couple of times Grant became too choked to speak as he tried to tell everyone what he'd told Meg and me earlier that day. Meg joined the dots with the tale of my 'break in', while I took over, saying that Ruby hadn't been in the garden while I'd been there. Grant finished, explaining what had happened after he'd called the police. If Ruby had been stolen, there was a slim chance of getting her back.

"I've searched everywhere. I've put posters up and I'm out leafleting too." Grant dabbed a stray tear with his sleeve. "What more can I do? I feel so useless."

Andy sighed. "I'm sorry. That's tough."

Meg's pen hovered over the clean sheet. "Let's get to work. We've got a dog to find."

Grant gave us a wobbly smile. "You're the first people to offer to help. My friends are too busy."

"With friends like those, who needs enemies?" Meg slapped his back, making him wince. "Anyhow, you've got us now. We'll find your pooch."

Chapter 19

The next day we all met up outside Becki's house in our walking shoes. Grant handed out his flyers and we set off in pairs: Becki with Keith, Grant with Andy, while Meg and I were a quartet with the dogs – although they did more to hinder us than help, pulling in the wrong direction when we bent to post the leaflets. The sun hadn't yet broken through the clouds, although there was a promised patch of brightness, leaving a chill in the air. I'd put on the usual jacket I wore for the morning dog walk, but goosebumps prickled Meg's bare arms.

She'd been unusually quiet so far. As we walked along, she turned to me. "No matter what we do, I can't see how we can find Ruby. She'll be long gone by now."

I grimaced. She'd voiced my thoughts, but I'd been buoyed by her positivity the previous night. Still, doing nothing wasn't an option.

"We may get lucky and find someone who saw something."

She shrugged. "I'll do the Facebook posts later. Grant doesn't use social media, so he hasn't got a clue." Then her expression became oddly wistful. "He's quite sweet, you know. Nothing like he is when he's around that Peter Drew."

I gazed at her. "Isn't he a bit old for you?"

"Give over!" She gave me a gentle shove. "There's only an eight-year gap. Anyhow, there's no chance of me liking him in that way. For a start, he's a florist. I have enough trouble with pollen as it is."

I chuckled and pushed open a creaking gate, watching my step on the concrete path intersected with cracks and tufts of grass, while Meg took the other side of the road. By the time we met up at the end of the cul de sac to head down an alley to the adjoining road, her contemplative mood had returned. "Grant mentioned something that made me think."

She fell silent.

Curious, I said, "Go on."

"I've been blaming myself for this war – if you want to call it that – with Peter. I thought that business with Hilda – you know, when she barricaded the road because someone had complained about her junk to the council – had just been one of those things. But it turns out that Peter was the one who called the council. Grant let it slip."

I tugged a batch of leaflets from my bag in preparation for the next street. "If we're honest, he started it with that holiday lets affair, but you haven't helped. But why would Peter complain about the outside of Hilda's shop making Beach Street look untidy? He doesn't care about us."

"It can be seen from certain angles in the harbour. One of his customers mentioned that it looked like an old scrapyard with all the junk outside, and it ruined the quaint effect for visitors."

I chuckled. "He did us a favour, then. It looks much better now. And we've got all the lovely bunting and decorations up, so that's another win."

"But Becki's business hasn't been the same since all those rumours about her being a fake. She's had loads of cancellations."

I squeezed Meg's arm. "As we said last night, it's only positive things from now on. Maybe we can do something else to promote Becki on the beach day."

We finished the leafleting and headed back to Becki's house. CC tracked us nervously from the leafy tree in the garden, which told us that the others had already arrived. Becki's door was on the latch, so we made our way inside. Her worktops were clear – her mugs hung from hooks in a row, all facing the same direction, while her tea, coffee and sugar pots were pushed to the back wall, behind a sparkling kettle. Her table gleamed, with not a crumb in sight. Even her huge Welsh dresser seemed to have had a makeover, with the books stacked upright and not a knickknack in sight. The smell of incense hung in the air, but it mingled with the fragrance of polish. I frowned. Since when had Becki been one for housework?

Meg nudged me and hissed, "As I said, she has a lot of time on her hands now."

While Becki bustled around the kitchen making us hot drinks, Andy updated us on the roads they had leafleted – and some potential news.

"A woman walking a dog saw us putting one of the posters up. She knew Grant—"

"One of my customers," Grant said.

Andy hesitated, as if waiting for Grant to say something else. When he didn't, he continued, "The night

Ruby went missing, she saw a hatchback opposite Grant's house with a man in the driver's seat and a woman beside him. She wouldn't have thought much of it, but when she walked past the car, they ducked."

"What kind was the car?" Meg said.

"She doesn't remember. She thinks it was silver, but it was hard to tell. But that's not the interesting part." He paused for effect. "It had a taxi registration plate on the back. No company name, though."

Meg let out a hiss of frustration. "So, it was just a taxi dropping off a customer."

"But thirty minutes later, when she came back down the road, she saw them again – the same people in the car."

Meg sounded bored. "So what? Maybe the woman forgot something, so they had to go back."

Andy rolled his eyes. "You're making this hard work! The car stopped beneath a streetlamp to let another car past, and the man and woman were wearing black beany hats. The driver put his hand to the side of his face, as if shielding it from view, and the woman was clutching something that wriggled. It looked like a puppy, but she assumed it was theirs."

Meg's eyes widened. "That's interesting. Why would they be wearing beany hats? It was warm enough that night for Becki to be wearing sandals."

Becki placed our steaming drinks on the table, her tongue poking out of the corner of her lips. She pushed my mug over to me. I took a sip, wincing as it scalded my mouth.

"That's a lot of taxi companies for the police to check," I said.

"I doubt they'll do that for a dog," Meg said. "That's down to us."

"Well, it must be someone who knew Grant had a dog worth stealing. A taxi driver would be ideal for that. I mean, they can travel about without people wondering what they're doing." Becki curled up on the chair next to Keith, tucking one foot beneath her leg. If I tried to do that, I'd end up with pins and needles.

"Who'll research the taxi companies?" Meg said. "I'm sorting out the social media side."

"I will," Grant and I said in unison.

"No," Meg told Grant. "I need to show you Facebook, seeing as you wouldn't let us contribute to the reward. Let Jenn do this. Andy, Keith and Becki can concentrate on our beach day."

"Beach day?" Grant frowned.

Meg made a zipping action across her mouth. "You're still the competition. So that's off-limits."

Grant sighed. "I don't know why all the Torringham traders can't work together."

"You've got your mate Peter Drew to thank for that. But you can be an honorary member of the Beach Street traders." She rubbed her nose. "Just don't come anywhere near me with your flowers."

♦

After spending a few hours on the computer searching for all the taxi companies in the area – only to realise that if I'd waited a day it might have been easier to phone the relevant department at the council – I joined Roo in the courtyard to get some air. The back door to the neighbouring shop stood ajar, and voices filtered out. I hesitated, debating whether to go back inside. I didn't feel in the mood for friendly chit-chat with my future competitor. But, if he was talking to someone inside, he'd probably left the door open to air his shop. I sat down on the old metal chair, with its flaking green paint, my previous neighbour had left behind. I'd always intended to sand and repaint the set, but it was on a long list of to-dos that never got done.

As Roo sat beside me, I rubbed the soft fur of her ears. Two hanging baskets lay on the ground by Dan's door. Was he putting them up out here? I groaned. It would be lovely to have a prettier outside space, but that meant he planned to spend time here – and I'd have to share my little courtyard. I'd known that was a possibility when I'd first got my little shop, but my former neighbour had rarely ventured outside, so I'd come to think of it as mine. Not that I'd done anything to make it nicer. I'd left that to nature. Pink valerian sprouted between the rocks in the wall – even though Meg had warned that the roots were invasive – and daisy-like flowers spread across the concrete paving. Among the dandelion leaves and small tufts of grass, a tiny violet lobelia grew in the corner, possibly from a seedling blown by the wind. But apart from a few wildflowers and weeds, the courtyard was surrounded by cliff-like walls of stone, the drainpipe and corners stained by algae where the sun never reached.

A man's voice echoed closer than before, and I jumped up, ready to scurry back inside. But I was too late. The door opened and my future rival – Dan – stepped outside, clutching an electric drill and two ornate brackets. His clothes and face were dusted with white, making his dark eyes gleam brighter.

He gave me an uncertain smile. "I hope you don't mind, but I wanted to give this place a splash of colour."

I shrugged, unable to voice my true thoughts. *Please don't spend too long out here – it's my safe space.* "I like flowers."

He nodded towards the ornate, but dilapidated, table and chairs. "Are they yours? I've got a set too, which I was going to put here." He pointed to the shaded wall beside his building.

"These? They were left behind by the last owner." Then, in case he thought that gave him the go-ahead to bin them, I added, "But I like them."

He scratched his head. "So how do you want this to work? I mean … what did you do before? Did you have that half and the owners of this place" – he jerked his thumb towards his shop – "have this part?"

I nodded. It was a lie, but that way I could keep my shabby garden furniture and he could turn his section into whatever he wanted. It also meant his bit would be in the shade for most of the day. That made me feel guilty, but I swallowed the urge to tell him the truth.

Roo ambled over to him, sniffing at his dusty trousers. "Okay." Dan bent to stroke her. "We'll stick to the previous arrangements. I'm not here to upset the apple cart."

But if he didn't want to do that, he wouldn't be opening a pet shop next to an existing one. A bitter taste rose in my mouth. Before I spilled any acid words I turned to go back inside, but he said, "I heard you're helping Grant find his dog. Can I do anything?"

I shrugged. It wasn't my place to refuse, even though I didn't want him joining our committee. He might be handsome with a winning smile, but staring at his face wouldn't pay my bills. Saying that, he had every right to come along. His shop was in Beach Street.

"Talk to Grant," I said. "He and Meg are leading the effort to find Ruby."

"Meg?" Dan frowned. "Isn't she the scary dog lady? I mean, the one who dresses up in a dog costume?"

"To do me a favour," I said tartly. Then I wished I hadn't. He might ask what it was all about, and I couldn't tell him that we were doing all we could to promote my business before he opened his. But he didn't say a word. Maybe my tone had warned him that my bite would be worse than Meg's bark.

I pointed to my door. "I'd better get back."

As I headed inside, he muttered, "I'll speak to Grant."

Chapter 20

It was Edna's usual morning to come to the shop, so I didn't have a single customer. But, strangely, Edna didn't turn up either. Was she ill? By eleven o'clock I got quite worried and pulled out my customer book to find her number. The phone rang until her answerphone clicked in.

"Hi, it's Jenn. I'm just checking you're okay," I said.

I'd meant to call the taxi companies the day before but, with Kirstie's customers in the morning, followed by a busy afternoon, I'd spent the evening slumped in front of the TV. However, with no customers and no Edna, I decided to make a start on calling the taxi companies. It didn't go to plan. When I asked if any of their drivers had a silver hatchback, I was met with confusion or suspicion.

"Has Steve done something wrong?" the first one asked.

"No. It's just that my friend left something in a silver hatchback taxi but she can't remember who she booked with or the taxi driver's name."

"If anything's found, we always put it in the lost property, love." There was a shuffling sound. "Has she lost a thong?"

He wouldn't elaborate on Steve's surname, saying it was a matter of confidentiality and if I had a complaint I needed to speak to the manager.

The next company refused to confirm whether they had any silver taxis, let alone tell me a name. The third was a one-man band with a white Prius, who could offer exceptional rates, much cheaper than Tootle Around Town, and he wouldn't kill me by speeding either. Something about the way he spoke about them made me skip down my list to find Tootle Around Town. A man answered in a gruff, unwelcoming tone. For some reason, my voice trembled as I gave him my sorry tale of a lost phone and asked about a silver hatchback.

"What a load of tosh! Come on, what's your real problem?"

"I … er … I, well, my friend thought she would recognise the name of the driver."

"So why's she not calling? I bet you're the one who's been complaining to the council. If you're planning on making up another story, don't bother. The council knows you're just a troll."

I hung up. My heart thumped as if he'd been shouting inches from my face, which was ridiculous; his anger hadn't been aimed at me, but at whoever was causing problems for his company. I went to pick up the phone to make another call, but decided against it. Meg would be much better doing this.

Instead, I made a start on replenishing the shelves and talking to my new friend, Syd the spider, who'd made his home behind the counter. He'd terrify my customers with his huge body and spindly legs, so I made sure to touch him when the doorbell jangled, to make him scurry to safety. But he had the whole place to himself until after lunch as my customers were hiding from Edna. Like buses, they appeared on the dot of two. By ten past I had three customers queuing behind Harry Martin. I'd been unable to source his usual type of seed, so he ummed and ahhed over which of the two other brands on offer would be best. He didn't want the birds leaving his garden in search of better stuff elsewhere. Behind all his deliberation lay loneliness and the simple pleasure of watching the colourful birds flutter by, so I didn't pressure him. I'd even offered him time to think while I served Linda, but he turned me down, saying he just needed a mo as he was in a hurry.

My phone began to ring. Not wishing to further slow his deliberations, I ignored it. After half a dozen rings it cut off, then it started again. An incessant, urgent sound. This time I went to take the call, but the answering machine broke in and Edna's voice sounded.

"Hello, dear. Thanks for your concern. I've been doing as you asked and spying on your competitor. I've got something interesting to report too." She chuckled to herself. "I'll tell you on Thursday. I've got to go now. Flossie wants a wee."

Why hadn't I changed the blasted answerphone for a newer model that didn't relay messages to an audience? As I faced my smirking customers, I flushed.

"A spy network, eh?" Harry beamed at me. "Is that to do with the laddie with the new shop next door?"

"I don't know." I winced. How did I make myself look innocent of all spying charges without making it seem as if Edna had gone mad? "I think she's trying to be helpful.

You know how kind Edna is. I think she's worried that I might lose customers when he starts up."

"It won't be long at this rate. I saw them bringing in boxes," Harry said.

"I think he'll be selling pet books too," Linda said. "I saw a box labelled with books. That's something you could consider."

The woman at the back of the queue gave an irate sigh and tapped her watch. I hadn't seen her before, but I'd gained quite a few new customers with all the publicity. "Along with speeding things up here," she said.

The other two stared at her. "This is Devon, not London," Harry said. "I'll be done soon enough." He picked up the bag of seed. "I'll take this. Put the change in the charity box."

He glared at the woman as he left, while Linda turned to her. "You go first, seeing as you're in such a rush."

As I rang the woman's items through the till, I gave her a sympathetic smile. But she didn't return it, or thank Linda for letting her go first. No doubt this would be her first and last time in my shop. She'd rather make a forty-minute return journey to the pet superstore than wait ten minutes – or she'd try my competitor when he opened.

When I totalled her goods, she shook her head. "This would be a pound cheaper up the road."

Linda leapt to my defence. "And you'd spend that in petrol."

The woman snapped open her purse, waited for me to give her the penny change, and huffed out of the shop with her bag.

As the door banged shut, the bell jangling goodbye, Linda pulled a face and shrugged. "She must have got out of bed the wrong side." Then she rested her arm on the counter. "So, what's this about Edna spying?"

Before I could say a word, the shop door opened again. Meg pulled down her hood and wiped her feet on the mat. The shoulders of her jacket were speckled by rain. She gazed back outside. "It's about to chuck it down." Then she brightened. "Hello, Linda, I've got your material whenever you need it."

"I was just finding out about Edna spying for Jenn," Linda said.

Behind Linda's back I mimed zipping my lip. When Linda turned back to me, I gave her a saintly smile. She frowned and looked at Meg.

"Come on, Meg. I know that if Jenn's up to something, you won't be far behind."

Meg sighed. "It's nothing, really. We're just trying to save Jenn's shop. Her business could go bust if the place next door takes all her trade. Edna's just trying to help."

"By doing what?" Linda said.

Meg paused. "By … making sure he isn't copying Jenn. She's doing all this brilliant stuff – the agony aunt…" She indicated one of the shocking pink tutus I'd ordered after Carla Jones had shown off her shih tzu at the dog show. "This pet clothing range, even the dog bedding is more interesting. Who wouldn't want a bone-shaped bed?"

'Nobody' was her answer. I'd had that since I'd moved in. It had since become a permanent fixture as I didn't have the heart to dump it. Meg had plainly not noticed it before if she thought it was a new style.

"She's not just selling here, you know." Meg had got into her stride with the sales talk. "She's even joined me on my stall at the craft fair. Last time, Becki and I were demonstrating training techniques."

Linda's face brightened. "I could do with some tips."

"We're doing dog yoga at the next one," I said. "Kirstie's leading a session."

"Oh, I don't know about that. It sounds a bit arty-farty to me," Linda said.

I stopped speaking and left the sales pitch to Meg. Hopefully, Linda would encourage her friends to support my shop. I knew she was an active participant in many groups, attending the local sewing bee, the art club and the book club. Josie, one of my customers, had invited me to that one, but I'd turned her down after hearing that some of their meet-ups could be a tad argumentative.

While Meg and Linda chatted, I served another regular, Paula. Roo recognised her as the treat lady, as she would always buy a large bag of dog chews, of which Roo took her fair share. Roo left her basket in the storeroom to sniff at her pocket. While Paula stroked Roo and fed her a few treats, she asked about my aunt, smiling when I told her that she was progressing well but it seemed increasingly likely that she would have to go to a care home.

"What will happen to this darling then?" Paula said,

giving Roo a vigorous rub.

When I hesitated, she glanced at me, her voice hardening. "You are going to keep her?"

"Of course!" I shot her an indignant look.

Until that moment, there'd been no certainty about it. But I'd found myself getting more attached to Roo. While I didn't appreciate her farting and snoring at night, it was no different to having a man in the bedroom. It would be nice to have a two-way conversation, but my relationship with Tim hadn't been that different. At least when I asked her if she fancied a tin of chicken and lamb for dinner, she'd bounce into the kitchen wagging her tail. Tim, on the other hand, would just grunt, "You decide." It was the same with TV. When I asked if Roo wanted to watch a film or another episode of *Death in Paradise*, she'd flick her tail and lick my hand. If it had been Tim I wouldn't have been asking; he'd hogged the remote control. Perhaps a dog was better than a man.

The bell above the door jangled again. Crikey! I'd never had so many customers in such a short time. When the man stepped inside, our mouths fell open in surprise. Dan! Had he come to check out the competition?

Meg broke the silence. "What are you doing here?"

Looking stunned, he stepped back. "Getting pet food. Edna told me off for buying it at the supermarket. She said if I was going to be a trader, I had to support the rest."

"You'd be better off doing that by not opening," Meg said, while Linda nodded.

"Er…" He scratched his chin. "I don't know quite what

to say to that."

He looked so uncomfortable, I couldn't help offering a friendlier welcome. "How can I help you?"

"I need kibble for my cat."

"You have a cat?" I fought to mask my concern. Anything furry with four legs – and not a dog – was fair game for Roo. It was bad enough having to share my courtyard, but while the owners would be staging pet shop wars, Roo and Dan's moggie would be fighting their own pet wars.

His knees cracking, he bent to join Paula, who fussed with Roo. "She's an eighteen-year-old blind, deaf moggie who never leaves the house."

Behind his back, Meg scowled. I ignored her and fetched two bags of dry cat food. As I put them on the counter, he got to his feet and surveyed the shop, bypassing Meg's fiery glare.

"It's a nice place you've got here."

"She's hoping to still have it next year too," Meg said.

He frowned and gave me a puzzled look. After choosing one of the bags, he took a ten-pound note from the back of his wallet. I noticed it was one of many.

"Put the change in the box," he said. He hefted the bag into his arms and gave me a smile. "Well, it was nice to see your shop. I'm going to be working in mine until late, but we'll keep the noise down. No doubt I'll see you at some point later." He bent to give Roo a farewell pat. "And this lovely one."

As he left, I popped his change into the box for the local

rescue centre.

"You didn't have to be that mean," I said to Meg.

"And you shouldn't be fraternising with the enemy," she responded.

For some reason, Linda's eyes gleamed with intrigue. It wasn't until later, when I replayed the scene, that I wondered if Linda had thought Dan and I were having illicit meetings. After all, he'd said he'd see me later. An innocent remark. He'd meant when I let Roo out to do her business in the courtyard but, knowing Linda, her imagination had plumbed the depths of a Mills and Boon novel. Enemies become secret lovers. But there was more chance of Meg getting together with Grant. Then I frowned. I hadn't thought about it until now, but had she been wearing lipstick when she'd come in earlier? And had that been a new lacy top beneath her jacket?

"No, not Grant of all people!" I muttered to myself.

I was being daft. I chuckled to myself, then slumped into my chair and gave Roo's ear a tickle.

"What do you think, Roo? I say there's no way Meg would be interested in Grant." But then, I'd thought the same about Becki and Keith. "Nah!" I shook the thought away. "Ridiculous. I'm going mad, Roo. Stark, raving bonkers."

As if in agreement, Roo licked my hand.

Chapter 21

Meg phoned me the next day to say that Edna had been taken into hospital and was in the ward next to my aunt's ward. She offered to drive us there so we could see Edna. Bone weary, after a day on my feet, I slumped into the passenger seat and inspected her.

"Another new top?"

She pulled away, not meeting my eye. When we stopped at the traffic lights, she turned up the radio, saying she loved the song. Strange, then, that she only knew a few words of the chorus, which she screeched with enthusiasm, mangling the rest. I snatched an inquisitive look at her glistening pink lips and her mascara-laden eyes. Diesel fumes blew in from the bus in front, but were soon masked by the apple-scented cardboard tree that dangled from her rear-view mirror as we drove away. Nothing other than her appearance had changed. Her dashboard was still thick with dust, except for a darker smear where, I guessed, a previous passenger had wiped their finger along the plastic. An empty plastic water bottle rattled between my foot and a scrunched-up crisp packet. And my seat was thick with dog hairs, the side window smeared by Amber's nose.

Meg drove up Main Road, past the line of B&Bs and out of Torringham into the countryside, where we wound through rolling fields interspersed with trees. The valley dropped away to one side, giving us a glimpse of the glittering sea and the boats cutting across the bay. My thoughts strayed to my auntie and Edna, both stuck inside the hospital, missing a beautiful day.

When the adverts blasted out, I turned the radio down. "Who's looking after Edna's dog?"

Meg chuckled. "Strangely, Becki is."

"How will CC deal with that? Flossie scares other dogs, let alone cats."

Meg shrugged. "Edna's neighbour said she couldn't have the dog, so she called Becki, who felt she couldn't refuse. She wanted to join us but couldn't leave Flossie alone."

"She should have asked Keith." I chuckled to myself. What a perfect reintroduction to the conversation I'd hoped to have earlier. Not pausing to give Meg a chance to think, I said, "So talking about men, how is Grant?"

Her mouth fell open. "Grant? Are you being serious?"

"Deadly," I said, although – going by the expression on her face – I was no longer so certain.

"There is nothing between me and that man. I just feel sorry for him. Anyhow, he's not my type and, I've told you enough times, he'll do my hay fever no good. I'm filled up to the eyeballs with anti-histamines as it is." She'd stopped at yet another set of traffic lights while making this speech, but now she forced the gear stick into first and roared away, tailgating the car in front. We made it all of a hundred yards before she braked hard for another red light.

"And another thing. I like my men to have something

154

about them. To be able to argue their own corner, not to sit beside idiots like Peter sodding Drew and let him get away with anything he wants." She gripped the steering wheel, her knuckles white. "Do you know that man still hasn't bothered with Grant? He phoned him last night to ask some weird question about gas services, but didn't ask about Ruby. What sort of friend is he? I mean, Grant's lost his dog and his best mate doesn't give one jot about it. That's why I'm so bothered. Grant deserves better friends than Peter."

I smiled to myself. If she hadn't moved on to her second rant, I'd have believed her. But the phrase 'the lady doth protest too much' sprang to mind. Not that I had a chance to say as much. Meg took off again and the G-force jerked my head back. Once she'd harried the car in front to move over to the 'slow' lane, she calmed down.

"This is a forty," I said.

"I'm doing forty-two."

"In five seconds."

"This Ruby business is bugging me. If we don't find her soon, she could be sold on, or worse. I've made a few calls to the taxi companies, but that Tootle Around Town you mentioned..." She prodded the steering wheel. "That's the one we want. I'm sure of it. They've got a terrible reputation in Berrinton. They come out to Torringham, so they'd know the area. What's more interesting is that Grant reckons he's seen one of their taxis dropping off a neighbour's daughter. He's going to speak to her later."

"Was it a silver hatchback?"

She shrugged. "It was four in the morning. For some reason the taxi pulled up outside his, rather than next door. The girl had been clubbing and was worse for wear, so she woke him up slamming the car door and shouting to the taxi driver. He can't remember the car. He just remembers watching her falling over."

"But the taxi driver wouldn't have seen the dog."

"Grant said he could have, as he carried Ruby out to check on the girl. She'd ended up in a bush in her garden and was having a job getting out. Grant's security light came on, so he could see the driver on his walkie-talkie, but the way the taxi was positioned, half hidden by his hedge, he couldn't see the actual car. He called across the hedge to see if the girl was okay, but she told him to bugger off."

"So do you have the driver's description?"

Meg grimaced. "Not much other than he was dark-haired. But we'll know more when Grant speaks to his neighbour. Let's check out Tootle Around Town after the hospital. Their base isn't far from there."

♦

Edna lay cushioned by pillows, her face grey and gaunt, her arm bandaged and a egg-shaped blackened bruise above her eye. The most perturbing part was her silence. She gave us a wan smile when Meg put a book and a box of chocolates on her bedside cabinet, but she didn't speak other than to say, "Flossie?"

"She's with Becki," Meg told her. "Don't worry about her. Just get yourself well."

"We're going to see her tomorrow," I said. "Becki's taking Flossie to her shop, but I said I'd walk her at lunchtime."

It would be impossible to walk Flossie with Roo. I'd never seen a dog so scared of one half its size but, when it came to Flossie, Roo was the dog version of CC, scuttling away with her tail between her legs.

Edna sighed and her eyelids fluttered shut. A few minutes later we heard her soft snores, so I told Meg that I'd pop to the next ward to visit my auntie, who was more talkative, but no less disturbing.

She welcomed me with a cry of "Letty!" – my older cousin's name.

The nurse came over and whispered, "She's having a difficult day." She bent down to Auntie Peg, raising her voice. "This is Jennifer. Where are your glasses, Mrs Harris?"

Confused, Auntie Peg gazed around. Her red-rimmed lower lids hung like those of an old basset hound, and below her glistening nose sat a droplet primed to fall. Her perm – her pride and joy – had flattened into a rumpled mess, but I daren't set about it with a hairbrush. Not unless I wanted a rerun of my last chaotic visit.

"Glasses? Did that man steal them again?"

"She's taken a dislike to one of the porters." The nurse chuckled. "We had a bit of a to-do when he came in

157

earlier."

My aunt's bony hand grasped mine. Her skin felt dry, as if it would crumple like tissue paper if I held it.

"Take me home. I want to go home. Where's my Letty?"

Her Letty was almost a thousand miles away, sunning herself in Spain, along with her husband, Bruce. They'd upped sticks and moved to Alicante, but if they took a plane to Exeter, it wouldn't be a much longer journey than driving from Torringham to London. I'd offered to collect them, but Letty and Bruce insisted they were too busy. Who would look after their poor dogs, Cassie and Benson? They couldn't bear to put them in kennels. Not in Spain, where they couldn't trust the staff to feed them a raw meat diet. Stuff Letty's poor mother. She could fester here in hospital. Meanly, I hoped the care home would be expensive and drain Letty's promised inheritance. That would serve them right.

"Letty's not here," I said. "They've found you a lovely place to live, near Torringham. You'll be able to see Roo as well."

There was little point saying that Roo wouldn't be able to live with her in the care home. She gave me a puzzled look. Had she forgotten about Roo? Since her fall, she sometimes reminded me of a cracked shell: her true self had gradually seeped out until little remained. Although some days were better than others, there was no way she would be able to cope with a dog.

Meg appeared at my side, giving my aunt a cheerful

smile. "Hello, Peg. How are you today?"

We spent another ten minutes with her, but the conversation looped into tangled threads leading back to the same knotty questions – are you taking me home, can you get my glasses back from that horrible man, where's Letty?. I tried to respond with patience, but she'd forgotten my answers within moments, leaving me unsure what to say next.

I brushed my aunt's cold cheek with a kiss. "We've got to go now. I'll come back at the weekend."

But for her, time had lost all meaning. She gazed past me to the window, where gulls wheeled in the sky and the sound of a distant siren filtered through. Nearby a trolley clattered along the corridor and laughter echoed from the nurses' station. No wonder she seemed so disoriented. This was hardly a restful place.

But, while it wasn't the same, I wished I could be in bed right now. I wasn't looking forward to an evening spent stalking taxi drivers, especially when something was certain to go wrong with Meg on the scene.

Chapter 22

Still grumbling about the exorbitant car parking charges – which I'd paid – Meg drove out of the hospital grounds, following the satnav instructions. When we passed McDonald's my stomach rumbled, even though I didn't fancy fast food. I'd taken a tub of leftover lasagne from the freezer that morning. By the time we got back, it would be defrosted and ready to cook in the oven while I took Roo for a brisk walk.

"How long do you think this will take?" I asked Meg.

She shrugged. "How long is a piece of string?"

I sighed. "We can't be all night. I have to walk Roo."

She glared at me. "A dog's life is at stake. Amber and Roo are tucked up in warm houses. Poor Ruby could be anywhere."

Chastised, I sat quietly while she took the back streets towards the town centre. She parked in an empty layby beside a row of shops a few streets from the main shopping centre.

"This is their office," she said. "Some of them go to the taxi rank in town but this is their quiet time, when the shops are closed and people aren't leaving the pubs yet, so I thought I'd try here."

I peered through the window into the taxi office. Beyond the blue cushioned chairs lining either side, a woman sat behind a glass screen, wearing a pair of headphones. A man waited. A customer, I guessed. One of the taxis must be heading back to pick him up.

Next door was a pizza parlour, its windows filled with photos of pizzas and menus, while on the other side was a brightly lit chip shop, with a flashing blue and red 'open' sign. The others in the row – a newsagents, a vape shop and a charity shop – were in darkness. The sign above another shop had been removed and a 'to let' board fixed above the door. I wound down the car window and rested my elbow on the frame. The pungent smell of fried food wafted in. My stomach rumbled. Goodness only knew when I'd get home to eat.

"I wanted to ask Edna about the shop next door," I said. "She went there on Tuesday. She said she had some news for me. She managed to broadcast it to the whole shop too."

Meg raised her eyebrows. "You had customers when Edna was in the shop? You lucky thing—"

"Not exactly." Although Meg had caught the tail-end of the incident, when she'd arrived to be questioned by Linda, I relayed the whole story to her, including the part about the rude customer.

"You'll have to ask her another day when she's more herself. She didn't wake up after you left." She gazed into her rear-view mirror. "Oh, hold on…"

In my wing mirror, I watched a black Prius purring down the road, its indicator flashing. It parked in front of us and the driver got out of the car. The taxi office door banged behind him. After speaking to the woman for a moment, he signalled to the waiting man and they got into the car.

"I didn't see your Facebook post," I said. "Did you mention the silver hatchback?"

She grinned. "It's had two hundred shares so far. Ruby is famous. Here…" She lifted herself from the seat to extract her phone from her back pocket. "Take a look."

After she put in her password and found her Facebook page, she handed the phone to me. Ruby gazed dolefully from the screen. Meg had used Grant's photograph. The messages ran into the hundreds. Even as I read them, more appeared. Most expressed sympathy and a desire to help, while others had ideas for what they would do to the dognappers.

"Nice." I grimaced after reading one particularly aggressive response. "Have you thought about deleting some of these comments?"

"Why would I do that? It's just people's ways of expressing themselves. You are a funny one, Jenn."

"There's speech and there's this…" I turned the phone to her.

As she read the few descriptive lines, she pulled a face. "Yuck! Much as I'd love to find the thieves, I think I'll leave their bits intact." She pressed her phone. "Gone."

A silver car passed, but it didn't have taxi plates.

"Is there any way we could speed this up?"

"Other than making a few dodgy calls to book a taxi, I can't see how," she said.

Even though she'd discounted it, I considered the idea. Then I decided against it. The drivers had a living to make, so it wouldn't be fair. Instead, I sighed, switched on the radio and slumped in my seat. Meg nibbled at a hangnail while checking out her Facebook page. Sniggering, she showed me a video with dogs grinning at the camera, hiding behind a wrecked sofa and other daft things.

"You ought to run a competition for the funniest video," she said.

"I don't know. What if people set up stunts and someone gets hurt?"

She rolled her eyes. "If you're that worried, put rules in place. Come on! It'll be fun. I'll post one of Amber."

"What's she done?"

"Nothing … yet." The 'yet' made up my mind. There would be no video competitions.

A silver car came into view. I nudged Meg and we watched as it slowed, pulling up behind us. From this angle, I couldn't tell if it was a hatchback, or see whether it had taxi plates. The driver walked past, his white shirt open at the neck, his belly hanging over his low, belted trousers, which sagged around his rear.

"He doesn't look fit enough to be a dognapper," Meg hissed as he pushed the taxi office door open. "His moobs are bigger than mine."

The man called something to the woman then went next door to the chip shop. Another car arrived, parking in the space in front. A silver hatchback with taxi plates! Meg and I nudged each other. The driver tooted at the man and gave him a thumbs-up.

"All right, Bob!" he shouted. "Getting the chips in?"

"Stan, my man!" Bob moved towards the car to speak to his friend.

Meg opened the glove box and pulled out a pad and a biro. As she scribbled down the car registration and other details, I strained to hear their conversation. I could make out the odd snippet from the driver, while Bob boomed like a town crier, often repeating his friend's comments, for which I was grateful. Nothing of interest, unless I wanted to know how little they'd earned so far but hoped to make up later. Then Bob asked how Sylvie was doing. I poked Meg's pad.

"Write 'Sylvie'."

I couldn't hear his reply, but the man on the pavement said, "Glad to hear about her and your Joe. My poor mum's not sleeping so well. It's her sciatica."

"Write 'Joe'," I instructed Meg.

The man inside the car spoke again, too muffled to hear, then my ears pricked up and I stiffened.

"No wonder! I've heard the bloody racket those dogs make!" Bob laughed, making his belly shake. "Have you thought about kittens? They're much quieter. Anyhow, I must be off. I'm starved."

I elbowed Meg, making her wince. But she mouthed to say she'd heard it too.

As he pushed at the door of the chippie, Bob turned back to his mate. "Sure you don't want anything, Stan?"

"Nah!" Stan got out of his car and straightened his thin tie. Like the other man, he wore a white shirt and black trousers, but his were crumpled. The taxi driver Grant had seen outside his house had dark hair like this man. First dogs, now this. Were we on to something? Stan sauntered into the taxi office, calling a greeting to the woman, who smiled. The glass door clanged shut, muting their conversation. He settled on a chair, folding one leg over his thigh and resting his head against the wall.

When Bob came out of the chip shop, carrying his dinner, Meg said, "Hold on."

She got out of the car and followed him into the taxi office. He sauntered past his friend and stepped through a door at the back, but Meg turned to the seated man and struck up a conversation. I wished I could lip-read. Instead, I settled for examining their body language. The man leaned forward, smiling, while Meg appeared quite animated. When she came out ten minutes later, she wore a broad grin.

"Got him!" she said.

"You know where he lives?"

She shrugged. "Not exactly, but I know he lives near Pengilley Farm. I asked if I recognised him – was he Sylvie's husband? He said yes. So I asked if she still lived in Berrinton." She grimaced. "That didn't go down too well. Apparently, she's never lived here – hates the place – but, luckily, he then went on to mention the trek back home each night and what a pain that is. When I asked where she's living now, he didn't like that either. He looked a bit suspicious until I said that I'd moved and assumed that Sylvie had too. But, nope, she's still out by Pengilley Farm, wherever that is."

"That can't be too hard to find. How many Pengilleys are there?"

"Fewer in Devon, but we'd be stuffed if he travels all the way home to Cornwall every night. That would be a bit like looking for a Smith."

Chapter 23

Pengilley Farm wasn't in Cornwall, thank goodness. But it wasn't close either, being tucked in the foothills of Dartmoor from what we could tell when we googled the directions. Even though we had shops to run, Meg decided that we should get up at four o'clock, as it would take an hour to get there. She couldn't imagine Stan, the taxi driver, would be up and about at five o'clock – not after an evening taxi stint. All we had to do was to look for his silver hatchback. Or that was the plan.

"Why don't we just report it?" I asked.

"The police won't thank us for sending them on a wild-goose chase. We need a bit more evidence."

"Just make sure we get back by eight," I said. "Roo'll need a walk before I open the shop."

As she drove out of Torringham, streetlights shone on darkened windows. The moon stayed hidden behind thick clouds, with not a star to be seen. We passed the odd car, one blinding us with its main beams, then we had a clear run through to the A38. Even the traffic lights worked in our favour, their luminous green beams greeting us as we trundled along.

Meg's imperious satnav directed us off the dual carriageway. Soon we were travelling through winding lanes, with hedgerows on either side, roofed by trees. As we climbed up a steep hill, I counted down the minutes until we reached our destination. But, when Meg turned the car into a narrow, bumpy lane, her headlights illuminating the grass sprouting in the centre, I became worried.

"Are you sure this is right?"

She shrugged and leaned closer to the windscreen, straining to see the road ahead. "Who knows?"

Her car engine struggled to manage what felt like an almost vertical climb, but when we reached the brow of the hill, I gazed nervously at the solitary light glowing deep in the valley below. I hoped her brakes worked. We'd need them.

I found out my answer moments later when a rabbit shot from the undergrowth, its eyes gleaming. Meg hit the brakes, tossing me forward, saved by my tight seatbelt. The car skidded, spitting grit from the tyres. When we stopped, we watched the rabbit bound across the lane then squirrel itself into the hedgerow on the other side.

"That was close," Meg muttered.

As we neared the bottom of the valley, a tall stone wall appeared to our right. Meg slowed the car to a crawl, the headlights shining on a sign: 'Pengilley Farm'. She unwound her window and leaned out. The glow we'd seen earlier came from a floodlight attached to a squat barn, but the rest of the farmyard lay shrouded in the velvet night.

"Do you think he lives there or further along?" Meg hissed.

"No idea." I'd assumed we'd find a house with a car sitting in the drive, rather than a metal five-barred gate with nothing to be seen other than a large, paved area with a barn. Our headlights brightened the road ahead, showing dried ruts made by a tractor.

"Perhaps you should keep going for a bit. There must be farm cottages somewhere."

"They're probably in there, at the back." Meg jerked her thumb towards the farm building.

But we drove on, the car jolting over potholes and clumps of mud, gravel crunching beneath the tyres. A few miles later, Meg slowed.

"Nothing," she said.

"Keep going," I said.

Another mile down the lane, we reached a gated field, with an entrance spacious enough for Meg to manage a ten-point turn. We started back, each inspecting our side to see if we'd somehow missed a cottage. When we arrived back at the farmyard, Meg switched off her car lights and crept the last few yards using the beam of the spotlight to pick out the entrance. She pulled up to one side of the gate and unclipped her seatbelt. "We can't come all this way and not check for his car."

Filled with unease, I got out, taking care not to bang the door shut. What if we were caught? Meg clambered over the creaking gate. Heart thudding, I followed, wishing I was anywhere but here. The ground was littered with dirt and straw, the smell of manure heavy in the air. We skirted the wall, keeping to the shadows, away from the spotlight. Another building appeared in the gloom – a huge metal barn with a padlocked door. Beyond that we could see the apex of a roof and a dim glow through a window of what must be the farmhouse. Would the occupants be getting up soon? A distant owl hooted, but I couldn't hear any farmyard noises: no cows mooing, pigs snuffling or cockerels crowing. Perhaps it was too early for them. I may have moved to Devon, but to a town renowned for its fishing industry. While herds of sheep speckled distant hills, there seemed to be more llamas in nearby fields than cows.

I hoped Meg understood farm routines better than me, because she was leading us down the garden path – literally. I tugged her sleeve and pointed across the courtyard to a building on the other side, but she shook her head and pressed onwards. By now I could make out the cottage's front door beneath a tiled porch. Two windows were on either side, one with the curtains half drawn. She ducked low. I crept behind her. Upstairs a light flashed on, piercing the gloom. The lawn turned green, dewdrops glinting. Meg darted away. I scurried after her, not spotting a bush overhanging the path. I stumbled, desperately stifling a gasp. Time slowed as the concrete grew closer. *Thwack!* I hit the ground. Winded, I lay there, pain shooting through my back and shoulder.

Meg grabbed my arm and hauled me to my feet, hissing, "Watch out!" She gazed at the window above, as if I hadn't spotted it, then shot away, leaving me frozen to the spot. A toilet flushed and water poured down the drainpipe. If I didn't move, whoever was upstairs might spot my shadow stretching across the lawn. I hobbled after her, my ankle smarting, my body contorted to one side in agony. She shook her head but didn't wait for me to catch up. Instead, she strode towards two cars parked by a hedge. I couldn't see more than shapes in the gloom, but I saw her hands rise and fall in frustration.

This time she signalled that we should move across the yard – to where I'd pointed earlier. The bathroom light shone on a drive that curved around a barn before it faded into the night. Wincing, I half trotted, half limped behind her, fighting back the urge to cry out with every step. As Meg dashed around the corner of the barn, a terrible yowl cut through the air and a cat dashed past, its hackles raised.

"Shit!" Meg's voice echoed in the silence.

As she appeared, wide-eyed, clutching her chest, a dark figure came to the upstairs window. When it creaked open and a man leaned out, Meg slammed me against the barn. I gritted my teeth against the pain.

"Who's there? Gill! We've got intruders again," the man called.

The window banged shut and Meg grabbed my arm. But I didn't need her help. A surge of adrenaline masked my discomfort. We sprinted past the cottage, past the barns, and threw ourselves over the five-barred gate. In the car I watched, panic-stricken, as two figures raced towards us. As they closed in, I pressed my foot against an imaginary pedal, desperately hoping we wouldn't get caught. Meg fumbled with the keys, turned the ignition, crunched the gear stick into first and wheel-spun away, her lights off. Moments later there was the crunch of metal. I shot forward, smashing into her dashboard. Every inch of me burned with pain. And fear.

"Shit!" Meg punched the steering wheel, slammed the car into reverse, then back into first. This time she switched on her lights. I fought not to beg her to slow down, although tears welled with every jolt and bump. When we crested the brow of the hill and she announced that she couldn't see anyone following us, my voice trembled. "Now can you take it a bit easier? I've done myself a massive injury."

"You should see my leg," she said. "I think that cat scratched me. I'll probably need a tetanus."

Chapter 24

We drove back in silence, except for my yelps when Meg's car lurched over a bump in the road or a pothole. Once back in Torringham, we checked Meg's car. The front wing was crumpled, the indicator casing smashed. After muttering something about the morning being a disaster all round, I staggered into the shop, apologising to Roo, who wouldn't get her morning walk.

I spent the day in agony, my head tilted to one side, barely able to press the till keys, let alone fetch items or pack my customers' bags. One customer felt so sorry for me that she insisted on taking over for an hour, while I lay on the settee willing the painkillers to do their job. At five o'clock I felt no better. Gasping at the pain, I stretched to bolt the shop door while Roo bounded around, desperate for a run. Instead, slowly, I opened the back door.

"You'll have to go out here. Sorry, Roo." My voice shook.

Dan appeared at his open back door, holding a watering can. His face fell. "Are you all right?"

Unable to move my neck, I turned my whole body around to face him. "Not really."

Roo raced over, jumping up at him. He tickled her ear while he surveyed me with concern. "You look terrible."

"Thanks." I didn't mean to sound rude, but I was tired, sore and not in the mood for conversation.

As I inched away, he said, "Can I do anything? To help,

I mean."

"Walk her," I half joked.

He beamed. "I'd love to."

For a moment, I felt bad. I'd coerced him into taking Roo out, but she needed it. A few steps around the courtyard wouldn't give her the exercise she needed, and I couldn't ask Meg. She had enough on her plate with her damaged car. And Becki was looking after Flossie. Thanking Dan, I hobbled upstairs to fetch Roo's lead.

As I handed it over, I said, "I'll keep my back door open. Just drop her inside."

He frowned. "Is there anything else I can get for you?"

I gave him a wry smile. "A new neck."

Roo woke me an hour later by licking my cheek. I opened my eyes to find Dan standing beside her, holding a plastic tub. "I hope you don't mind, but I've brought you some soup. I'm not sure it'll fill you up, but it's easy to reheat. I can feed Roo before I go."

I tried to move my head, but a bolt of agony shot down my spine. "Please. The dog food is in the fridge, the mixer on the side. Use the rest of the tin."

I inched back into the cushion, listening to the chink of metal and the clip of Roo's claws on the floor. Dan chatted to her while he sorted her dinner. I liked that. She would too. She often cocked her head to one side when I talked. Sometimes I swore she understood me, but then she'd do something daft, like bringing her ball to me when I asked if she missed her mum (my auntie), and I'd sigh and roll it across the floor.

Dan came back, hovering by the lounge door. "Look, this might sound odd, but I'm free all day tomorrow. My workmen are finishing up. If they need me, they can give me a call. Can I help you out? I'd be really happy to walk Roo again and man your shop. You can't work in that condition."

"A trial run before you open?" I tried to conceal my tart words with a smile. To be honest, I no longer cared whether he was a competitor. No way would I be able to open my shop. Stiffness had crept through my body. Just the tiniest jar and the fiery pain was back. "You don't have to do that for me, though."

"I really don't mind." He gave me a sympathetic smile. "Till training is always useful."

"Thank you so much." This time I gave him a proper smile. "I really appreciate it, but can I ask a favour? Please don't steal my customers."

He gave me an odd look, but crossed his heart. "I won't do anything to harm your business."

♦

At five thirty the next day, Dan bounded up the stairs, telling me that the shop had been a pleasure to run and he'd take Roo out. As he unhooked the lead from the coat rack, he grinned. He had a lovely smile, and a cute dimple.

"Do you know that some of your customers are quite mad?"

Thanks to the prescription tablets the doctor had agreed

over the phone and Becki had picked up for me, I'd managed to sit up, but it hurt to turn my head.

"Tell me about it." It was a rhetorical statement, but he proceeded to do so.

"One of your customers accused me of doing away with you. Apparently, I've been looking to take over your shop all along. Another wouldn't stop going on about it being a queer sort of spy operation, when the spied upon became the spy. She wouldn't elaborate." He scratched his head. "Does any of that make sense to you?"

It did. I kept my face blank, although I wilted inside. "I have some interesting customers." To change the subject, I pointed to the remote control on the floor. "Please can you pick that up? I dropped it."

"No problem. Can I get you a cup of tea or a coffee?"

I gazed at him. He was doing all this for me, even though I'd been so unfriendly to him. "Thank you for helping, especially when I've hardly been kind to you."

"You haven't been terrible. Not like your mate, Meg, although Grant swears she's an absolute wonder."

"That's how I got hurt." When he gave me a confused look, I explained. "We were trying to find Ruby. Meg and I staked out this taxi company and found a driver with a silver hatchback. We overheard him and a friend talking about dogs, so Meg went in and questioned him further. He mentioned this place in the middle of nowhere. Pengolley or Pentally…" I paused to think, but it wouldn't come to mind. "Or something. Anyhow, we went there in the early hours of yesterday morning, when it was dark.

To cut a long story short, I fell over, the farmer chased us, and Meg smashed up her car."

Dan pulled a face. "After all that, you didn't find Ruby?"

I went to shake my head, but my neck twinged a warning. "Worse, it looks like that taxi driver was having Meg on. Sending her on a wild-goose chase for some reason. She googled the farm on satellite view and it's just what we saw. There's nothing else around for miles. The farmer didn't look like the taxi driver either. Much older."

"Did you give the police this man's details?"

"I think Grant has. But Meg wants us to follow him home when he finishes work one night. How, I don't know – he'll probably go straight home from his last job."

Dan's brow puckered. Then his lovely brown eyes lit up. "I've an idea. We just need to find a young pedigree dog, like Ruby." He pointed to the tatty armchair in the corner. "Mind if I sit down?"

I squirmed, hoping my bank statements weren't on view. I'd cleared up the mess on the coffee table, but it hadn't moved far. "Dump the paperwork over there. I never know where to put it."

"First I'll put the kettle on and make you that promised drink. Now, is it tea or coffee?"

Chapter 25

The next morning my neck felt much better. When Dan offered to take Roo for a walk, I told him there was no need, but he pointed out that a bit more rest would do me good. After all, what were Sundays for? I spent most of the day tottering around my flat, restless with cabin fever, so I decided to take Roo for a stroll around the harbour. Meg insisted on joining me, holding Roo's lead in case she pulled too hard and damaged my recovering neck.

When I told her about Dan's idea, she gave a grudging shrug. "I guess it could work. But, what I want to know is, why are you letting your competitor run your shop? Sainsbury's wouldn't let Tesco do that."

"Sainsbury's has thousands of workers."

"You could have asked me." She sounded hurt.

I laid my hand on her arm. "You've got a business to run – and a car to mend."

She pulled a face. "The insurance company is sorting that. I told them I drove into a wall because I didn't see it hidden behind a hedge."

I grinned. "The truth, then."

We paused to let some tourists past. They were identifiable by the way they shuffled along, looking at the scenery rather than where they walked. Laughter echoed, mingling with the cries of gulls who soared above or perched on the rooftops, their watchful eyes trained on unsuspecting visitors. Meg gazed up in consternation, obviously remembering her last incident with a gull.

"I wish I'd brought an umbrella. I don't want to ruin this top."

Before I could comment on her new outfit – yet another! And the now regular dash of lipstick and mascara – a spiky-haired woman called Meg's name. She waved her over to where she sat in a group outside the pub. I'd assumed they were tourists as a camera sat in the centre of the table, a huge thing with a long lens. Stifling a groan, Meg plastered on a smile and led me to them.

"I was just telling my B&B friends about your shop," the woman said.

"Great!" Meg beamed. "I could always do with new customers." She tugged at my sleeve, drawing me close. "This is Jenn. She owns the pet shop."

"We're a dog-free zone, sadly." The man with sand-coloured hair gave me a warm smile as he leaned across to stroke both dogs. If he didn't have a thick band of gold on his finger, I could have quite fancied him.

He nudged the woman beside him. "What about your friend? The one with the deaf dog."

There couldn't be many people with deaf dogs in Torringham. "Laura?" I said. "I know her and Bessie. They come in my shop."

"We're getting a dog tomorrow." The woman on the other side of the table smiled. "A gorgeous little Cockapoo. We've just sold our B&B, so it's the right time."

Meg's ears pricked up. So did mine. But she spoke

first. "A Cockapoo? Can we borrow it?"

The woman looked alarmed. "I-I don't—"

"You can bring it with you. It's just that a friend of ours had his dog stolen and we need an expensive dog to attract attention. We tried to get him back ourselves but…" She jerked her head towards me. "Quasimodo here managed to get us caught."

The woman with the spiky blonde-tipped hair chuckled and surveyed me with amusement. I rolled my eyes. I may have tripped over a bush, but Meg had been the one who'd screeched when the cat attacked her.

The woman shook her head. "I don't—"

"There'll be no risk to your dog, I promise." Meg placed her hand on her chest. "You'd be doing a really good deed. It might prevent yours from being stolen too."

The woman's eyes widened and she darted a worried look at the man beside her.

When Meg passed me the dog leads, put on her sweetest smile and headed across to the other side of the table, I knew the woman had no chance of refusing. Twenty minutes later, we wandered away with her agreement to lend us her dog.

Meg wore a broad grin. "When I saw that Shona, I thought 'Uh-oh'. She's the bolshy one from the book club. Honestly, if she was stuck alone in a ten-acre field, she'd have an argument with the scarecrow."

I chuckled. Talk about pots and kettles. I considered pointing out they could be twins, but decided against it.

"The black lady with the colourful headscarf is her

partner, Kim. I think she keeps Shona on a tight rein and out of trouble. I've seen Josie and her husband around – not to speak to – but I've only seen the other couple once or twice." Meg chuckled to herself. "It worked out better than I could have anticipated. Let's get a drink at the Lord Mountfield. My shout. I could do with a bit of thinking space. This time that taxi driver is not going to get one over on us."

♦

So much for needing space to think. Within five minutes of buying our drinks and nabbing a table outside – which wasn't easy, when people dived on them like gulls each time one became available – Meg typed a message on the Beach Street traders' WhatsApp group, inviting them to join us. A secretive smile lit her face as she typed another message, but when I asked what that was about, she tapped her nose and changed the subject by sniffing the air.

"Those chips smell delicious, don't they?"

When I nodded, she said, "We'll have to order a bowl of them when the queue goes down."

Her smile widened when her phone buzzed. She picked it up, frowned, and typed another message. Then she put the phone face-down on the bench, her expression shuttered when she turned back to me. I got my answer when Grant appeared, strolling beside Dan.

Meg blushed. "I asked Grant, as it's his dog. Dan was

with him, so I said they could both come."

I watched them saunter towards us. Grant was animated, his arms waving. Dan's grin told me that he was listening to a joke or a funny story. If he hung around with Meg for too long, he'd have tonnes of them. They edged between the benches. When Dan seemed surprised to see me, it was my turn to redden.

"I'm feeling better," I said before he could utter a word. "The painkillers and this…" – I waggled my vodka and diet Coke – "have worked wonders."

"I told you not to drink it too quickly!" Meg gasped. "I'm not sure you're meant to be having alcohol."

I shrugged. "At least the pain's gone again."

Grant reached into the pocket of his trousers and pulled out his wallet. "Who'd like a drink?"

"Not Jenn," Meg said, before I could speak. "Get your own. If we get into rounds, it'll become a nightmare."

None of the other traders had responded to the invitation – not even Becki, who rarely turned down the opportunity to go out. But perhaps she couldn't. Not with Flossie – although her son could look after the dog for an hour or so.

"We'll probably get something to eat too," Dan said. "I'd be happy to buy you—"

"Chips," Meg said. "A bowl each would be perfect, thanks."

Grant and Dan went inside to join the queue. Grant came out first, putting his beer on the slatted table and hitching up his trousers before sitting down. Dan appeared a few minutes later, sipping at his pint.

"Mind if I sit here?" he said to me.

Meg rolled her eyes. "Where else are you going to sit, unless you want me to shift up so you and Grant can get cosy?"

Once seated, he gazed across to the bay where a fishing trawler chugged out to sea from the quay. "Nice view."

"Grant is lovely, if I say so myself." Meg chuckled. Beside her, Grant squirmed with embarrassment, but he darted a surreptitious glance at Meg, then another when she twisted around to look at the view.

The Lord Mountfield was the best pub in Torringham to catch the late evening sun and the gorgeous sunsets. The sea sparkled beneath a hazy sun. Nearby, yachts and motor launches nestled in the marina, while boats dotted the outer harbour, bobbing on their swing moorings. In the channel between them, a trawler chugged past the incoming pilot boat. One of the workers often came into my shop. He'd told me that he and his colleagues made regular trips taking pilots to or from the huge tankers that crossed the English Channel or to escort ships into the bay.

"Do you know about the pilot boat?" I asked Dan. When he shook his head, I told him about my customer.

He laughed. "So you have some normal customers then."

Meg scowled. "Just remember, they're hers."

"Let's not talk about work," I pleaded. The last thing I needed was Meg getting defensive about my business. I was worried enough as it was.

A waiter interrupted us, placing two bowls of chips on the table. "The other orders will be a few minutes," he said.

While we ate, Meg raised the subject of Ruby, explaining that we'd managed to sort a Cockapoo and a date – this weekend. The waiter returned and put steaming plates of fish and chips in front of the men. Below the table, Roo nudged me, but she couldn't have the salt-laden chips. Instead, I pulled a few dog treats from my pocket and gave her and Amber one each. Unable to stomach any more, I pushed my bowl to one side, making sure to place it beside the umbrella pole so the gulls couldn't swoop in. My neck had started to hurt so I stood up, straightening my back.

"The lifeboat's coming in," I said. "I'm just going to watch it. I won't be a mo."

As I bent to unhook Roo's lead, I gasped in pain. Meg shot me a look of concern. "I'll come with you." She took both leads and shielded her eyes. "Oh, that's interesting. It looks like they're towing a boat."

We stood by the harbour wall as the lifeboat headed towards the adjacent pontoon. Moments later Grant appeared leaving Dan to watch over their lunches, but when Dan followed him over, Meg's face fell. "Please tell me that you've finished your food."

Dan looked surprised. "I've just come over for—"

"Rookie error!" she screeched, shoving the leads into Dan's hand and dashing towards our table. A herring gull had pulled Grant's fish onto the table and was pecking at it.

"Oh!" Grant's hand shot to his mouth.

"I guess it's beans on toast tonight." Dan looked rueful as the gull flitted over to the harbour wall to wolf down the fish.

Furious, Meg sprinted to the bird, her fist raised. "I'll get you for nicking Grant's food!" she shouted, but the gull flew away, settling on the roof above.

Behind her another gull swooped onto the table. Meg spun around, launching herself at the bird.

Dan folded his arms and chuckled. "There's no need for TV comedies. Not when we've got Meg. She's pure gold." Then he nudged Grant. "What you said earlier … I think you'll find the feeling is mutual. She seems very protective of you."

Chapter 26

After work on Saturday, we chose to meet at Keith's house because Becki had said he had a Hive with a security camera. I couldn't see it, so he pointed it out and showed how his mobile beeped when someone came onto his property. He had a little bungalow, similar to the others on his estate, with a one-car driveway and narrow, well-tended flowerbeds filled with annuals on either side of the pathway and below the low wall fronting the pavement.

Even though he worked with fish all day, a lovely smell greeted me in the hallway. There was a squeak and a little device squirted a vanilla scent. My peel-off freshener had hardened into a green pebble long ago. Maybe I should invest in one like his for my lounge, especially after rainy dog walks, when the smell of damp dog infiltrated every soft furnishing.

While it was clean and tidy, Keith's house couldn't be called modern. The painted beige woodchip wallpaper, salmon-coloured carpet and mahogany dining furniture put paid to that. But his kitchen had been refitted and the units gleamed white against the glazed navy subway tiles.

"Nice!" Meg's eyes widened in appreciation.

He beamed. "All my own work." His doorbell rang and he hurried away.

Becki bustled around his kitchen, looking at home. As agreed, she'd left Flossie with her son.

Meg darted a glance at me and chuckled. "You know

where everything is, then, Becki?"

Becki stuck her tongue out and reached into a cupboard, counting out seven mugs which she put in a line by the kettle. She'd tied her hair back, but thick strands hung to each side of her face. An inch of brown crept from her roots, dull against the pink and blue. Was she growing her dye out? That would be a shame; I liked her cheerful colour.

The sound of cooing came from the lounge. We peered through the doorway to find Grant, Keith and Dan huddled around Josie, who clutched the most adorable Cockapoo. The little mite wriggled in her arms, his bright eyes full of excitement.

Josie turned to Meg. "You promise that what we're about to do won't cause any harm to him whatsoever?"

"Cross my heart." Meg mirrored her words with actions.

Grant swallowed, his eyes glistening. "Thank you for doing this. I miss my Ruby so much. It's probably too late to get her back, but I have to try."

Josie met his gaze. "We've only had Charlie a few days and already I can't imagine how I'd feel to lose him."

"It's awful," Grant's voice trembled. "I have no idea if she's alive, dead, or being mistreated. If I ever get her back, I'm turning my garden into Fort Knox."

We settled in Keith's lounge – Grant next to Josie on the settee, Dan on the other side of him, Meg in the armchair, while Becki, Keith and I pulled up chairs. Above us the clock ticked. When Keith had booked the taxi, he'd insisted it had to be Stan, as he'd driven a friend the previous week and had told Keith he'd be safe with him. That had stunned the woman into a silence that lasted so long, Keith had to check she was still on the line.

She'd told him that they didn't usually assign drivers, but if he could make it eight o'clock rather than seven thirty, she'd oblige.

We chuckled as he told us the story. "You'll probably find that he's speedy Gonzalez," Meg said.

Keith's eyebrows rose and his face paled. "I hope not. I'm a twenty-mile-an-hour man."

Becki patted his arm. "You'll be fine. Just think of Ruby."

"I'll buy you a pint for this," Grant said. "After I collect you."

At five past eight, a car horn tooted. Keith stopped drumming his nails on the wooden arm of his chair. Josie mirrored his worried expression as Becki went to take the sleeping puppy from her arms.

"I'll hold him tight," Becki assured her.

Keith slipped his arms through his jacket, grimacing. He'd been quiet since Meg had told him about Stan being a fast driver. But all he had to do was sit in a taxi telling Stan about his gorgeous new puppy. As he disappeared outside, Becki followed with Charlie in her arms. Unable to contain her curiosity, Meg dropped to all fours and crawled into Keith's bedroom. I didn't know what Keith would make of us being there, but I followed, kneeling beside her to peer out from behind his curtains.

Becki dashed down the path, calling for Keith. He turned, put his hand to his mouth and said, "Oops! I forgot my keys."

"You'll need them for later. I'll be doing the night shift, remember?"

"Will do." He paused to pet Charlie and got into the taxi. After a brief conversation with Stan, the car roared away.

I gulped. "Oh dear! Lewis Hamilton has nothing on him."

We crawled back out to find Becki coming back in. She caught us down on all fours. Looking puzzled, she shook her head. "I won't ask what you're doing down there."

Dan came into the hallway, hitching up his collar. Although it was nearly June, a chill wind swept through the open door. He waited while Grant thanked Josie, who wished him luck finding his dog. While Dan and Grant headed to Berrinton to pick up Keith, Becki took Josie home, leaving Meg and me to watch TV. While it was unlikely that Stan would return tonight, he might decide to drive past at some point to check out the house, and we wanted to be part of the action.

An hour later, the men returned. Keith turned off all the lights and drew the lounge curtains, leaving us with a lamp in the corner that cast a cosy glow across the lounge. Then he fetched a bottle of wine from the kitchen and poured us all a glass. Although I wasn't keen on red wine, I sipped my drink while he recounted his exploits.

"That Stan is a terrible driver." He clutched his chest.

"Twice he nearly rear-ended cars. I kept up my charade, telling him that my mate had said he drove slowly, and you know what he said?"

Keith waited for us to shake our heads before elaborating. "He reckoned it must have been rush hour, as he didn't believe in speed limits. After that nightmare, I made Grant poodle back." When his mobile dinged, he checked it. "Just a van going past. I've made Grant park on the other side of the road and I've reset my camera, so it picks up movement in the road. I might regret that at three o'clock in the morning."

"So what did you tell Stan?" Meg asked.

"What we agreed. After Becki had made sure he'd seen Charlie, I spent the whole journey raving about my wonderful new puppy. Told him it cost me four figures, but my wife was determined we'd get a proper pedigree. No mongrels for us." He winked at Sam, who glowered back.

"She's not a mongrel, she's a Heinz," she said. "Roo's the mutt."

"Leave Roo out of this." I gave Meg a playful shove.

"Roo's beautiful," Dan murmured. "I love going into the courtyard to find her there."

Keith and Grant frowned. They clearly didn't realise we had a shared courtyard. I didn't get a chance to explain either, as the conversation rewound back to Stan.

"So, do you reckon he'll come back tonight?" Meg took a sip of her wine and scowled. "No offence, but this isn't for me."

"I've got a bottle of Pinot Grigio in the car, if you'd prefer that," Grant said.

Meg nodded. "Please. I prefer a drier wine."

When Grant went to retrieve his bottle, we watched his progress on Keith's phone, sniggering as he stooped in front of his wing mirror to smooth his hair.

"What's he up to?" Meg said.

Becki chuckled. "Preening himself for you."

Bottle in hand, he sauntered back across the road, making the phone ding again, while Keith returned to Meg's earlier point – which we'd all forgotten – telling us that it was unlikely Stan would be back later, but he might try over the next few days. "He reckoned that he doesn't finish until five in the morning at weekends, so he's hardly likely to come around then. But he might have been trying to trick me. After all, I'd just told him that my house was empty with an expensive puppy home alone."

A thought nagged at me. I'd voiced it the other day – but Meg had been adamant that there was something dodgy about Stan and he'd mentioned dogs. Still, it was a possibility we had to consider.

"What if Ruby's thief isn't Stan? The police must have investigated him by now. Have you spoken to them, Grant?"

"They said they were following all leads."

"I think we should still keep checking other avenues. Just in case."

Meg sighed and took the fresh glass of wine that Grant handed to her. "You're right." She yawned, not bothering to cover her mouth. "I'll start making phone calls to the other taxi companies on Monday. We've got the craft fair tomorrow, so we can ask around and see if we can find other potential leads."

Chapter 27

Kirstie had put a tarpaulin out, upon which she laid her yoga mat in the shade, away from the hot sun that prickled my skin. She'd also brought along her pooch, a well-behaved black and white collie that looked like a pirate with a dark patch around one eye. On command the dog lay down on the mat, his ears pricked, eyes bright with curiosity. She fiddled with her mobile phone and soon the sound of plinking water and pan pipes filled the air.

"This will be interesting," Meg hissed as Kirstie lay down beside the dog and started gentle stretching exercises, working first his back legs then his front.

Tourists strolled past, barely glancing at the pair, as if dog yoga was an everyday occurrence. I couldn't believe the dog's control when a family walked past clutching open boxes, from which they snaffled chips. One of the children dropped one and a gull swooped down to pick it up, flapping away with it.

Meg nudged me, her eyebrows raised knowingly. "Three, two—"

A squeal ripped through the air, then there was a crash as the upended box hit the ground and a second gull fled the crime scene. The child stood mute in shock then began to wail as gulls dived around her, plucking her dinner from the ground.

"Gerroff!" Andy stamped his foot but the gulls just skittered aside, refusing to move far from their lunch.

The family scarpered with their howling child, leaving chaos in their wake. I grabbed a bag and set about clearing up the mess. Unperturbed, Kirstie continued with her yoga. As I wiped my greasy hands on a wet wipe, I watched her kneeling on the mat, her dog's paws on her shoulders.

"I can't say I fancy trying that with Amber," Meg said. "Their mouths are almost touching, and I've seen the places Amber likes to put her nose. Do you really think this is going to encourage people to come into your shop?"

I shrugged. "I asked Kirstie the same thing and she said that it didn't matter either way. This would be a good training session for Cyprus."

"For *who?*" Meg pulled a face.

"Cyprus. She got him from a foreign rescue organisation when he was a pup."

"Good thing she didn't get him from Cockermouth, Crapstone or Penistone."

"It's pronounced Penny-stone." I sighed. "Anyhow, Cyprus is a country, not a town."

"Hungary, then. Can you imagine? *Hungary, are you hungry?*" she called in a high-pitched voice, causing a visitor to look at us in surprise.

Andy wandered past carrying taster pieces of his daughter's freshly baked millionaire shortbread. They were meant for potential buyers, but Meg pinched one, popping it into her mouth. It bulged at the side of her cheek as she grinned. Spitting crumbs, she said, "As it happens, I am."

Kirstie had moved to lie down beside Cyprus. She pushed herself up, forming an upside-down V with her bum in the air, while her clever dog stretched out his front paws, planting his rear end in the air too.

"I wouldn't mind trying that with Roo," I said. "How long would it take to teach her, do you reckon?"

Meg pursed her lips. "I wouldn't mind being able to do what she's doing full stop. I'd end up with my boobs in my face and my belly hanging down."

Meg wasn't plump, but I could see her point. With Kirstie's lithe body and her long neck, she looked so graceful. In comparison, Meg and I would be like Geraldine in the ballet scene in the *Vicar of Dibley*, lumping around, looking anything but serene.

A spiky-haired woman came over to us.

"Isn't that your friend, Shona?" I asked Meg. "Ask her if she's heard anything more about Ruby."

While Meg went off to talk to Shona, I handed out leaflets for Becki's shop – her business hadn't recovered since Peter had instigated the damaging rumours – and ones offering a reward for information on Ruby. From where she stood at our stall, Becki caught my eye and pointed to a woman in lightweight sports clothing, who stood watching Kirstie.

I headed over to the woman.

"I'd be interested in doing that," she told me.

Hiding my surprise, I handed her a flyer about Kirstie's services. "Go over and have a chat to her. She won't mind."

The woman looked doubtfully at Kirstie, who'd resumed her 'bum up' position. I led the woman over and knelt beside Kirstie, mirroring them with my head on the ground, backside in the air, to advise Kirstie that she had a customer. Gracefully, she got up, patting Cyprus on the head and telling him to lie down. He lapped at a bowl of water then did as she had asked, while I ambled away, wondering what I was doing wrong with Roo.

After a few minutes Meg returned from her chat with Shona, giving me a rueful shake of her head. "Not a dickie bird, but she's going to ask around." Then her eyes widened. "Look at that!"

I turned to see Shona taking two squares of millionaire shortbread from Andy's tray. She wolfed one down and gave Andy a cake-filled grin. Just like Meg had done to me earlier.

"Greedy mare." Meg scowled. "Those B&Bers are always on the lookout for freebies."

Behind them the pub tables were full of people eating and drinking beneath umbrellas. Many had caught the sun, their noses crimson, white lines crisscrossing their reddened shoulders or backs. A waiter sidled between the groups, collecting glasses. My throat felt parched, so I headed back over to the stall and fetched my bottle of sparkling water. It gave a satisfying hiss when I twisted the lid. As I glugged the water, I spotted Dan sauntering towards us wearing sunglasses, his beige chino trousers crisply ironed, a jacket slung over his shoulder, even though the sun blazed, glinting on the windows of the colourful cottages tiered around the harbour. I touched my too-warm shoulders and wished I'd worn a long-sleeved top rather than a thin T-shirt.

Kirstie touched my arm. "I'm going to take Cyprus home. It's getting too hot for him."

I picked up the leaflets outlining her training services. "I'll keep telling people about you, although there's not so many locals out today."

She smiled. "That woman has signed up, so I'm pleased."

As she walked away, Dan ambled over, wafting the scent of aftershave, his sunglasses concealing his eyes. A hint of dark hair peeked between his unbuttoned shirt collar. For a moment, I imagined him bare-chested on a beach, looking trim in a pair of shorts. Blushing, I glanced away.

He didn't notice or, if he did, he hid it behind a charming smile. He lifted his jacket. "I don't know why I brought this." Then he noticed the leaflets I held. "May I?" As he scanned it, a cute dimple cut into his cheek and he chuckled. "Dog agony aunt? I know someone who could do with that."

"Are you talking about me?" I said.

He laughed. "No, Roo's lovely. My friend's dog, on the other hand – talk about a nightmare."

Meg ripped the leaflet from his grasp. "No, you don't!"

Startled, Dan's mouth gaped. I snatched it back from her and pushed it into his hand.

"Meg! That's—"

She glared at him. "Don't think you can offer a dog agony aunt service in your place too. That's Jenn's idea."

He scratched his head. "Believe me, that's the last thing I'd want to do."

"Oh!" Meg placed her hands on her hips. "Not good enough for you, is it?"

Muttering an apology, I pulled her away. "Don't be so rude. I thought we were all friends now."

Dan had gone to talk to Becki. What must he think of me? One minute he was helping in my shop, taking Roo for a walk while my neck healed, and the next moment my best friend was attacking him for reading a leaflet.

Meg tracked my gaze. "When is he opening his shop, anyhow? He's taking his time sorting it out."

I hesitated. "I haven't asked. I don't like to talk business with him. It doesn't feel right."

"If it doesn't feel right, that's probably because it isn't," she said sharply. "Look at him. I mean, *really* take a look."

We turned in Dan's direction. He'd hooked his jacket back over his shoulder, holding it in place with his index finger, and pushed his sunglasses up to rest in his hair. Becki grinned at something he said, her head coyly to one side. She picked up one of her heart-shaped rose quartz crystals from the table and signalled for him to move closer, cupping her hand to whisper in his ear. If I didn't know Becki better, I'd say she was flirting with him. But she wouldn't do that. She was just being her usual friendly self. Anyhow, she was a one-man woman and wouldn't do anything to upset Keith, who was at home in case Stan appeared.

"So?" I said.

Meg huffed at me. "He's suave. Too good to be true. He's wrapping us all around his little finger, and he knows it."

"But he's Grant's friend."

Her face soured. "Has it ever occurred to you that none of us actually knows him that well? He's bought a pet shop next to yours, yet he rarely talks about it. He's even had the windows whitewashed so no one can see inside, but he's been in your place working and getting to know your customers. He's made friends with Peter, then Grant. When Ruby goes missing, he's suddenly in our faces, there to help."

I tried to butt in, to tell her I disagreed, but she steamrollered me into submission, holding out her hand to show she hadn't finished and talking over me.

"You said yourself, it might not be Stan. What if the thief is closer to home? I mean, no offence, but what better person to sell dogs than someone in the pet shop business? And what better way to make sure you don't get caught than by being buddies with the ones searching for the dog? It was Dan's idea to trap Stan. Who says he isn't winding us up by sending us on yet another wild-goose chase?"

"One of our own creation," I blurted when she finally took a breath. "Grant spotted the taxi outside his house that night and we followed up the lead. Anyhow, I can't agree with you about Dan. You need to give him a chance."

Pursing her lips, she pointed at me. "We'll keep on Stan's case, but I'm going to watch Dan very carefully from now on."

Chapter 28

The beach day had been postponed by a week as we hadn't time to do the necessary work. When Becki popped in on Monday lunchtime to arrange an impromptu committee meeting to discuss it the next night, she found me groaning in discomfort and slathered in aloe vera, my shoulders and arms glistening and scarlet, and pale circles around my eyes from my sunglasses.

She wore a colourful kaftan that I hadn't seen before. Unlike me, she had a healthy glow – her nose and cheeks dappled by freckles after being in the stall's shade the previous day.

"What's this?" Becki picked up a small box from the counter and turned it around to examine it.

"It's a GPS tracker that attaches to a dog's collar. I had a customer request it. I bought two, just in case." I shrugged. "You never know, someone else might want one."

Even though she'd put her reading glasses on, Becki squinted as she read the packaging. "Oh, that's a shame. You have to sign up for a contract, or else I'd consider it for Flossie. She's proving to be an escape artist. With that, and CC who's permanently up the tree now as he's terrified of her, it's all becoming a bit of a nightmare. I can't wait for Edna to get back home."

I wished I could help out, but there was no way Flossie could stay here. Not with Roo.

"How about I put the kettle on?" I said.

She checked her watch. "I can make it a quickie. I have a reading at two."

While I bustled around the kitchen, she leaned against the counter examining her nails. She didn't speak until I held out her coffee, which she took from me, then put on the side.

"Keith hasn't seen Stan's taxi," she said. "That ding on his mobile phone is doing his head in. He says he's going to have to realign the camera so it's just on the drive. It'll still pick up anyone going into the garden – that's if this Stan actually ever comes back."

I surveyed her over the rim of my cup, recalling what Meg had said. "Do you think…" I hesitated and reformulated my words. I didn't want to make it sound like I thought Dan was capable of stealing Ruby. "Meg thinks it might be someone closer to home."

Becki gazed out of the open window. From her angle, she'd see little but blue sky and puffs of cloud. But a breeze drifted in, bringing with it the distant cries of gulls above the drone of cars.

I kept going. She'd assume that I'd changed the subject, not realising the link between my comments. "What was Dan talking about yesterday? Did he ask you about Ruby?" Was that too obvious? "Or when he planned to open his shop?"

After Dan and Becki finished chatting, he'd given me a friendly wave and strolled off in the opposite direction. For some reason, I'd felt a disappointment I barely understood.

"I asked, but he didn't give me a straight answer. He's waiting on workmen, who promised to come back dreckly." We shared a smile, knowing the pain that came with that word. "If he can't get them to come on time, no one can."

"Why do you say that?"

She shrugged, her fingers wrapped around her mug. If I hadn't felt so morose, I'd have admired her latest nail artwork. "It's interesting watching how he works. He doesn't talk about himself; he asks questions, makes you feel special."

My sense of gloom deepened. So he was like that with everyone. Not just me. Ridiculous. It wasn't as if I liked him, was it? The kitchen darkened as a cloud covered the sun.

"What's wrong with that?"

"I didn't say there was anything wrong. Just that he's charming. Before I knew it, I was telling him about my business, the types of crystals I sold in my shop, my son refusing to get out of bed before noon. But after he left, I realised that I'd found out nothing more about him other than his troubles with his workmen. Yet it's usually me who listens rather than talks." She chuckled, her perceptive eyes surveying my glum face. "You're being quite defensive about him."

"Not really," I said. "How's Keith?"

"I've already told you. He's fed up with his mobile going off at all hours. His customers think he has a mistress as he can't tell them why his phone keeps dinging. It won't be long before someone comes into my shop to tell me they think he's two-timing me. Anyhow…" She put her half-full cup on the side. "I have to go. Don't forget – seven tomorrow night at the Fisherman's Rest."

She left me feeling miserable. Sighing, I poured her tea into the sink, not caring that it splashed the sides. Becki's words bothered me more than I could believe. As I washed up, a voice filtered up from the courtyard. I peeked out of the window to see Dan chatting to Roo as he fondled her ears. She laid her head on his lap, gazing at him in adoration. I didn't mind Roo liking him so much – it was lovely for her to have more company – but I felt unsettled at the thought of Dan being a charmer.

In my landing hung a tapestry with the embroidered words, 'To thine own self be true'. If I had to be honest, my true self was shaded in green. For Becki that would mean life, renewal and nature. Whereas for me it stood for jealousy.

♦

I arrived at the Fisherman's Rest to find the committee members seated outside beneath the shade of a wooden canopy. Thank goodness. While my sunburn had faded, my damaged skin was peeling, and hung like cobwebs from my shoulders. I'd chosen a loose cotton top with long sleeves, but my arms itched beneath the fabric. I fought the urge to scratch them.

Keith's phone sat in the centre of the table, reminding us that we were still waiting for Stan's hoped-for visit. But, since Keith had moved his camera to focus on his empty driveway, it had remained silent. Beside him, Meg sat with her pad, twirling her biro and drumming it on the tabletop, impatient to get started. She'd pushed her sunglasses into her hair, strands curled untidily around the lens. Tonight she wore an old pink T-shirt with a rippled love heart on the front. Usually I wouldn't notice, but she'd taken more care with her appearance lately. Each day had become a maiden voyage for another top or a pair of trousers.

Then I guessed why. Grant hadn't been invited, or Dan, as Becki said we were here to talk about the beach day, and nothing else. We'd had to put back the proposed day once because of searching for Ruby, and we didn't want to do it a second time.

"Let's get down to business." Becki prodded Meg's pad. "Can you find the previous sheet? We'll see if anyone has actually done anything yet."

"Who put you in charge?" Meg pouted, but she dutifully flicked through the pages to find the notes from our previous meeting.

After a shame-faced few minutes, where Meg listed what we'd agreed, and we admitted to having done nothing, we settled down to an animated discussion about balloons, music and shells. Keith promised the latter – he would ask one of his restaurant customers to save scallop shells for us. Then we could make wind chimes or string them across our shops. Andy would make beach-themed buns, I'd buy in more seaside and pirate dog wares, while Sam would bring out Torringham tea towels. We'd add any other bright ideas on WhatsApp.

Within moments of Meg putting away her pad and pen, our conversation turned to Ruby. When Meg voiced her doubts about Stan, Keith frowned.

"But you were the one who heard him mentioning dogs." He shook his head. "I know that the police haven't found anything yet, but I think you were on to something. There's definitely something shifty about him. We need to give it another go. Find out where he lives."

"But how?" Meg said. "Short of tracking him around Berrinton, what can we do?"

Tracking? The word sparked a lightbulb moment. I gasped, and all heads turned in my direction. I grinned and raised my drink to them.

"I have the perfect idea."

Chapter 29

Grant agreed to pay for the GPS contract, so I donated my dog tracking device to the cause. After downloading the app, he did a trial drive around the countryside with Becki and the tracker, leaving Meg and me with his phone. Every ten minutes we got a call from Becki asking us to tell her where she was and all but once – when they went out of GPS range – we were able to pinpoint their location.

As Keith had to be the one going in the taxi again – we thought it would look odd if another person asked for Stan to take them back to Torringham – it had to be Saturday night. I grimaced at this. Although the tracker battery would last for days, I didn't like the idea that a customer might happen across the device down the back of Stan's rear passenger seat. Who knew what drunken revellers did? If they were sick, Stan would have to clean the back seat, or they could drop money and find it while searching.

"Can we make it as late as possible?" I pleaded.

Keith raised weary eyes to mine. "I have to get up at five every weekday to go to the fish market, and you want me to go to bed at that time on my one day off?"

"It's for Ruby." Becki smiled and laid her hand on his arm. "And besides, we'll all be up with you."

From the look on Meg's face, she hadn't considered that. Neither had I, but we couldn't expect Keith to go through the pain alone.

As he picked up the phone, he frowned. "What excuse

can I give? I mean, where would they pick me up? It's hardly like a fifty-year-old would be clubbing until three in the morning."

Becki shrugged. "Ask to be picked up from Purple Paradise. They have an area for over-twenty-fives where they play nineties music."

Keith looked aghast. "Purple Paradise. Are you kidding? You've picked the local druggies' hangout – the one place in Berrinton that no one in their right mind goes."

"But you won't be inside." Meg rolled her eyes. "You're just making it look as if you have been."

"I'll need a stiff drink if I'm getting in that man's cab again."

We could hear the taxi dispatcher's voice filtering from the phone. Again, she sounded incredulous that Keith wanted Stan. Finally she regained her composure and chuckled.

"It'll have to be two o'clock. And it'll cost you thirty-five quid at that time."

"I-I..." Keith stuttered but, from the end of the table, Grant gave a thumbs-up. He'd cover the cost.

"Okay."

♦

Saturday rolled around. After spending the evening at Meg's flat drinking tea and watching the clock tick, I had an inexplicable urge to find a kebab shop when we got to

Berrinton. After dropping Roo off, I got into Meg's newly mended car to find that a layer of dust no longer covered the dashboard, while the plastic bottle in the footwell, the crumpled tissues and empty sweet wrappers had been cleared away. But an empty sandwich carton had already been discarded on the floor and a disgusting smell pervaded the air, one the freshener dangling from her rear-view mirror couldn't mask. I wrinkled my nose. Meg chuckled.

"That's Amber. She loves to roll in stuff. Thank a fox for that stink."

Puzzled, I gazed at her. Amber had looked pristine when I'd been in Meg's flat earlier. "She smelled fine to me."

"I showered her. But with all the palaver, I forgot about the blanket in the car."

Grimacing, I rolled the window down. If Keith thought his journey would be bad, ours would be ten times worse.

We arrived at Keith's house, where I sprang out of the car, flapping my hand in front of my face. "I don't think I can get back in there. Can't you get rid of the blanket? Put it in Keith's back garden or something."

Without asking Keith, she took the blanket from the back seat, holding it gingerly between finger and thumb, well clear of her clothing, and dumped it beside Keith's garage door, telling me she'd pick it up later. We followed Becki inside, wiping our feet on the mat, to find Grant huddled at the dining table and Keith nowhere to be seen.

Becki rolled her eyes. "He was fretting about looking

out of place among all the partying youngsters, so I've had to go back to the house to borrow a couple of Nathan's tops. I found the biggest ones I could find, but…" She shrugged. "I'm not sure what they'll look like."

Grant pulled a sorrowful face. "I'm sorry you're all having to go to this bother on my behalf. It should be me going in the taxi."

"You can't." Becki put her hand on his shoulder. "If Stan did take Ruby, he might recognise you."

As Keith walked into the room, a strong scent of aftershave wafting around him, I stifled the urge to giggle. He looked ridiculous in a too-short black hoodie. It hung, unzipped, over a grey shirt which hung loose over his jeans. He tugged at the tight sleeves, trying to pull them to his wrists, but failed. "How do I look?"

"Nice!" Meg said without a hint of sarcasm.

Grant raised his eyebrows, but didn't say a word.

Keith slipped the hood over his head. "At least no one will recognise me."

"I don't know why you're worrying," I said. "You are allowed out at night."

"Believe me, no one in their right mind would want to be seen at Purple Paradise," he growled. "The last thing I need is a rumour going around that I'm going after young girls or something."

♦

Although Grant would return from Berrinton with Becki

– Meg and I had volunteered to follow the tracker when Stan finished his shift – I offered to sit in the back of Becki's car on the way there. Grant gave me a grateful smile, probably assuming I'd gone out of my way to give him time alone with Meg. But I had to confess, my overriding concern was the smell in her car. I felt a bit guilty, especially when Meg glared at me. I guessed she didn't want Grant to see behind her façade of dainty tops, freshly washed hair and careful make-up. Even though she'd removed the blanket, we hadn't thought to leave the car windows open to get rid of the stench. I was sure she'd come up with an excuse, though – she'd probably blame me for treading in something.

Becki drove, while Keith sat beside her, fretting whether he'd survive the journey back in Stan's taxi. Even at this time of night, cars whizzed past us, some with beams so bright they blinded me. Hedgerows turned to racing green, then faded back to grey. Distant hills loomed, silhouettes against the sky. We moved on until I spotted the sea below, the lighthouse beaming bright. Berrinton's colourful promenade lights twinkled in the distance. Above us, a hazy aura surrounded the smiling moon, casting a silver glow across the sea. Stars glittered in the inky sky, the North Star shining brighter than the rest. Nearby I found the Plough – the only constellation I knew. My ex, Tim, had been able to name most of them, drowning me in names and shapes I could never remember.

Becki indicated left, taking the bypass to Berrinton,

even though Grant and Meg had gone straight ahead, taking the coast road. We reached Berrinton and parked near the harbour. Waves lapped against the sea wall and yachts bobbed in the marina, their masts gently swaying. Although it was one o'clock and most of Torringham had been asleep when we'd left twenty minutes earlier (Keith had been impatient to leave), young people thronged the streets. Women tottered on impossibly high heels. Music filtered from a nearby bar and shrieks and laughter filled the air.

A family wandered by with a child in a pushchair, incongruous among the revellers. The young boy rubbed his eyes and yawned. I couldn't help copying him. We headed across the road and into a busy side street, where the smell of fried food hung in the air and a noisy crowd clustered outside a brightly lit takeaway. Across the road a neon sign flashed the words 'Purple Paradise'. Outside stood several bouncers watching a straggly line of clubbers. Crikey! Did people go *into* nightclubs at this time in the morning? Not for the first time, I felt older than my years. We waited a distance from the crowd. A chill breeze cut through my jacket. I hugged it tight, shivering in sympathy for the women in their strappy tops and the lads in their thin shirts.

Soon Grant and Meg joined us. She held a cone of ketchup-splattered chips, a sheen coating her fingers. I pilfered one without being invited, and soon regretted it. But when she offered another, I shrugged and took it. The chips might be greasy, soggy and hard in the centre, but they were food.

At twenty to two – far too early – Keith hitched his hoodie over his head, gave Becki a peck on the cheek and the rest of us a thin-lipped smile, and traipsed across the road, his shoulders sagging, his head low.

"Poor Keith," Becki whispered.

We stepped back into the shadows. A black taxi drew up and a couple jumped in. As it pulled away, we spotted Keith talking to a young man, similarly clothed in a dark hoodie.

"Oh look! He's made a friend," Meg cooed.

As the time edged towards two o'clock, the two men were still talking. Grant checked his watch for the tenth time in as many minutes and suggested we walk a bit further away, just in case Stan spotted us.

"We can keep track on here." He held out his phone to reveal a blinking circle on a map. Zooming in, we could see the GPS pinpointing Keith's exact location.

We moved down to the bottom of the street, out of sight of the road, but still able to see Keith and his new friend. When Keith and the lad strolled towards the road, we stepped from the pavement to catch sight of a silver taxi, its indicator flashing, its rear brake lights glowing. The lad took the front seat, while Keith slipped into the rear.

"What is he doing?" Becki raised her hands and turned to us, her expression anxious.

Meg gave her a reassuring smile. "You'll probably find he knows that bloke. He's probably from Torringham."

"I hope so." She glanced at Meg and me. "You will be

okay with us leaving you here, won't you?" She looked back up the road, frowning.

Grant handed Meg his phone. "Thanks for doing this. Drive carefully. I've already cost you a fortune."

Meg tutted. "We're big girls, you know."

Becki clutched Grant's arm. "Do you mind if we run back to my car? I don't know why, but I have a bad feeling about this."

Chapter 30

Meg and I strolled back to her car, holding Grant's phone while we monitored Keith's progress. The taxi had taken the coastal road out of Berrinton. If Becki had waited a moment longer, we could have told her that. I tried calling her number, but it just rang out.

"She's probably got her phone on silent." Meg scowled. "And we've got Grant's phone, so we can't tell her not to take the bypass."

The flashing blue dot moved into a side road. Meg frowned and looked at me. I shrugged. "Maybe there's roadworks or something."

The dot started to move again, going back towards the main coastal road. It turned towards Torringham.

"Look, they're heading under the railway bridge." The phone screen shone on her face, lighting her devious expression. "This would be perfect for stalking a partner having an affair. Hide it in the car when the husband says he's going to see his grandmother overnight and bang, you've nabbed him! He's booked into a hotel in Blackpool."

"Or it could be misused by a controlling partner who wants to keep tabs on his other half."

She grimaced. "That's true. We'll stick to stalking taxi drivers."

As I stood by the car park pay machine, rifling through my bag for change, Meg held up the phone. "I think it's jammed. The dot's not moving and it hasn't done for a few minutes now."

"Give it another minute," I said. "It might be the GPS signal."

We got into her car and she handed me the phone. The blue dot still hadn't moved. I frowned. If it was the GPS, the app would tell us it had no signal. I shut down the app and restarted it, but the dot still hadn't moved. Either the car was at a standstill or the tracker had malfunctioned.

I clicked my seatbelt into place. "We'd better go and see what's happening."

Meg crunched into gear and we set off, past the red, green and blue lights strung along the promenade. They reflected on the dappled sea. Opposite, restaurants sat in the gloom but for a few backlights by the bar areas. Like Torringham, this part of Berrinton had gone to bed.

We followed the coast road, my curiosity turning to concern. Had the tracker been thrown out? Or, more likely, had Stan's taxi broken down? Ahead of us was the iron railway bridge. Once we'd rounded the corner, we'd find out the reason for the delay. As we closed in, blue lights flickered against the brickwork and on the beach huts beyond. Keith's fear must have been realised – there'd been an accident! Darting me an alarmed look, Meg steered the car around the bend, where a police car blocked our path. Beyond, three other police cars surrounded a vehicle. In all the chaos, it was hard to make out its colour. At least there wasn't an ambulance. Yet.

A policeman appeared, signalling for us to turn around,

but Meg ignored him and drove into a small side road that led to a line of guesthouses. Bumping the car up a kerb, she pursed her lips.

"It looks like the taxi Keith's in."

"Are you sure?"

She shrugged. "There's only one way to find out." She jerked her head towards the policeman who'd tried to block our path. "Just don't let him see us."

We stepped out into the chill of the flickering blue night. Voices echoed above the tinny sound of a radio receiver and the nearby sea lapping against the shore. We tiptoed over the bumpy grass, sticking to the shadows behind the beach huts. Ahead, headlights cut through a gap between the huts. Tufts of grass tangled our feet as we sidled through, shielding our eyes from the dazzling glare. We stepped onto the pavement, beside the boxed-in taxi. It took me a moment to focus on the scene. Bright floaters the shape of headlights scorched my vision. Meg gasped.

"They've got Keith!"

Keith was being led by two police officers towards one of the cars. He cut a solitary figure – subdued, shell-shocked. What on earth had he done? Stan stood by his taxi, throwing his hands in the air and shouting at a policewoman, but all but a few bellowed words were muted by the surrounding racket.

"…wrong man!"

The policewoman pointed to his taxi and pushed him away. Again, he lunged forward, his mouth a square of anger. Crikey! My hand leapt to my mouth. Was he going to hit her? She jabbed towards his taxi, and then to the police car. He was being told to get in his taxi or to join Keith. But why were they taking Keith, not Stan?

The policeman who'd told us to turn around appeared beside us, his mouth a grim line.

"I told you—"

I butted in. "That's our friend, Keith. Why are you taking him away?"

"You need to leave," he said.

"We can't go without our friend," Meg said. "He's done nothing wrong."

"Your friend is being taken to the station. I suggest you go home. He'll contact you if and when he is ready to leave."

"If and when?" Meg screeched. I put my hand on her shoulder to calm her down, but it didn't work. "You can't take him. He's done nothing wrong!"

The policeman shepherded us back to Meg's car, repeating his standard lines. We couldn't see Keith. We had to go home. Meg walked backwards, pleading with him, while I tugged at her sleeve, worried that we'd be arrested too – especially after what had happened to Peter Drew when he'd shoved that policeman. Finally, we reached her car and Meg slumped into the seat.

As she turned the key in the ignition, she muttered, "Becki's going to kill us."

In silence we headed towards Torringham. We should be stalking Stan, following the tracker. If he had stolen Ruby, we needed the cover of darkness for our search. But

Keith was now our priority. I clenched my fists in frustration, unable to believe that we'd been thwarted again. Then I dialled Becki's number. Yet again it rang without being answered.

"For goodness' sake!" I hissed. I waited before giving it another go, then waited another minute before I tapped redial again. Giving up, I put my phone on one thigh, Grant's on the other, and rested my elbow against the door to gaze outside. Gone was the suburban sprawl. The headlights picked out a stone wall, ivy, pink and white valerian tufts. A canopy of dark trees loomed ahead. I sighed. Another fruitless night – worse. It was a disaster. The digital clock on the dashboard glowed. Almost three o'clock. I rubbed my eyes and yawned.

Meg's headlights illuminated the sign for Torringham and the planters filled with flowers, reminding me to check the blue dot on the GPS app. Sure enough, Stan had headed back to Berrinton. Or … I had a worrying thought. What if Keith hadn't managed to put the tracker down the back of the car seat before his arrest? That would mean I was following his route. I searched for the police station on the map. It was nowhere near the harbour where Stan – or so I hoped – was currently heading.

My phone buzzed. Becki. I gulped. How would she react? While it wasn't our fault, I felt strangely guilty.

I answered. "Hi. It's Jenn."

"I've had fourteen missed calls. Is everything okay?"

"Not really. There's—"

"What's happened? Have you had an accident?

Where's Keith? He's not back yet," she gabbled, not giving me the chance to speak. "Are you at the hospital?"

"Becki! Shut up and listen!" Meg hollered.

Becki went silent.

"Keith's at the police station. He's been arrested," I said.

"Police station?" she gasped. "W-why?" I heard her mutter to someone, her voice incredulous. "Keith's been arrested!"

As Grant's exclaimed "What!" carried down the line, Becki said, "Why?"

"We don't know," Meg yelled over me.

I put the phone on speaker – even though Meg had heard our conversation without it – and held it between us. "We saw him being taken away by the police. They left Stan behind. The policeman said they were taking him to the police station."

"Which one?"

That stumped me. Was there more than one in Berrinton? I answered, hesitantly, "Berrinton?"

"We're on our way," Becki said.

Meg had pulled into a bus layby at the top of Main Road. She reversed into someone's drive to do a three-point turn.

"What's the point of us going as well?" I said.

She glared at me. "We can't leave him there."

Chapter 31

They released Keith at eight o'clock the next morning. When he stumbled, haggard, into the reception area, Becki pounced on him, hugging him, patting his back.

"Let's go." Meg yawned and slapped my thigh.

"Hold on," I said. "We need to find out what happened."

But Keith had no idea. The police hadn't pressed charges. They'd given little explanation, other than to say they'd got the wrong man. It seemed that Keith's fellow passenger was the wanted one – perhaps the nightclub bouncers had called the police after seeing him leave in Stan's taxi? – but the police hadn't realised that the man had got out when the taxi had dropped him off in a side road. That explained the unusual detour Meg and I had seen on the GPS app.

"Why did they want him?" Meg frowned. "He looked nothing like you. Surely they could see you were much older."

"Thanks!" Keith wiped his hand down his face, pulling the corners of his red-rimmed eyes downwards. Swollen pouches of skin hung beneath. "I shouldn't have agreed to let him go in the cab with me. He'd mentioned something about a skunk, but I thought he was making a joke about a lad's stripy shirt."

"Skunk!" Meg snorted. "You thought he was talking about an animal?"

Keith gave a wry smile. "I'm an innocent."

Becki slipped her arm through his and drew him outside. After three hours sitting on hard plastic chairs in the reception area, my legs had stiffened but, as we walked, the numbness faded and the warm morning breeze blew away the claustrophobia of the stuffy waiting room. We strolled past Victorian terraces, Becki and Keith leading the way back to where we'd parked our cars in a side street.

"Roo will be wondering where I am," I told Meg.

She gazed at me, her face pale. "So will Amber, but there's one thing we need to do before we go home."

I sighed, but didn't complain. She tapped Grant's arm. "Do you want to go in Becki's car or ours? We've going via Piddlingford."

"Piddlingford?" He frowned. I pulled his mobile from my pocket. I hadn't given it back to him yet.

"The GPS is showing there. We'll just drive past to check it's definitely Stan's car on the drive and nothing odd has happened, like someone finding the tracker and taking it home. Then we'll come back."

"You don't need to go to all this trouble for me," Grant said. "You both look exhausted."

Meg shrugged. "So do you, but it's just an extra forty minutes or so out of our way. At least we're not going miles to that Pengilley place."

♦

Stan's silver hatchback sat on a gravel driveway beside a moss-covered concrete path. His house was at the end of a terrace which stood apart from Piddlingford village. Perhaps they'd been farmworkers' cottages at some point. Not that I could see a farmyard. The houses were surrounded by fields that rolled down towards the bypass. He'd parked his taxi beside a long garage with an asbestos roof, the doors the same green as the gutters and front door of the house. A slate-grey peeked from beneath the flaking paint. Meg reversed her car, so we were hidden behind a tall privet hedge. The three of us stepped out to be greeted by a gentle birdsong, unlike the brash cries of the gulls in Torringham.

Stan's hedge ended beside a fence that surrounded a field. His garage obscured our view of his back garden, but I could make out a larger-than-average wooden shed with a felt roof. Goosebumps prickled my arms. Perhaps Ruby was tucked in there. Meg pointed to a wooden sign further down the road, her finger following a worn track that crossed the field, away from the house.

"A public footpath." Her face lit up. "We'll have to bring Roo and Amber for a walk later. If it looks interesting, we can come back tonight."

"Don't do that!" Grant frowned. "What if they get stolen too?"

For a moment, Meg looked worried – I did too – then she shrugged. "Loads of people must walk this way." She pointed to a distant woman with an Alsatian. "Look! She's fine."

I pursed my lips, not wishing to point out that few people would want to take on an Alsatian. As the woman got closer, what I'd thought was a red hat was revealed to be a headscarf. We headed back, dawdling so we could get another view of Stan's place. But even that wasn't enough to satisfy our curiosity. Back in the car, Meg drove up the road, using the junction of a cul de sac to circle around, telling us to keep our eyes peeled when we passed the house again. To our surprise, the woman with the Alsatian turned into Stan's driveway. A blonde ponytail hung below her headscarf and the bottoms of her green wellies were caked in dirt. It was unlikely to have come from the fields, as we hadn't had rain for over a week.

"That must be Sylvie, the wife he mentioned when he was talking to that man outside the taxi office. And maybe that's the dog."

Had the men mentioned one dog or several during their chat? I couldn't remember. But I felt more certain than ever that Stan didn't have Ruby in the shed. Surely we would have heard barking or another clue that she was there. Also, the woman would be walking Ruby with the Alsatian – unless the bigger dog was likely to attack Grant's little one. But if Ruby had been taken by Stan, she'd probably been sold by now, to someone unscrupulous enough not to care that she was microchipped, and that a scan would reveal her true owner. I grimaced. Unless the chip had been removed. I'd seen horror stories about that on Facebook.

"That puts the cat among the pigeons." Meg groaned.

"We won't be doing any midnight rescue missions. Not with that huge thing barking the place down."

Grant leaned forward, putting his hands on the corners of the front seats. "That woman … I've seen her before. She came in my shop. I'm certain of it." He scratched his chin. "She returned later to buy a bunch of daffodils. I didn't think much of it at the time, as all my customers loved to stroke Ruby. Now I think about it, she said she'd just moved to Torringham and wanted to know where I exercised Ruby, so I told her that I lived next to the park." He scowled. "I shouldn't have given too much information away, but it seemed such an innocent question. She also asked if I was going to breed from her, as she said she was thinking of getting a Pomeranian."

"From the sound of it, she managed to do precisely that," Meg said dryly.

Chapter 32

When we got back, I fed Roo and took her for a brisk walk, then decided to have a nap. As I tucked myself under the duvet cover, she cocked her head to one side, confused. Before I knew it, I woke to find it was three thirty. I grabbed my trousers from the floor and pushed my feet into them, bouncing to help ease them over my expanding backside. I really had to cut down on the cakes. After brushing my teeth, a hasty wash and swiping my hair with my hairbrush, I went through to the kitchen, where I found my mobile phone on the side showing four missed calls, all from Meg.

When I phoned her, she sounded irate. "We said three o'clock. I've been banging on your door for the past half hour."

I yawned. "Are you outside?"

"I've gone back home."

"Give me five minutes."

As I unhooked Roo's lead, she vaulted over the coffee table – too impatient to go around it – then circled me in excitement, frustrating my attempt to clip her harness on. Once out in the alley, she strained at the lead to reach Dan, who stood chatting to Peter Drew. Dan smiled and called Roo over. I didn't fancy being stuck next to a scowling Peter, so I pointed towards Meg's shop to tell him I didn't have time to stop.

Peter interrupted me. "We were just talking about

Dan's plans for his pet section."

Surprised, I gazed at him. Had he just spoken politely? That was a first. Then it occurred to me that it was an odd thing to say. What else would a pet shop have?

"You must be looking forward to a little competition," Peter continued.

Dan frowned. "I didn't see books on pet care in your shop."

"There's a few, but not many. Books aren't one of my big sellers." Using an expression Meg favoured, I added, "So fill your boots" before leaving them.

"See you at the opening ceremony," Peter called to my retreating back.

Thank goodness he couldn't see my face. He must know I hadn't been invited. I didn't care about that – we hadn't invited Dan to join in the beach day preparations – but... oh no! If Dan had booked his event for the same date as ours, all our efforts would be wasted. Customers would flock to his shiny new shop, not mine.

Meg huffed when I reached her, and prodded her watch. "I'd could have had another hour in bed. And I could have got a parking ticket."

I shrugged apologetically and opened the rear door. A wall of heat hit me, so I waited a moment to let it dissipate before patting the rear seat to encourage Roo into the car. We set off, Meg studiously ignoring Dan and Peter as we passed them. I did the same, but made it less obvious by ruffling the heads of the panting dogs.

By the time we reached Piddlingford, Meg had

forgotten my misdemeanour, laughing about the previous night, even though it had been anything but funny for Keith. She drove past Stan's house, parking in a cul de sac a short walk from his house. Stan's taxi wasn't on the drive. Without it there to hide the tufts of grass sprouting through the gravel and the slatted wooden gate that hung from its hinges, the house looked even more unkempt.

Meg didn't pause to look, but strode ahead, clutching the ball she'd brought, even though Amber was a one-way dog with balls – happy to chase, but not to retrieve them. We clambered over the stile, while the dogs slipped through a gap at the bottom.

As we followed the footpath away from the house, Meg hissed and flapped her hand at me. "This way!"

"But…" Then I realised that she was right. There was no point doing this if we stuck to the footpath.

Meg tossed the ball towards the two-metre-high chain-link fence at the back of Stan's garden. Amber sprinted across the uneven grass, chased by Roo, but neither picked up the ball. Instead, they trotted over to sniff at Stan's fence. I realised in dismay that an old cloth had been hung at the shed windows, hiding what lay inside. I checked we weren't being watched. In the distance the bay was dotted with boats and a tanker shimmered on the horizon. To one side lay Berrinton, to the other the impressive Shadwell Point headland. Torringham nestled out of sight, tucked behind woodland – although I could just see the lighthouse at the end of the breakwater. Stan would see this wonderful vista each day, along with the patchwork of rolling fields ahead and the hazy purple peaks of Dartmoor in the other direction.

Below us the field sloped down to a hedgerow, where a stile led to another field. Someone was walking there. A man? No, it looked more like a woman, although it was hard to tell. Then I spotted a dog. I nudged Meg.

"Is that her?"

Squinting, she shielded her eyes with her hand. "Yes!" She turned to me, grinning. "That means no one's at home. Stay here and keep a look-out."

Before I could respond, she dashed across the grass and over the nearby stile. Nervous, I yo-yoed between surveying the house and the field. The woman had moved behind the hedgerow, but her Alsatian zig-zagged across the field as if searching for something.

Meg pushed open the gate, which juddered against the path, and tiptoed into the garden. Her back pressed against the wall of the house, she slid around the corner and peeked through the kitchen window. I sighed. The leather strap of Amber's lead bulged from her back pocket. How would I get both dogs safely out of the field if something happened? Worse, the top window of the adjoining house was open. What if the neighbours looked out? From upstairs, they would be able to see beyond the straggly hedge between the gardens. At least the Alsatian still hared around the field, although he was closer now.

Meg darted past the kitchen door and flattened herself against the wall beside the patio window. My heart pounded, echoing in my ears. My legs felt like jelly. She peeked inside, then became bolder, cupping her hands against the pane. Amber nosed at my feet, reminding me that I stood there in full view of the neighbours. I picked up her ball and tossed it away. She gambolled after it, followed by Roo.

Meg hurried across the lawn, ducking beneath a washing line strung with socks and shirts. She reached me and pointed to the large wooden shed.

"I don't think Ruby's in there." She brushed away a strand of moss that dangled from her fringe. "It's too quiet. But I'll check. I've tried the garage – it's locked, but I could see through a crack at the bottom of the door. There's nothing but junk inside."

When she darted over to the shed, I moved further around to get a better view. She gazed inside, then shook her head at me. As she disappeared around the corner, to the front of the shed, I raised my hands heavenward in frustration. If there was nothing there, what on earth was she doing? The crackle of tyres sounded. Stan was home.

"Meg!" I hissed, although she must have heard him too.

A door squeaked. Had Meg gone inside the shed? In the car, Stan leaned over the passenger seat, as if opening the glove compartment. Too late, I realised that if I could see him, he could see me. He sat up, and our eyes met. I dashed along the fence line to conceal myself behind the cover of the shed. A car door slammed and gravel crunched.

"Meg!" I whispered. But there was no answer.

"Oi!" Stan yelled. The gate scraped against the path,

there were footsteps, and he appeared at the fence, his chin jutting, his fists clenched. He wore a stained T-shirt. "What are you up to?"

"N-nothing…" I couldn't think what to say. "My dogs. I was looking for their ball."

It lay a short distance away, next to a concrete fence post. Traitorous Amber must have picked it up after all and dropped it beside me, before wandering off with Roo to sniff something in the middle of the field. As I stooped to retrieve it, Stan's dirt-smeared jeans were in my eye line. A strange stench wafted from him – an animal smell, but not manure. Too strong for just one Alsatian. No matter what Roo did – even after rolling in fox poop – I didn't smell like that. The stench oozed out of every fibre.

I nodded towards the dogs. "I best be off."

Frowning, he lifted a filthy hand and pointed towards the footpath. He looked like a gardener or a mechanic, not a taxi driver.

"You should be sticking to the footpath."

I turned to where he indicated, groaning when I saw the woman striding towards us with her Alsatian. How would Meg get out with that dog around?

"I will," I said.

He looked hard at me. I've heard that the eyes are the windows to the soul, but there wasn't a spark of light in his grey eyes. He pursed his lips. "Well, go on then."

I hurried away, avoiding the woman, who glared at me. Perhaps she'd seen me talking to her husband, or maybe she was upset that I'd been trespassing. Hesitantly, Amber followed us, but she kept turning back to look for Meg. At the bottom of the field, I climbed over the stile and into the neighbouring field. What should I do? I'd left my friend stuck in a shed. Somehow, I had to get back without raising suspicion. If only I'd headed back to the road, rather than going this way. Should I call Meg? But what if her phone wasn't on silent? But, even trapped in the shed, she could still text me. I checked my phone just in case, and was dismayed to find I had no signal.

Nearby the dogs burrowed in a hedgerow, tails wagging. No doubt they'd picked up the scent of a rabbit or another creature. When I called to them, Roo backed out, her tongue lolling, but Amber didn't appear.

"Amber!" I slapped my legs. "Come on!"

Twigs snapped and the hedge shook, giving away her position. Rolling my eyes in frustration, I walked over, to find Amber ensnared by her collar deep inside the thicket.

"Great!" I hissed and gingerly stepped forward. Brambles tore at my jeans. As I moved deeper into the hedge, they tangled my feet and scratched my arms. Carefully, I reached down to unhook Amber. She looked at me with mournful eyes and tried tugging herself free.

"You got yourself into this," I said as I pulled at the prickly branch. "Ouch!"

Blood welled on my thumb. I sucked it and attempted again to manoeuvre my hand between the evil barbs. Once she was freed, I kept hold of Amber's collar as I fought my way backwards. Brambles clawed at her coat, shredding my clothes and skin. Crimson welts appeared on my arms.

Finally, I was out of the hedge and back in the grassy field. Amber dashed to freedom, greeted like a long-lost friend by Roo, while I hooked myself from a tenacious strand. I turned and went back the way I had come. The dogs followed me. Walking along, I kept one eye on Stan's house. Meg was nowhere to be seen. When we reached the stile by the road, a car roared past. Knowing it was a bad idea – but it would be worse if one of them got hit by a car – I threaded the lead through Amber's collar and clipped it onto Roo's. My temper frayed as the daft mutts tried to squeeze through the small gap in the stile together, but eventually I persuaded Roo to come through first.

We hurried up the road. I didn't dare to look as we passed Stan's drive. Once I'd put the dogs back in the car, I'd go back for Meg. Then I jerked to a halt, slapping my head in exasperation. Stupid! Meg had the car keys, which meant I had no choice. I had to risk calling her. Two signal bars lit the top right-hand corner of my mobile. She answered after one ring, sounding strained.

"Meg!" I hissed. "Where are you?"

"In the car." She sounded as if she was in agony. "Where are you?"

"I'll be two minutes. Hold on."

I rounded the corner to the cul de sac, thankful to find Meg sitting in the passenger seat, her door open. She clutched a crumpled tissue to her face, grimacing. "I've bust my ankle."

"How did you do that?" I asked.

"Jumping over the fence. You'll have to drive back."

She pushed away the excited Amber and plucked the blood-stained tissue from her face, leaving a fragment glued to an ugly wound on her cheek. "Sodding nail got me in the shed." Then her eyes widened. "You don't look much better. What happened to you?"

"Your dog. I had to rescue her…"

She ruffled Amber's head. "I heard something interesting, though. When Stan's wife came back, he said, 'I told you not to shit in your own back yard.'" Meg pursed her lips. "I remember that word for word, because it's an expression my thieving ex-boyfriend used."

"What does it mean?" I said.

"Listen. Then Stan's wife said, 'Torringham's hardly our back yard.' And he said something like, 'Well, it's close enough. First, we had the pigs here—'"

Confused, I said, "Pigs?"

Meg rolled her eyes. "Police… Have you never heard that expression?" Not waiting for an answer, she ploughed on, imitating Stan's gruff tenor and lightening her tone for his wife's. "And now that woman's hanging around.' Then she said, 'Stop being daft, she's just walking her dogs.' I didn't hear any more, as they went inside. Thank goodness their Alsatian didn't sniff me out." Meg frowned. "I did find something in the shed, though. A dog crate – too small for an Alsatian and, by the look of it, it's been used recently." She wrinkled her nose. "It stank."

"He did too!" I said. "He smelled really strongly of

animals. It was weird. We'll have to ask Grant if he could track where he'd been."

Meg sucked air between her teeth, her face contorted with pain. "Sadly, I won't be going anywhere today but home."

Chapter 33

After my stressful weekend, I longed for the calm of a day spent serving customers. The constant rumble and scrape of things being shifted around in Dan's shop didn't bother me. I guessed it meant he was unpacking boxes. Soon he'd open and all but my most loyal customers would head next door – if only to assuage their curiosity. I hoped he didn't plan a price war. My bank statements were looking healthier and the headache of which bill to prioritise had gone. Freedom from money worries was a wonderful feeling.

The shop bell jangled. Kirstie strolled in, looking her usual serene self. She gave me a smile and pointed to the storeroom. "I'll make myself at home. I have a Labrador coming who has an eating issue, so I'd advise you to barricade your treats."

She'd made a rare joke, albeit a poor one, but I chuckled politely. As she went to say something, Meg poked her head through the door. I gave my spider friend, Syd, a nudge and he disappeared into a crevice in the skirting board. An ugly scratch still lined Meg's cheek, but she brushed away my concern, pointing out that my arms didn't look much better. While Kirstie went into the storeroom to get ready for her client, Meg limped over to my chair and sat rubbing her ankle.

"Grant's been watching the tracker. Before Stan came back, he went out past Craggsfoot."

"Where's that?"

"It's a hamlet about three miles from Piddlingford. The GPS showed him going there from his house and back again, so it doesn't look like a taxi run. Grant googled it. Looks like a smallholding with a few barns. Hopefully, the tracker's battery won't die and we can see if he returns there tomorrow."

"Down, Archie!" A screech echoed in the alleyway. Seconds later, the door crashed open and a panting black Labrador appeared at the end of a taut lead, hopping like a kangaroo on his back legs. Behind him, his owner gritted her teeth, fighting to hold him back. When he saw the shelves stacked with dog treats, the crafty dog stepped backwards, loosening his lead, then twisted around and whipped his head free from his collar, before making a dive for my tray of filled bones.

"Archie!" She went to grab him, her fingertips millimetres from his neck, but he snatched a bone and bounded away, bashing into a shelf. Tins crashed to the ground, rolling in all directions. Archie bolted, his tail between his legs. He sprinted through the open door to my flat, and thumped up my stairs. I rushed after him, certain that I'd seen him heading into my lounge but, when I stepped inside, Archie wasn't there. I didn't bother to check behind the settee or go into my bedroom. If he'd come in here, Roo would have come out to greet him. Through the open door, she surveyed me with guiltless eyes from on top of the duvet. Too stressed by Archie's disappearance, I didn't reprimand her, but went in search of the missing dog. On the landing, I found Meg hobbling up the stairs, but a dark shape had caught my attention: Archie had discovered the defrosting chicken leg I'd tucked at the back of the kitchen worktop, away from Roo's prying nose. He stood with his feet on the worktop, stretching to reach the plate, the discarded bone at his feet. Even though he was a puppy, he was taller than Roo, although he hadn't filled out yet. At the rate he ate, it wouldn't be long before he did.

"Archie!" I shouted. Too late. He jumped down, the chicken leg hanging from his mouth. The plate tilted precariously then fell and smashed on the tiles, firing shards across the floor. Archie's eyes widened and he dashed past me – his tail between his legs and my tea in his mouth – back down the stairs.

Chasing him, I passed Meg, who gasped, "I tried to grab him."

Taking the stairs two at a time, Meg staggering behind me, I arrived back in the shop to find Archie's owner chasing him around. As Archie bounced around in glee, the chicken leg in his drooling mouth, to my horror, Roo slipped past me and joined in with a joyful bark.

"I'll get this," Meg said, taking up a 'star' position in one aisle, while I stood in the other. But Archie proved a slippery beast, ducking under our hands, smashing into shelves, and darting from the toppling packets. Muttering repeated apologies, his red-faced owner tried again to seize him, but he skimmed past her outstretched fingers, aided by Roo, who shot in between them.

"Roo!" I bellowed, but she ignored me.

Archie dropped my chicken leg in favour of another bone, and Roo snatched it up, tossing it into the air jubilantly. My dinner had become the dogs', but that was the least of my worries. At this rate, I wouldn't have a shop left. Archie's swishing tail cleared another shelf and packets fell onto the floor, then he abandoned the slobbered-over bone in favour of bird seed. Meg grabbed the box, tearing it from his mouth, but he sprang away, bashing into his owner, who tried to corral him in the corner. Just when I thought we'd got him, my treacherous Roo sprang between them and Archie vaulted over her to freedom.

Kirstie appeared beside me, raising a hand to her mouth as she surveyed the scene. She must have been safely tucked in the loo, which is exactly where I'd bolt myself when this was over. If only to get some peace.

"What on earth ... I thought a bomb had gone off." Her voice was steely. "Stop chasing the dogs. They think you're playing with them. Jenn, get Roo out of here!"

Roo pricked up her ears and dropped her spoils. She allowed me to take her by the collar, leaving her partner-in-crime tearing at a box of gravy bones. As Archie's owner stood shell-shocked, not daring to move, Kirstie took the lead from her. Before I knew it, Archie's collar was back on and he followed Kirstie meekly into her consulting room.

"I'm so sorry," Archie's owner said for the zillionth time.

Keeping a tight hold on Roo, I shrugged. What else could I do? She wouldn't be seeing Kirstie if she didn't need help with Archie.

"I'll help you clear up," Meg said.

"I'll put the kettle on first. I think we could do with a brew."

After barricading Roo in my lounge – jamming the door so she couldn't lever it open while Archie was downstairs – I made the drinks and took them into the shop. Meg had made a great start, putting the tins in the right place and the undamaged packets back on the shelves.

As I opened the door to give Kirstie and Archie's owner their tea, the woman apologised again. "I've just been telling Kirstie about his eating disorder. He doesn't stop. We've got a house rabbit. He doesn't touch her but he follows her around all day eating her poop. Everything and anything." She lifted her hands in frustration. "I don't know what to do with him."

"I'm here to help with that," Kirstie said.

Behind her, Archie lay on the blanket, his tongue lolling, his chest heaving. His tail flapped against the floor, but he didn't attempt to get up, gazing at me with his gorgeous, doleful eyes. Who would have guessed that just a few minutes ago he'd been wrecking my shop?

I closed the door and left them to talk in privacy. Meg had put my chicken next to the till, wrapped in tissue, beside a pile of punctured and ripped boxes smeared with saliva.

"I don't think it's chicken tonight," I said.

"It's just one dinner. That poor woman must spend her life fighting him off her food." She scooped bird seed into a pile and grinned. "At least there's a silver lining. She doesn't need a hoover when she's got Archie. Maybe we should call him out here to finish clearing up."

♦

Kirstie stood with Archie and his owner as I fitted him with a new harness. He wouldn't be able to slip out of this one. He seemed a changed dog, but I spotted him darting a glance at Kirstie before looking mournfully at my stacked shelves.

"Rome wasn't built in a day," Kirstie said. "I'll come to your house on Thursday and we'll do some more work."

I didn't charge Archie's owner for the packets of bird seed, even when she offered. She insisted on paying for the bones, though, as Archie would eat them. Before leaving, she apologised again. When I smiled and said there was no need to worry, I meant it. I'd regained my sense of humour. The shop would live to see another day.

"You'll need to keep Roo away from my next customer," Kirstie said.

The doorbell jangled and Dan strolled in. Chuckling, I turned to Kirstie. "Is he dangerous, then?"

She gave me an odd look, said hi to Dan and wandered back to her little room.

Dan slipped his hands into his pockets and gave me a rueful smile. "Peter blabbed about my opening event before I had a chance to invite you."

"Keeping the competition at arm's length?" I lightened my sarcasm behind a grin.

He frowned. "You're not offended about the pet books, are you?"

"Believe me, that's the least of my worries."

He pointed to the broken packets on the counter. "Supplier issues?"

"Archie issues." I stuffed the packets on the shelf below the till and wiped my hands down my trousers. "At least the shop survived."

"Ah! I see," he said, although he couldn't possibly have guessed what had happened – unless he'd heard the pandemonium through the wall. "I'm opening on Saturday evening. Bring your friends."

The evening? So he wouldn't be using our beach day to entice my customers away? That made me feel a little better, although I dreaded what would happen the following week. Would I have any customers left?

I was about to jokingly ask if the invitation included Meg when a jingle alerted me to my next customer. But I didn't need the bell. The dog took one look at Dan and started a ferocious yapping, his lips drawn back to his gums. Dan stepped back, almost tripping, but the little dog didn't let up. He looked like such a sweet thing, with fluffy golden fur and pointed ears. I could imagine that many a person had been fooled into trying to stroke him, but his appearance was just a trap to steal their fingers.

"I'll get Kirstie," I said to the dog's owner, although Kirstie must have heard her customer arriving.

"Kirstie?" the woman frowned.

"Our dog agony aunt."

When the woman gave me a puzzled look, I said, "You know, the dog trainer you booked."

"Oh no, that's not me, duck." She stooped to pick up her dog, bringing the bared teeth closer to my face.

Dan pointed to the door. "I'd better be off."

As he scarpered, the woman chuckled and tickled the dog's throat. "That's why I'm not training him. I never have to worry about queuing with my little one around."

Chapter 34

That night I sat in the Fisherman's Rest nursing half a pint of lager. Meg wore a flowery dress and strappy sandals. She'd styled her bob in loose ringlets, which I vowed to copy one day – if I could be bothered. My favoured routine involved a quick swipe with my hairbrush and a dash of mascara. Grant sat next to her, beaming with excitement as he told us that Stan's taxi had gone back out to Craggsfoot again that afternoon.

"Where is he now?" I asked curiously.

Grant checked his mobile and grimaced. "A warning came through on the app to say that the battery needed recharging. Now the GPS isn't picking up the tracker, so I think it's died. But the last I saw, less than an hour ago, he was at his house."

"Maybe it's his night off." I took a sip of lager. "Are you going to the police?"

Meg glanced up. "Why would he do that?"

I frowned. "Because it's the most sensible course of action. You don't seriously think we should go there, do you?"

Her expression told me she did. I turned to Grant. He was reasonable. He'd agree with me about the best way of getting Ruby back, but he stunned me by shrugging.

"We have no proof. What if Stan was visiting his aunt or a friend? I can't imagine the police would be happy turning up to find I'd wasted even more of their time."

"So what are you planning to do?" I said 'you', even though I knew this would involve me.

Meg grinned. "Are you free tomorrow night?" She gave Grant's arm a squeeze "We're all going to get Ruby back."

As she spoke, Dan stopped by the table, wafting a hint of aftershave. He stooped to stroke Roo and Amber, who nuzzled his legs, then looked up and gave me a wide smile. My smile flickered with uncertainty. Had Grant and Meg invited him, or had he just been passing and spotted us? When he pointed to our drinks and asked if we wanted another, I guessed it was the former. Puzzled, I glanced at Meg, who held out her glass. I thought she didn't like Dan. The last time they'd met at the craft fair she'd been downright rude to him, yet here she was, beaming a saccharine smile as she accepted his offer of a glass of white wine.

Grant got to his feet. "I'll give you a hand."

As the men went to the bar, I nudged Meg and asked the question I'd been thinking.

She smiled. "He's Grant's friend. If you can put your animosity to one side, so can I. If I want to be with Grant, then I have to accept his friendship with Dan." She chuckled. "But you can be my buffer. There's only so much I can stomach in one night."

"You and Grant, then…?"

She flushed, put her finger to her mouth and nibbled her nail, leaving me hanging in suspense. "We … er … might be a little more than just good friends."

"Last night?" I sniggered like a schoolgirl.

The colour in her cheeks deepened. "He took me out for a thank you meal because I busted my ankle."

"You didn't embarrass him, then, like you did to me?" She looked confused, so I elaborated. "You know, when you told Peter Drew that we were lovers."

"Ah!" she said. "No. We had a lovely night, although we did bump into that idiot when we were at the Lord Mountfield. He walked in, spotted us, and stomped out. It was hilarious, although Grant didn't feel the same way. At least it's spurred him on to do the one thing I've been on at him to do."

"What?"

"He's putting himself forward to be chairman of the Torringham Traders."

I gasped. "What? What will Peter say?"

"Grant's already been nominated by several others. Mick, the butcher, says we need someone to bring the traders together, not keep up the 'them and us' situation we have at present."

Dan and Grant came back with the drinks. When they sat down, I turned to Grant. "Meg's been telling me about your planned coup."

He took a swig of his beer, wiping away his frothy moustache with the back of his hand. "To be honest, it wasn't my choice. Mick and a few of the others wanted someone with a foot in each camp." He grimaced. "Apparently, both the Beach Street traders and those in the High Street trust me."

"How does Peter feel about that?" Dan asked. Meg fired him an angry glare, but he batted her away. "It's a sensible question."

Wincing, Grant sucked air between his teeth. "He's not happy. He thinks that Meg has turned me."

"On?" Meg burst into hoots of laughter, and heads swivelled in our direction. Grant flushed the brightest crimson I'd ever seen, but he seemed secretly pleased.

Dan's dark eyes glinted with amusement and he grinned, a dimple creasing his cheek. His white shirt and teeth set off his golden tan. Our gazes locked and I felt a strange burst of anticipation. Hope of something more? I longed to stay in the moment, but discomfort made me look away. There was no point. He'd switch on his lovely smile to make anyone feel good. It wasn't just for me.

Grant cleared his throat. "What time are you planning your opening ceremony on Saturday?"

His change of subject worked.

"Six o'clock. After the beach day has finished. I didn't want to step on your toes."

"A good thing too. Otherwise it wouldn't be fair on Jenn," Meg said.

Grant and Dan frowned. Hadn't they considered the impact on my business?

Meg took a glug of her wine and grimaced. "This is sweet, not dry. Did you think I needed sweetening up?"

"I can get you another." Dan rose from his chair but Meg flapped him away, so he settled back down. This time he spoke to me. "Are you doing something on Saturday,

247

then?"

Meg rolled her eyes. "Have you forgotten she's with us working on the beach day?" Then her eyes glinted. "Were you thinking of taking her out or something?"

Dan's frown intensified. "I don't understand. Why would my opening affect Jenn?"

Meg harrumphed. "If you haven't worked that out by now…" She shrugged. "Anyway, let's not talk business tonight. We've got more interesting things to discuss."

Chapter 35

The next evening, we drove out to Craggsfoot. Dan sat beside me. We'd invited Becki, but she turned us down, saying she didn't want to leave Flossie. I suspected that she and Keith were worried about the possibility of another stint banged up in the police station. Grant had insisted that we took his car in case Stan recognised Meg's, although he'd owned it for less than a week. Even though the air conditioning was on full, it did little to blast away the cloying new-car scent that clung to the fabric. I rubbed my chilled arm, feeling the prickle of goosebumps even though the sun blazed through the windscreen. In the front, Meg's hand rested on Grant's thigh. He looked odd in jeans – somehow too casual, compared to his usual chinos or suit trousers. Unlike Meg, who'd worn one of her new tops for some reason, I'd put on an old T-shirt and jeans. We may have agreed to call the police if we found anything suspicious, but I knew my impulsive friend too well, and I wanted to be prepared.

We passed Stan's house. Groans filled the car as we spotted his empty driveway. Hopefully, since it was six o'clock, it meant he was doing a taxi shift and we wouldn't find him at Craggsfoot. Grant poodled through Piddlingford, keeping below the speed limit. When Meg asked him to put his foot down, he sighed, saying that 30mph was the threshold, not a target. I chuckled to myself. It was the sort of thing my dad used to say. I guessed the old saying about opposites attracting had some basis to it. What else could have drawn feisty Meg to a man more suited to a pipe and slippers? I glanced casually at Dan, who seemed lost in thought. Maybe that's why we didn't get on. Like me, he was the owner of a pet shop. Like me, Dan loved animals. While I felt for Auntie Peg, I couldn't help but be thankful that Roo couldn't live with her at the care home. I loved having Roo with me and I'd miss her if she'd had to leave. No longer did I care about the pungent smells, her snoring and the dog hair that clung to the furnishings and drifted like tumbleweed across the kitchen tiles. I went to pluck a hair from the leg of my jeans, then changed my mind. It was better on me than on Grant's pristine mat.

As we drove away from Piddlingford, the lane narrowed and stone walls closed in on each side. Soon we moved beneath a tunnel of trees, then headed up a steep hill. When Grant's satnav directed us left, he hesitated, gazing in dismay down the rutted track.

"I told you not to bring your car." Meg sounded as if they'd been married for twenty years. "Mine would handle it better."

"How?" Grant turned the wheel in the direction of the lane.

"It's done it before. When we went to Pengilley Farm."

Grant chuckled. "We won't mention how that went. Let's hope my car doesn't end up like yours."

"It was just a little owie."

He tried – and failed – to hide a smirk. I did too. I'd

seen Meg's bumper and her smashed wing. But if she wanted to pretend it had been a tiny bump, I wouldn't argue. Ahead of us, tufts of grass sprouted along the centre of the lane. Meg and I had jolted along a similar track on our trip to Pengilley Farm. We passed a thatched cottage then two Victorian terraces, each with an empty driveway.

After we'd been driving for what seemed an age – not helped by Grant's snail pace – Meg said, "Nearly there." She tapped the satnav to turn it off. "No need for this."

Grant slowed even further to a crawl. I wound the window down, grateful to feel warm air on my face. Beside me Dan sat with gritted teeth, a muscle bulging on his jawline. His fingers worried the hem of his shirt but, when he saw me looking at him, he smiled.

Meg pointed ahead to where we could just make out a corrugated roof beyond a clump of trees. "That must be it. Go past and we'll see if we can find somewhere to park."

Grant snorted but drove on, passing the yard with its chained, padlocked five-barred gate. Beyond it lay two squat metal barns. I heard a faint howl, which became a clamour of barking.

"Crikey!" Meg hissed. She turned to me, looking apprehensive, although her eyes were wide with excitement. Grant's knuckles whitened as he gripped the steering wheel, his profile tense, his face pale. Ahead lay a small layby, rutted by tyres, the mud hardened by the sun. He squeezed the car against the hedgerow, and branches squealed along the paintwork. When he stopped, Dan got out of the car. I shifted along the back seat, accepting his hand to help me out.

Grant seemed frozen, then Meg nudged him. "Come on. Let's get this over with."

We headed back down the lane, Dan leading the way, while Meg held Grant's hand. The breeze carried the sound of yapping to us. Even though the sun beat down, the hairs on the back of my neck prickled. When we reached the gate, I turned to the others.

"Should we call the police?"

Meg shook her head. "Let's check it out first."

Before I could respond, Grant surprised me by vaulting over the gate. He landed on the other side, brushing his hands together and, without checking whether anyone was around, strode across the hardstanding towards the barns. Meg copied him. Dan and I shrugged and followed, although my legs quivered with nerves and I kept a wary look-out in case Stan or his Alsatian appeared. Straw littered the paving, blowing in the wind, but there wasn't the farmyard smell of manure I had expected. Instead, a foul odour hung in the air, like the one that had clung to Stan when I last met him.

I reached Meg by the first barn. She tugged at the padlock, then dropped it in frustration. It clanged against the metal door, sending the dogs inside into a frenzy of baying and howling. The stench had become terrible, almost acidic, making my eyes water. I held my arm to my nose.

"How many are there?"

"Loads by the sound of it," Meg said.

"I'll call the police." I pulled my phone from my pocket, thankful to see I had a signal. She put a hand on my arm. "Not yet." Then she turned, as if to speak to Grant, but he'd disappeared, along with Dan. Puzzled, we headed to the corner of the barn, where we found Dan and Grant striding towards us, grim faced.

"There's no way in," Dan said.

"Nothing's impossible," Meg told him. She gave Grant a thin-lipped smile. "I told you we'd need it."

Before I could say anything, she and Grant sprinted away. Exasperated, I said, "What's she up to now?"

Dan didn't answer. He scratched the side of his face, his brow creased. "I hope we find Ruby in there."

I knelt to peek through a tiny gap in the bottom of the door, grit biting through the knees of my jeans and digging into my palms. The stench made me gag, but I forced myself to stay there. My eyes swam with tears. Slowly, I made sense of the gloom. I could see straw and the glimmer of a metal cage, but the angle frustrated me. I got to my feet, brushing my knees, and grimaced at Dan. "I can't see much."

Meg and Grant sprinted over, red-faced and breathless. He clutched a crowbar. So much for our plan to call the police if we saw anything suspicious. I set my unease aside, understanding his desperate need to find Ruby.

He levered the crowbar beneath the fastening and hefted himself against it, his face strained, his teeth clenched. The metal bar bent but refused to yield. When Dan held out his hand, Grant stepped aside. Dan pushed hard, puce with effort, until the bolt caved. There was a loud snap, which sent the dogs into a frenzy, and two screws fell to the ground.

Meg tugged open the door, then blanched at the horrific scene inside. A terrible stink hit us like a wave. When Meg clutched her chest and retched, I fought not to do the same.

"Go…" Whatever Dan had been about to say faded away into a stunned silence.

Pens and cages lined the sides of the barn, some no bigger than crates, filled with layers of filthy straw. Some of the dogs inside clawed and jumped at the bars, desperate for freedom, while others cowered at the back, showing the whites of their eyes. I went inside. In one cage, tiny puppies nestled beside their mum, whose dull eyes assessed me. I couldn't tell her breed, her filthy coat was matted and tangled, and she had patches of bare, raw skin. I'd seen it before, but on pictures of mange-ridden foxes, not pedigree dogs, which these must be.

Grant's shoulders jerked as he walked down the row. He must be crying, but I couldn't hear his sobs over the cacophony. Meg hurried after him, laying her hand on his shoulder.

Dan's face shimmered through my tears. I couldn't speak. A huge bubble of hurt choked me. Who would do such a thing to these poor creatures? Holding up my phone, I pointed outside. He followed me. As I called 999, a man shouted, "Oi!"

"Go!" Dan hissed, pushing me away.

As I raced around the corner of the building, I spotted

Stan's taxi parked at the entrance. It seemed incongruous that such a clean vehicle should be here. But who would suspect a taxi driver of stealing dogs? I hid behind the barn, pressing my finger to my ear to mask the noise of the dogs and the shouting, but I had to move further away to hear the operator.

Meg hollered, "You disgusting piece of—"

"Police, please!" I gasped. "It's an emergency."

I gave little detail on the dogs, just saying that we'd found a puppy farm and we thought that our friend's stolen dog might be there. The call seemed to take an age. Impatient to get back, I mouthed a silent 'Come on…'. Whatever was going on outside the barn, it didn't sound good. Shouts rose above the howls. Meg shrieked.

"They need to come now! Someone's going to get badly hurt!" I yelled down the line, then I shoved my phone in my pocket and raced back. Stan was surrounded by Meg, Grant and Dan. Stan tried to shove past them, but Dan pushed him back.

"This is private property," Stan yelled, jabbing his finger towards the lane. "You need to leave! My mates will be here soon. We've done nothing wrong."

We? So this wasn't a one-man operation. I tingled with fear. If Stan had managed to call his friends, no doubt they'd arrive before the police. Then we'd be in for it. At least they wouldn't be able to get the dogs away in time, and the police would see the terrible conditions for themselves.

"My dog was on private property too!" Grant's anger

stunned me. I'd never heard him raise his voice before. "You stole her!"

"Lies!" Stan spat. He lunged at Grant, but Dan caught his arm and wrestled him to the ground, holding his arm behind his back. For a moment I gazed at Dan in admiration, then I realised I needed to help. I dived on Stan's flailing legs. Meg joined me, grasping one leg while I held on to the other. Stan twisted and kicked out, but we clung on, leaving Grant and Dan to deal with his upper half. Thank goodness Stan wasn't a huge man, although he was muscular – more than I expected from a man who drove a taxi all day.

It seemed an age until we heard a distant siren. It gave Stan a renewed impetus and he kicked out, throwing me off. As I scrabbled to regain a hold, his foot smashed my cheek, firing a bolt of pain across my teeth and face. Gasping, I grabbed his leg again.

"Are you okay?" Meg panted.

I couldn't answer. My mouth had filled with the metallic taste of blood.

Then the siren merged with another. Finally a police car pulled up outside. Two officers clambered over the gate and into the yard. Dan moved away to allow one of them to grab Stan, but I clung on. As Stan was hauled from beneath me, I fell to one side.

Dan knelt down. "That looks nasty. You might need to go to A&E."

I tried to smile, but couldn't. My cheek throbbed, and my mouth felt thick and numb. I let Dan take my hand and help me to my feet. Giddy, I staggered back, but he caught me.

"Sorry," I said, but I couldn't form the 's'.

Another police car arrived. While Grant and Meg went over to speak to a policewoman, Dan led me over to a rusty metal tank beside a trough, where he sat me down. "From what I recall, you didn't come away too well the last time you went looking for Ruby."

I tried to smile, but it hurt. I looked over into the gloomy barn, where the shadowy dogs still howled. Hopefully, they'd soon be freed from their awful jail. My wounds would heal soon enough. I just hoped theirs would too.

Chapter 36

Dan fussed around my kitchen while I lay on the settee trying to stop Roo from licking my swollen face. The pain had subsided into a dull ache, but Roo's nose managed to find the most painful spots. A sense of gloom filled my flat. We may have saved countless dogs from a life of abject misery, but we hadn't recovered Ruby. The police had promised to go after Stan's wife, Sylvie, after Grant had told them about her interest in the dog and Meg had recounted the conversation she'd overheard.

When Dan came in carrying two steaming mugs, I shifted so I could take the hot chocolate from him. Angling the cup towards the unbruised side of my mouth, I slurped the froth at the top, while Dan perched by my feet, stroking Roo.

"Thank you." It still hurt to speak, but at least my words made sense now.

He shrugged. "My pleasure."

"Not just for the drink, but for all your help. You have enough on your plate getting your shop ready to open."

His brow creased. "Do you mind if I ask something?"

I shook my head.

"I … er…" He trailed off into silence, biting his lip. Then he took a deep breath. "What is it with you and Meg and my shop? Do you have a problem with books?"

Books? I tried to work out what he meant. Of course – he planned to sell books about pets among his other wares.

I sighed. "Meg's worried, and I am too, that you'll put me out of business."

He frowned. "But how?"

What a ridiculous question. But I answered it politely, as best as I could with my swollen mouth lisping the words. "Two pet shops next door to each other means one will suffer, which will be mine, especially when it isn't visible from the road. It wouldn't be so bad if you'd picked a shop in another street. But it's too late now."

"Two pet shops?" His frown deepened. "But…" His eyes widened. "You don't think … but … who said it was going to be a pet shop?"

I put my hot chocolate on the coffee table, away from Roo's flapping tail. "Peter Drew told everyone. Apparently, it's good to have a bit of competition. But…" I cast a glum look at my bank statements and bills – all paid – piled on the armchair. "I can't see how." Then his words hit me. "So, is yours a pet shop or not?"

He scratched his head. "No, it's not. But why would Peter say that? He must have known what everyone would think."

"He wouldn't care about you – he only cared about hurting us. So—"

"I'm surprised you're still talking to me. That goes a long way to explaining why you run hot and cold, while Meg freezes me out. Grant keeps saying what a lovely person she is, but I couldn't see it myself." When he caught the expression on my face, he added, "No offence."

I gave him a wonky smile. "None taken. You've only

said the truth." I settled into the cushions, trying to look nonchalant, although curiosity ate at me. "You haven't said what your shop is going to be. Why the big secret? I mean, you've still got whitewash on the windows."

"You only had to ask. I would have told you." He chuckled. "But I kept the interior hidden for the big reveal. Do you want to see it? That's if you're up to it."

Intrigued, I eased myself to my feet. He led the way downstairs. Above the courtyard, stars littered the sky around a crescent moon. He opened his back door, snapping on the light to reveal a tiled corridor with a small kitchen to one side, a toilet and what seemed to be a storeroom on the other. A stairwell rose into the darkness. As he unbolted the door to the shop, I held my breath in anticipation.

A shaft of light from the corridor lit up a beach scene. Puzzled, I stepped past him, to see what looked like a miniature mountain ahead. He turned on the lights – not the blinding brightness of the corridor, but subdued lighting that illuminated rows of books, encased within bookcases showing scenes from around the world. He flicked another switch and the window display lit up. It was a town of model houses, with books perched between them. There was a French chateau, a Swiss-style chalet, a row of Tudor houses, even a village of straw huts. On one side, towering above a hill of books, stood Neuschwanstein Castle, which I recognised after seeing it in *Chitty Chitty Bang Bang*. It was unusual, but strangely effective.

He gave me a wry smile. "It's a bookshop, but one that specialises in travel."

"I've always wanted to run a bookshop, but my ex preferred a pet shop."

I headed over to the mountain I'd spotted earlier. Up close I realised it was not much wider than the other bookcases, but squatter with carved sides and a pointed snowy top. Inside it were books on mountaineering, rock climbing and hill walks. A section on travel around Devon featured a large cut-out of a beach scene – familiar from old-fashioned railway advertising posters – while the bookcase had been decorated with painted carvings of nearby sights of interest. Shadwell Point and its squat lighthouse protruded at one end, while a trawler cut through huge waves at the top.

"My friend created all this."

"It's incredible," I whispered in awe.

I turned and spotted children's books in a bookcase made to look like the gingerbread house that had entranced Hansel and Gretel, its sides and top decorated with fanciful cakes and sweets. Beside it sat a small table and two chairs while the walls behind showed paintings of scenes from fairy tales: Goldilocks, Red Riding Hood and Alice in Wonderland. Above, fairy lights twinkled. Magical.

The pet section was framed by a kennel frontage, with carvings featuring playful dogs and cats. I noticed a grey and white dog with blue eyes.

"Roo?" I chuckled.

Dan grinned and pointed to a cat. "And that's my Maud."

"Oh!" I glanced at Roo, who sniffed around the counter. It looked like a typical bookcase but, on closer inspection, I could see that the books had been sculpted and painted. "Will your cat be okay with Roo here?"

"Maud's in the lounge. She's been staying with a friend while this place was being renovated. It wouldn't have been fair on her with all the workmen and banging going on. She's on her last legs as it is."

I attempted a sympathetic smile, but winced in discomfort and instead patted his arm. "Your place is stunning."

He pointed to an old oak door to the side of the counter. "That goes through to your shop – it's from when they were owned by the same person. We found it behind a piece of plasterboard, but it was too lovely to cover. You'll have the same on the other side."

"Maybe, but I doubt we'll find out. I can't afford to lose the shelving space and you won't want lots of dogs in here."

"They're welcome. That's for our furry friends." He pointed to a cushion tucked in an alcove beneath the pet books. "Talking about pets, can I help with your shop tomorrow?"

I shook my head. "I'll be fine, but thank you. You have enough to be getting on with here."

"It's finished, apart from cleaning the windows, and I'll do that on Friday," he said.

"You've done so much for me and I…" I flushed, remembering all the times I'd been mean to him, when he'd done nothing to deserve it. "Well … I haven't exactly been nice to you."

"Let's keep that in the past. Anyhow, I really enjoyed working in your place last time, even if your customers said odd things about me being a spy." He gave a throaty chuckle. "But of course they would! They thought I was opening another pet shop – no thanks to Peter. You wait until I see him."

Chapter 37

I had never been so thankful that Dan was helping in my shop, although I don't know if he felt the same. I wasn't ill enough to hide away in my flat but, with my puffy lips and bruised, swollen cheek, we'd agreed that I would sit in the storeroom when customers came in. I had a mound of paperwork to do, so it wouldn't be wasted time. I'd pulled the chair to the other side of the counter, so I could dart unseen into the storeroom when the doorbell jangled. It worked well for the first customer but, when someone tapped on the window – from where I stood, I couldn't see who – Dan shot me a worried look. "It's Edna. She's pointing to the door."

Becki had told me that Edna was back home after spending a week at her sister's after being released from hospital, but I hadn't expected her to be back to her usual routine so soon. Judging by the expression on Dan's face, he didn't fancy dealing with her alone, but he signalled for me to go.

"I can't leave you with Edna," I hissed.

"You may as well," he said. "I have a feeling she may become a regular at mine soon enough."

"Are you sure?" I said, feeling even more guilty for persuading her to spend a morning or two in his shop when it opened. But I didn't feel guilty enough to hang around. Much as I liked Edna, I couldn't face a barrage of questions about my face.

In the storeroom, I knelt beside the closed door to peer through the keyhole – it was hardly spying if it was my own shop – intrigued to find out why Edna had knocked rather than come inside.

I heard Edna's voice. "Thank you. I can't carry my Flossie and open it, not with this sling."

She waddled inside, huffing, and lifted her arm for Dan to take the dog. He obliged, asking, "What can I get you?"

I chortled to myself – he'd expect her to ask for dog food or to buy something, but I knew better.

"You've moved the chair. I like it better where it usually is. Where's Jenn?"

"She's not well," he said.

"I heard what happened. How is she?"

"A bit sore, but she's fine. Just resting."

"Send her my love. It sounds a rum business. Poor Grant. I couldn't imagine what I'd do if someone stole my Flossie."

She patted her lap to show him she wanted her dog back. "Jenn usually gets me a nice cup of tea and a few biscuits."

I chuckled at her cheek.

Dan scratched his head. "Okay. I'll see what she's got."

"I prefer chocolate digestives," Edna called to his retreating back, even though I'd never offered her them before. "Or jaffa cakes. Actually, if she's got any cakes, that would be better."

I rolled my eyes. Dan would probably find my stash of chocolate brownies – bought from Andy's bakery – and give her one of those. They weren't cheap, but they were worth the price. So not only would I have no further sales this morning with Edna back, but I'd be minus two pounds on the huge slab of cake (Andy's daughter didn't stint on the sizes).

When Dan returned, Edna didn't express her delight at having my fancy brownie in place of her usual plain digestive. No doubt she didn't want to let on that it wasn't the norm. Curious, I peeked through the spy hole. He'd placed a plate and cup on the counter beside her. With Flossie in her lap and her arm in a sling, she sipped her tea and nibbled at the brownie in turn, brushing away the crumbs that Flossie didn't lap from her skirt and scattering them on my floor. As she ate, she talked, spitting yet more crumbs.

I got up from the floor and returned to work. Soon I was absorbed, my mind muting the one-sided conversation. When my bladder twinged, I groaned, regretting the three cups of coffee I'd drunk to get a caffeine boost this morning. Soon the urge became more persistent. I fidgeted with discomfort. It was impossible to access the toilet without going through the shop, so I couldn't leave without Edna finding out that I'd been hiding from her. Twenty minutes later my gentle wriggle had changed to a stand-up-and-cross-my-legs urgency. Ridiculous. I was a grown woman. As I squirmed, the years seemed to fall away and I remembered having to jump up and down outside the bathroom when I was a child, hollering at my dad to hurry up. It had never worked.

Suddenly, Edna shrieked. I dashed over to peek through the keyhole. She stood, clutching her chest, pointing to the wall. She must have seen Syd. At her feet stood Flossie, hackles raised and growling. Panic-stricken, I wrenched open the door.

"That's Syd! Leave him alone!" I shouted.

My heart dropped when Flossie pounced on a black thing skittering across the skirting board. Syd! I was too late! But still I tried to save my spider friend, prising open Flossie's jaws and scraping his broken body from her tongue. Gently I wiped the mess onto my palm. Flossie nosed at the mangled blob, but I pushed her away. She sat down, panting, giving me an open-mouthed grin. Bits of Syd's legs clung to her teeth.

"It was only a spider, dear," Edna said.

My voice wobbled and tears threatened to spill. "Some people say the same about dogs."

Just then my stomach cramped, reminding me of my urgent need. I shot upstairs, taking them two at a time. Unceremoniously, I dabbed Syd onto a piece of tissue. Before going back into the shop, I laid him among the geraniums in one of Dan's hanging baskets – still on the tissue, as he was stuck fast – and left him fluttering in the breeze.

Back inside, I found Dan kneeling beside a sobbing Edna.

"Are you okay, Edna? I'm sorry if I upset you."

She twisted a crumpled hanky in her trembling hands.

Her face was streaked with tears. "You didn't want to see me. You hid from me."

Dan's anxious gaze met mine. It was true. I hadn't felt up to listening to Edna all morning. What could I say to defend myself? I pointed to my cheek. "Dan took over the shop. I didn't want you to see me looking like this."

She glanced up and her eyes widened. Had she not noticed my face when I'd been attempting to rescue Syd from Flossie? Of course – I'd been angled to one side. Her tears subsided and she dabbed her eyes.

Raising a tentative hand to my face, she said, "Does it hurt?"

"A bit."

"Sally Arnold told me you'd all been in the wars. She heard it from Barbara Drew." When he heard Peter's wife's name, Dan grimaced, but Edna didn't seem to notice. She started to regale us with the latest gossip. "Barbara phoned Grant to beg him not to stand for chairman of Torringham Traders, but Grant said that Peter wasn't fit for the job."

I couldn't imagine how that conversation had led to Grant telling her about our rescue attempt, but I didn't need to ask. Edna elaborated. "That's when Meg grabbed the phone. She and Grant seem to be getting quite close." She eyed Dan and I, as if we could also be potential lovers, then seemed to think better of it. "Anyhow, Meg told her off. Said she shouldn't be bothering Grant at this time of night when he'd had one hell of a day. That she and Peter hadn't bothered with him since he'd lost his Ruby and he deserved better friends than that." Edna put on an indignant voice. "'Well, I never!' Barbara said. 'What gives you the right to speak to us like that, you jumped up good-for-nothing?' They were her exact words. Then Meg started shouting and told her that you were injured, Grant was in bits, and she and Peter were sitting on their big fat..." – Edna dropped her voice to a whisper – "arses." She resumed her usual tone. "...doing nothing but spouting malicious gossip to all and sundry."

"Barbara said that?" I would have expected her to retell the story, omitting any references that cast her and Peter in a less than positive light.

"Well, that's where Sally comes in. She was around their house. It was her who encouraged Barbara to call Grant ahead of the committee meeting. It's an emergency one or something. She didn't need to listen to hear every word. Meg was like ... her words, not mine ... a megaphone."

"That's why I came round, struggling with Flossie and my poorly arm." Edna's wide eyes met mine, making me feel worse than ever. "I had to see how you were doing."

Chapter 38

I'd spent the afternoon wavering between feeling terrible about hiding from Edna and realising why I'd done so. But Edna had made me pay for it by staying another hour, joining us for a sandwich lunch – which, I hoped, wouldn't become her usual routine. When I'd noticed the time ticking towards one o'clock, I'd offered to carry Flossie to the bus stop, but Dan had insisted that I sat down while he went with them.

He'd come back, grinning, to find me slumped on the chair. "I helped her onto the bus. I watched it leave too. She's definitely gone."

I sank my head into my hands and groaned. "I'm such an awful person."

"You're not," he said. "Look, I know we said we'd give you a rest from customers today, but if everyone knows about your face, why don't you come out with me tonight?" He chuckled. "We could give Syd a send-off."

"That's not funny." I slapped his thigh. "Believe it or not, I was fond of that spider."

He raised his eyebrows. Did he think I was joking? Sensibly, he didn't ask. At five thirty, after a busy afternoon, he offered to drive us to Penfold Cove to take Roo for a walk, saying it would make a change from Torringham. He gave me a concerned look. "Are you up to it?"

I waved him away, feeling daft that I'd thought I

needed to hide away from my customers. While they'd fussed over my bruised face, they hadn't asked too many questions. One had congratulated me on my bravery, leaving me perplexed as I hadn't told him what had happened, until Dan pointed out that by now most of Torringham would know the full story.

Within minutes of turning the shop sign to closed, we headed out of the door. I hadn't invited Meg or Becki to join us. They'd be getting ready for the Torringham Traders meeting, where Dan and I should be. But Meg had insisted that I recuperate, rather than coming along to what promised to be a confrontational affair. Part of me was disappointed not to be there but Meg had assured me that Grant had more than enough support. For the first time in a year, the Beach Street traders would be there. Meg and Becki had promised to join us at the Fisherman's Rest later to celebrate Grant's success. Or so I hoped. It would be lovely if all the traders started working together again. But I couldn't believe that Peter would go quietly. He hadn't got his revenge on us after the police carted him away from the gas works debacle.

Dan steered the car down a steep road lined by large houses with manicured lawns. He glanced at me. "Penny for them?"

I shrugged. "I was just thinking about Peter."

"Don't," he said. "I still can't believe he told everyone that I was starting a pet shop. I could have been run out of town before I even opened."

"You nearly did. But..." I smiled at him. "Strangely,

it's worked out brilliantly. Thanks to my friends and all the publicity, business is booming." I hesitated. "Look … I know we kept you at arm's length, but why don't you open earlier on Saturday? You could take advantage of the crowds."

Dan turned the car into the car park. The sun dazzled on windscreens, brightening the colourful huts surrounding the beach. Families huddled around car boots, their children wrapped in towels, buckets and spades by their feet. Soon the car park would empty. After I'd bought a parking ticket, we headed away from the beach – where no dogs were allowed throughout the summer – towards Penfold Cove.

We panted up a slope, then walked across a large, grassy plain interspersed with trees and surrounded by hedgerows. Benches dotted the edge where the land slipped away, becoming jagged rocky outcrops against which the waves lapped. I directed us to the back of the field, where we passed an old stone building camouflaged by brambles and ivy. Ahead Roo chased a spaniel in circles, swinging around so the dog sprinted after her.

"They're having fun," I said, but Dan seemed lost in thought.

"This business with Peter … I … er…" Floundering, he bit his lip. "Do you think people will blame me? Think I was siding with him? I did try to tell you, but you didn't want to talk about it … but it's my fault too. I didn't say much about my plans. If anyone asked what my shop was, I told them, but few people did." He scratched his head. "I thought it was odd, but people obviously felt embarrassed to mention my shop, thinking they were betraying you."

He spoke in a matter-of-fact way, then his voice became wistful. "The thing is, if I'd been more open about it, this could have been resolved ages ago. But my friend created something so special with the carvings that I felt like a parent at Christmas, wanting to keep it a secret so I could see the looks on people's faces when we did the big reveal." He chuckled. "Does that sound big-headed?"

"I don't think so."

"Think?" He smiled, but his eyes pleaded for reassurance. It took me aback. I'd always assumed he was confident.

"I love your shop. I thought it was amazing. If it was mine, I would have opened the doors ages ago just to show it off. I guess that would make me more big-headed than you."

We went through a kissing gate. Like an old hand, Roo led us down the rutted path. I took care over the uneven stones, but I could feel Dan's hand hovering close behind me in case I tripped. It was sweet of him, but unnecessary.

We walked in silence down the steps and onto the beach, where pebbles crunched beneath our feet, dropping in ridges towards the sea. A few hardy souls braved the water, even though a cool breeze had picked up. Rocky outcrops enclosed the cove. Opposite stood a ruined building with moss and algae covering it. Behind it, wooden steps disappeared into woodland that rose to the brow of the steep hill and stretched along the craggy headland.

"Do you fancy sitting for a while?" I said.

I chose to sit in the middle of a slope, carving a hollow in the stones to make a seat. As I squirmed to make it more comfortable, Dan wore a wide grin. Chuckling, he perched beside me. "I won't say what it looks like you're doing."

I loved to hear the shush of the sea, but Penfold Cove brought new sounds: the clink of tumbling stones dragged by the waves, the sound of laughter, and the yap of excited dogs chasing pebbles into the sea. But no gulls. Maybe there weren't enough tourists here to feed them. As Roo padded along the shoreline, jumping away from the incoming tide, I spotted something black peeking from beneath the sea. A rock? Or a seal? It moved, its head becoming a familiar shape. It turned inky eyes in our direction, then raised its pointed nose towards the sky once again.

Two swans glided near the shore – a now familiar sight in Torringham harbour, but less so here. Close by, a man launched a stick into the sea. His dog splashed into the water, paddling out to retrieve the stick. Hadn't the owner spotted the swans? But before I could mention it to Dan, something crashed into me from behind. Paws clawed my shoulders, the weight pushing me down. Roo? I tried to shove her away, but she was too heavy.

A woman's cry cut through the air. "Archie! Down!" Pebbles chinked nearby. "Archie! Get here *now!*"

The weight lifted. I looked up to find Dan hefting a

black Labrador from me. Not the Archie, surely? One look at his owner confirmed my suspicion. It was the woman who'd brought him along to the agony aunt session. Archie's tongue lolled as he all but grinned at me. I smiled back. While he might have wrecked my shop, at least he hadn't murdered my spider.

"I'm so, so sorry." The woman's hand flew to her mouth, her face draining of colour. "He's hurt you!"

Archie wriggled in Dan's arms, his tail wagging, his eyes bright with excitement.

"I can't believe he's done that to you. Are you okay? I'm so sorry," the woman gabbled.

Confused, I checked my clothing. No damage other than a smear of mud on my top. "He didn't hurt me."

"But your face!" She gazed at me, wide-eyed. Then she reddened. "Oh dear. You're the lady from the pet shop. Oh gosh. What must you think of us?"

I got to my feet. "Honestly, he's fine. Just a bit lively. Kirstie will have him sorted in no time. And this…" – I pointed to my face – "is the result of an accident yesterday, nothing to do with Archie."

I rubbed his silky coat and was rewarded by a slobbery tongue across my face – thankfully not my injured side. After making a dozen more apologies, his owner led Archie away.

I shook my head as he raced off. "I think Kirstie's got her work cut out with that one. She doesn't know the word 'down'."

"Who? The dog?" Dan said.

"The owner." I chuckled. "But, it's clear Archie doesn't either."

Chapter 39

We had an enjoyable stroll back before picking up fish and chips, which we ate in our courtyard sitting at my rickety table and chairs, as Dan's pristine set lay in the shade. That was something else I'd been stupid about. I promised myself we'd switch them around another day. If we hadn't told Meg and Becki that we'd meet them later, we would have stayed there chatting – Dan told me wonderful tales about his travels to New Zealand, Peru and Japan. It was lovely to hear him talking about himself rather than asking questions about me.

We arrived at the Fisherman's Rest before our friends. Not wanting to risk people asking what had happened, I'd positioned myself so my swollen face couldn't be seen by anyone else – although, if Edna was right, most of them knew already. Even though there was plenty of space, Dan pulled his chair close to mine as he told me about his time motorcycling around Vietnam and Cambodia. I couldn't imagine him on a motorbike.

Then we heard Meg, shouting, "My honour is my word!" to laughter.

Our friends rounded the corner and headed over, grinning. Meg chose one of the free chairs, leaving the other for Becki, while the men pilfered spare chairs from surrounding tables. Dan and I shifted our chairs together to make more room. Our arms touched. I buzzed with anticipation. Grant volunteered to buy the first round, saying that he owed everyone a drink for their support. He included Dan and me in the offer because, he said, we'd been through the wars for him.

The mood became subdued as we remembered that, despite all our efforts, we hadn't been able to find his Ruby. Perhaps we never would. But as he and Keith walked to the bar, Meg chuckled and set about regaling Dan and me with a run-down of the meeting. Although the others had all been there, they listened, joining in when she forgot bits.

"Peter gave a speech." Her eyes glinted with amusement. "About honour and how he'd been there for all the traders in Torringham. That got him heckled, especially when Gary from the café pointed out that Peter had tried to get the council to change the designation of some of the Beach Street shops when they came up for sale." She rubbed her fingers and thumb together. "Gary said it was interesting that Peter's developer mates would be the ones making the money if the shops were turned into self-catering lets."

"Gary from Hollacombe's Café by the harbour? You'd have thought he'd want to keep the trade around the High Street so tourists go past his place."

Meg shrugged. "Loads of the traders were on our side. And I now hold the honorary position of girlfriend of the chairman of the Torringham Traders."

"Girlfriend?" I raised my eyebrows. "It's official then."

Meg blushed and dropped her head coyly. Then, true to form, she ruined the romantic moment. "It's a shame about him being a florist. I've told him he'll have to sell paper flowers."

Becki leaned to one side so Keith could place a tray on the table. "Do what I do and just steer clear until he's had a shower and a change of clothes."

A sudden thought flitted through my mind. Dan would smell of new books. There was nothing nicer than that. Except, perhaps there was. Dan's aftershave wafting through the air, like it did now.

Keith frowned. "Are you moaning about my job again?"

Becki patted the chair beside her. "Of course not. I get all the benefits of the freshest fish and a lovely man. What more could a woman want?"

Placated, he pulled out his chair and sat down. Grant joined us a moment later, tucking his wallet into his back pocket. He sipped at his beer, eyeing me over the rim of his glass. "We've invited all the traders to join in the beach day celebrations. I hope you don't mind."

"Why not?" I said. "The more the merrier, if they have time to prepare for it. I've been trying to convince Dan to open his shop in the morning too, to make the most of the day, rather than waiting until the evening."

Meg put her drink down and glared at me. "Why?" She glanced at Dan. "No offence, but you'll be competing with her and she needs the money."

Dan chuckled. "None taken. Who says I'll take Jenn's trade? For all you know, I could be taking yours and opening a sewing shop."

Meg snorted. "You've called it The Rover's Return. It's obvious that it's a dog's name and nothing to do with crafts."

"Travel, perhaps?" He beamed at her.

"Don't be daft." She waved him away. "Anyhow, If Jenn's fine with you opening, I'm not going to argue."

I loved my friend for being so supportive, and longed to tell her the truth. As the conversation moved back to the committee meeting, I hissed at Dan. "Why didn't you tell them? You'll have to take that whitewash off before Saturday."

He chuckled. "I enjoy winding Meg up. Look at her."

I did. Although Meg seemed absorbed by the discussion around plans for future meetings, her face switched from a smile to a scowl each time she glanced at Dan. On, off, on, off. I couldn't help laughing.

"Hot and cold, just like you said about me."

Dan's gorgeous eyes locked with mine. "Believe me, you're just hot."

"That's smooth." I chuckled, embarrassed.

Meg's previous words popped into my mind. I hoped she wasn't right about him being a charmer. But I brushed away the thought and basked in the compliment. A corny chat-up line. But weren't they all?

Dan glanced up. Peter Drew and a few of his buddies had arrived, seating themselves nearby. After his friends exchanged smiles with our table – except for Meg and Peter, who both remained stony-faced – they sat with their backs to us. I recognised two of them from the first time

I'd seen Dan, when he'd been drinking with them in the pub. I felt for him. He hadn't chosen to take sides.

"You can go over and say hello," I whispered.

He grinned at me and squeezed my arm. "It's fine. I'm a big boy now. Anyhow…" He looked from me to where he was hemmed in by Becki on the other side. "I don't think I'll be going anywhere soon."

Peter glowered at us. I ignored him, but Meg couldn't help sticking out her tongue.

"Put it away," I said. Too late.

Peter strode over to us, his jaw bulging, his fists clenched. Was he about to hit someone? Grant's eyes widened and he stood up. On the other side of our table, Andy did the same, while Becki put her hand on Keith's thigh. I didn't need to worry about Dan – not that I got the impression he'd want to participate in their bun fight – as he had no room to stand up, let alone join in. But no one thought about Meg, who jumped to her feet, chin jutting.

"You!" he growled and jabbed his finger at her. "You're the cause of all this."

Grant put his arm in front of Meg. Peter's face reddened. "I don't know what you see in that bloody witch," he told Grant. "It must be some kind of spell or something, because it couldn't be anything else. I can promise you one thing…" Spittle clung to the corners of his mouth as he brandished a trembling fist. "She may have started it. But I'm going to finish it."

He stomped back to his table, where he sat muttering and shaking his head.

Sighing, Grant sat down. "Did you have to do that, Meg? He's all about prestige and he's just lost – in his eyes – his position at the top of Torringham society. You know, and I know, that's not the case. But you don't need to mock a man when he's on his knees."

Meg gave him a contrite look, kissed his cheek and, without a word, went over to Peter.

Grant put his head in his hands. "What is she doing now? I can't watch."

"I'm sorry, Peter," she said in a voice loud enough for the whole area to hear. "It was wrong and childish of me to stick my tongue out at you. I know that you must feel hurt and I wouldn't want to do anything to make you feel worse. I can assure you that I'll put everything behind us."

"Well, I won't." Peter's mouth twisted in disgust.

"I *will*," Meg said. "We all need to start working together."

Before he could answer, she hurried back. Grant gave her a grateful smile, while the others looked impressed. But I had a feeling she'd dealt herself a winning card. Later, when Dan managed to escape to the toilet and the others were chatting among themselves, she leaned over to me. "Did it work?"

"What?"

"When I said sorry to Peter. The gossip machine will broadcast my abject apology, so if he does or says anything against us in future, he'll look bad." She licked her finger and held it in the air. "Another goal to me, don't you think?"

Chapter 40

Beach day arrived, bringing with it a carnival atmosphere, even though the clouds above threatened to dampen our festivities. As I headed back after Roo's morning walk, I found Hilda directing operations. Her nephew had brought his Punch and Judy show to set up outside her shop, while her children and grandchildren strung scallop shells between lamp posts and over shop doorways. Hilda had managed to source a child's plastic clam sandpit, and had filled one half with sand and the other with water. I couldn't imagine anyone using it, though, not with the sea a short stroll down the road.

I'd hung shells across the entrance to my alley. I'd also brought some of my wares out to sell on the street, as I'd done on our promotion day. Once again, the cheerful dog neckerchiefs fluttered in the wind, alongside a stack of pet toys shaped like ice-cream cones and a few leads embroidered with boats. But my imagination hadn't stretched to other seaside-themed pet products. It was all very well getting stock in for today but, if it didn't sell, I'd be stuck with it. At least Hilda had loaned me one of her family again, Warren, so I could talk to people and try to drum up business.

I'd hidden my bruises beneath a layer of foundation, which meant I'd had to liberally apply mascara and lipstick to stop myself from looking pasty. Although I'd tied my hair into a scallop-shell-topped bun – which matched my shell necklace – my flowery top and shorts could be classed as everyday beach wear. Unlike Meg, who'd outdone everyone with her grass skirt, off-the-shoulder top, garlands of flowers around her neck and shells in her hair. She sashayed along the street welcoming the trickle of visitors, that soon became a steady stream.

Dan emerged from his front door, giving me a smile. "How are you doing?"

He'd removed the whitewash on his shop windows during the night, covering them instead with blue drapes patterned with boats and lighthouses, so his bookshelves and window display remained hidden from view. All for Meg's benefit, I guessed, as I knew he was looking forward to seeing her expression when she realised that it wasn't a pet shop.

"I still don't know why you didn't open today." I moved into the safety of his porch and off the crowded street. "You would have done a brisk trade."

He nodded at a family who stepped out of Andy's bakery, cramming iced buns and doughnuts into their mouths. Andy had also sourced a candy-floss machine, and the sweet smell drifted towards us. I watched two children who strolled past, sticky fingers picking at the pink strands. Then I sniggered. "You didn't want to get your shop dirty ahead of your opening, did you?"

Dan's eyes twinkled. "Okay, you've found me out. I appreciate that people are on holiday, but I've put up a sign asking them not to bring food into the shop. I'd like to ease myself in too, rather than spend the day pointing at the sign."

Intrigued, I said, "Yet you don't mind dogs?"

"Dogs don't smear ice cream and jam into the pages of books. Believe me, I learned that lesson after working in another bookshop."

"Just pray that Archie's owner isn't a book lover." I chuckled. "Anyhow, what about tonight? Won't you be serving drinks?"

"Fizz, but people don't tend to throw that over the books." He grimaced. "Now I've said that... But an accident's different to people simply not caring."

Just then a truck heaped with manure pulled up alongside us. The stench overpowered the smell of cakes and sugar. The driver wound down the passenger window and shouted, "I've got a delivery for..." He picked up a crumpled sheet and frowned. "This can't be right."

I took the sheet from him and showed it to Dan, my eyes watering from the smell. "It's Meg's shop."

"Are you sure you've got the right place?" Dan said.

The driver's frown deepened. "Well, he read the address out twice. He paid half and said he'd pay the other half after I'd delivered this."

Down the street, Meg stood chatting with Hilda outside Becki's shop. I caught her eye and waved at her. Puzzled, she hurried over.

"This is for you." I pointed to the manure.

Gaping, she shook her head. "Sodding Peter Drew."

Soon Hilda joined the animated discussion. I moved away, leaving them to it.

"How much for the other half?" I heard Hilda say. She rifled through her bag and pulled out a purse, which she snapped open and handed the driver a wad of notes. "Deliver it to my Jim. He'd be glad of it … Don't you worry about him who ordered it. We'll deal with that bugger … I'll give you Jim's address." She tapped Meg's shoulder. "You sign for it, then it's job done."

The truck pulled away, leaving us in a fug of diesel and manure. Hilda popped her purse back into her handbag and tottered over to us, slapping her hands together. "Peter's as daft as a brush." She chuckled. "If he'd wanted a proper job, he'd have best been asking me." Her mouth became a grim line as she spotted Mrs Hollacombe trundling down the pavement, spilling holidaymakers onto the road. Her mobility scooter was decked out in bunting. Adverts offering a 'beach day' offer of a free cup of tea with every meal in her son's café adorned the sides. While Dan and I leapt back to the safety of his doorway, Meg scarpered into the road.

Only Hilda stood her ground. She held out her hand forcing Mrs Hollacombe to brake, stopping inches from her feet.

"Don't you be running our customers off the path," Hilda said.

Mrs Hollacombe glared at her. "You know I'm not allowed on the road."

Hilda put her hands on her hips. "Well, it's the road or the High Street. You're not ploughing that thing through here."

Neither woman moved. When Mrs Hollacombe folded her arms and leaned back in her seat, Hilda's expression tightened. "Are you moving it, or not?" She signalled to Meg. "Go fetch my Linda."

Mrs Hollacombe's eyes widened. "There's no need for that, as you well know." She turned the wheel and bumped down the kerb, then whirred away, tooting her horn and scattering tourists who wandered in the road.

"What was that all about?" Dan scratched his head. "Surely someone in a mobility scooter needs to get through?"

"Mrs Hollacombe drives at breakneck speed," I said.

Meg laughed. "Do you remember when she almost flattened Hilda a few years ago?" Then she added, "She won't be doing that again."

Further down the street, a gas van drew up near Meg's shop. I assumed the driver was stopping to collect something from one of the shops, but Meg sighed. "What *now?*" She stormed away to accost the driver.

"Do you want to go over?" Dan's voice suggested it was the last thing he fancied doing.

Even from where we stood, we could see Meg's mouth wide with anger. She flung her arms in the air. When Hilda joined them, I shook my head. "I think some things are best left to the professionals."

Dan nodded to a potential customer who examined one of my embroidered leads. Her silky coated greyhound sat panting by her side. "You deal with her and I'll put the kettle on."

When he reappeared having made three teas – one for my helper – we sipped our drinks in peace. A crowd had formed around the gas van, blocking our view of Meg and Hilda. I felt for the poor man. Whatever business he'd been about to undertake, it wouldn't be happening today.

A while later, Meg appeared, her cheeks flushed, her body taut, clenching her fists. "Just you wait until I get hold of that man. I'll wring his bl…" She glanced at a family hovering nearby. "Neck."

"Who?" Dan said, unnecessarily.

"Peter flaming Drew. He only tried Hilda's trick, although not as well, and called the gas board saying there was a leak. Thankfully, we've proved there isn't one, but…" Looking distracted, she stopped mid-sentence, her eyes widening. "Seriously? Can't that man think of anything original?"

The hordes and the van had moved on. Many of the tourists had headed off to the beach or to the restaurants, cafés, and fish and chip shops, leaving locals to make the most of the children's activities and the treats on offer. It meant we had a clear view of a pizza delivery bike parked by the kerb outside Meg's shop. The rider was lugging a stack of boxes through her door.

She growled, "I'm going to kill him."

"Don't do that!" Dan said, but she sprinted away.

Grimacing at each other, we hurriedly tucked our mugs in his porch. After calling to Warren to keep an eye on my wares, we dashed after Meg, rushing into her shop to find her manhandling the lad outside.

"I am *not* paying for things I didn't order!" she yelled.

"B-b-but what will my boss say?"

"Tell him he shouldn't accept an order for ten pizzas without payment."

The lad's shoulders slumped and his voice trembled. "I-it's only my second day."

Dan reached into his back pocket and pulled out a wallet stuffed with notes. I stared at him in astonishment. What was it with everyone having bulging pots of money to hand? If I unzipped my purse, I'd only find a few coppers and bits of fluff.

"How much are they?"

"One hundred and twenty," the lad told him.

Dan's eyebrows rose but he counted out the money and handed it over, giving the lad an extra fiver. So much for me thinking he was stingy when he'd given Heidi a 2p tip in the Fisherman's Rest that night. Dan split the boxes into two piles, saying we'd deliver half to the traders at our end of the street, and Meg could distribute the rest to the others.

"Cheers," she said, in the dourest possible tone. When I gave her a quizzical look, she sighed. "Look, it's lovely of Dan to buy these. It means it's sort of backfired on Peter too. But it's only twelve thirty. What else has that idiot got up his sleeve?"

Chapter 41

Within minutes of the last pizza box being handed out, Dan shot off, saying he wouldn't be long. Twenty minutes later, one of Hilda's grandchildren came over with a message from Meg asking if I could help shut her shop. Did she mean now or at closing time? But, when I asked, the messenger had no idea. Thankfully, Dan reappeared, so I asked him to keep an eye on my bits and pieces outside while I went over to Meg's.

Inside her shop I found her assistant, Sarah, looking perplexed. She had no explanation other than, "Meg took a phone call, told me to get you to help close up, then disappeared."

I called Meg's number, but she didn't answer. When I tried fifteen minutes later, it went straight to answerphone. Either she'd turned her mobile off or her battery had died. While we brought in Meg's wares and the trestle table, my mind was working overtime. Peter had promised revenge. I thought those silly stunts he'd pulled earlier had been the worst of it, but what if he'd taken it one step further? The idea seemed ridiculous, but I couldn't help worrying. When Sarah left, I phoned Dan to say I wouldn't be back for a while. Then I sat by Meg's till, drumming my fingers on the counter. In the street people wandered past, most of them ambling towards the harbour. As time moved on, the shadows lengthened. Sunburned families began to head in the other direction, lugging bags and crabbing buckets. Usually, day-trippers would go back to the car park via the bustling High Street, rather than take this longer route. It seemed that our beach day had worked. But I couldn't feel happy. Not when I had no idea what had happened to Meg.

In the end, I decided to lock up, leaving a note to ask Meg to call when she returned, and taking Amber with me. First, I hurried over to Becki, but she was as clueless as me. As I left her, I fixed on a smile. Dan had to make a start on his opening night and I'd promised to give him a hand. If he thought I was anxious about Meg, it might spoil his special evening.

When Dan spotted me, I gave him a breezy, "Hi!"

"How's Meg?"

I waved him away. "She hasn't come back yet, but I wouldn't worry too much. She'll let me know later." Still keeping my tone light, I couldn't help asking, "I don't suppose you know where Peter Drew is?"

Dan reddened. "Have you heard about that already? I was going to tell you."

"What?" Fear made my voice sharp.

"About going to speak to him. Wasn't that what you meant?"

When I shook my head, he winced. "I went around to see Peter. That's why I went off before you had to go to Meg's. All that palaver this morning was getting out of hand. I told him it had to stop."

But it hadn't, or else Meg wouldn't have vanished like that. I was just about to say so when Dan added, "He had plans for other daft stuff, but I made him cancel it all. I left him under no illusion that if anything else happened, I'd be forced to tell everyone something I know about him. I'm not usually one for blackmail, but … well…" He shrugged. "Let's just say, as long as we can keep Meg under control, he won't do anything else."

"You're certain about that?"

"That was the deal – unless Meg restarts this nonsense."

"But how do you know something about him that we don't?"

Dan tapped his nose. "Let's just say that we share a mutual friend who knew I was thinking of putting an offer on my place. He introduced us after advising me to speak to Peter before doing so. According to him, if anyone knew business, Peter did. But our friend is a bit of a blabbermouth and told me a lot more, including a few pieces of gossip Peter would have preferred me not to know."

At least his answer meant Meg's disappearance wasn't down to Peter. Perhaps one of her relatives had been in an accident? Whatever the reason, I'd have to wait until she returned to find out. I was about to say as much when Dan said, "Don't ask me about Peter's secret. I'm never going to spill. I've promised to stay silent and, as long as he keeps his part of the deal, I will."

I gave him a wry smile. "I'm intrigued. But I understand." Our friendship had blossomed to the point where I felt comfortable giving a coy, "Maybe in a decade or so I might be able to wriggle it out of you."

"A decade?" He chuckled.

"All good things come to those who wait."

He scrutinised me. "I hope that's true, because—"

Warren poked his head from the shop, calling, "Jenn, you've got a customer on the phone. They said they needed to speak to you."

Before rushing away, I told Dan I'd give him a hand after I'd walked the dogs. He needed to get on and so did I. But I wished we'd had five minutes more. I would have loved to know what he'd been about to say.

♦

Warren agreed to hold the fort while I took the dogs for a jog around the block. I didn't usually make a habit of running, being a bit self-conscious about my boobs, but this was the most efficient way of exercising the dogs in the shortest time. My mind worked as fast as my legs, running through all the possible scenarios, worrying about Meg. When my phone beeped, I came to a halt, praying it would be her. I cupped my hand around my screen so I could read it in the glare of the sun, and heaved a sigh of relief. It was. Thank goodness!

We're okay. Please feed Amber. See you later. X

Twice I tried to call her back but, as before, the answerphone cut in. It couldn't be her battery if she'd managed to text, so either she was trying to avoid me or there was another reason. Baffled but a little happier, I clipped the leads back onto the dogs and we made our way back home. After I'd paid Warren and locked up the shop, I fed Amber and Roo and left the back door open, so they could lie in the courtyard while I helped Dan.

He'd managed to get everything done. He just had the glasses to fill – which he would do later – and platters of nibbles to put out on a table by the arched doorway that had once led through to my shop. His kitchen was more spacious and modern than mine. Like Keith, he had gleaming white units. He didn't have tiled surrounds, but laminated boards several shades lighter than his slate-grey work surfaces. An American fridge sat in the corner. How he'd got it up the narrow stairs, I had no idea. As I opened it, Dan appeared in the doorway, holding my phone.

He held it out. "Looks like Meg. I wasn't being nosey, but the notification popped up."

I read the message. *On our way back. Be a couple of hours. X*

Who was 'our'? Unless… I tried her mobile, frustrated to get the answering service again, then called Keith, but his phone just rang a dozen times before I was directed to his florist shop's voicemail. I gave up and followed Dan down the stairs with two of his shop-bought platters. As I handed them to him, I chuckled. "Are you going to bar people from touching the books after eating?"

He grinned. "Didn't I say that you're on nursemaid duty? You can go around wiping greasy fingers."

Laughing, I pretended to smack his hand, but he surprised me by taking hold of mine. "I'm glad you're here. I have to confess, I'm nervous about tonight."

"Are you?" I'd always thought of him as a confident person. But once again I'd been proved wrong. Just as I'd worried when Meg called him a charmer when, in reality, he was simply a decent, kind man. He'd done so much for me – whereas I couldn't say the same. Luckily, it wasn't too late to make amends.

He grimaced. "It's been such a strange few months. I hope tonight goes well."

"It'll be great. People will love this place. It'll be fantastic to have the best bookshop in Torringham next door too."

"The only one."

"It's a shame you kept those drapes up to hide it from Meg. It would have been nice to show off your window display today."

He laughed, his eyes twinkling. "I can't tell you how much I was looking forward to seeing the expression on her face. I was going to borrow a few of your dog bits to put by the door to wind her up when she came in tonight, but there's no point now."

I smiled at him. "Trust Meg to ruin your plans. You never know, she might get here in time. How long have we got until everyone arrives?"

Dan shrugged, a flush rising to his cheeks. "What I was going to say earlier—"

The door banged behind us and a voice called, "Are we early?"

Sighing, Dan checked his watch. "It looks like it's not

meant to be." Leaving me flummoxed, he strode over to the door to let the first revellers in.

Chapter 42

By nine o'clock the party was in full swing. Although Dan's bookshop was spacious, the scent of bodies filled the room – aftershave, perfume, alcohol and other smells. I wrinkled my nose as I passed a man in a jumper, who bent close to a woman who leaned away from him. As Dan refilled people's glasses, I wryly recalled my opening. Tim and I had unlocked the door, said, "Ta-dahhh!" and then sat for hours waiting for our first customer. After that, we had our first serious discussion about promoting our shop. Since it was tucked away, it was necessary. Something I'd forgotten until Peter had let me think that Dan was opening a pet shop. Thanks to him, I'd again put more effort into marketing – and had reaped the rewards.

Most of the guests were fellow shop owners, many from the High Street or the harbour, in addition to Beach Street. I recognised a few people from the Fisherman's Rest, including Heidi. Then there was Josie, who'd loaned us her Cockapoo in our attempt to entice Stan. She stood in a group with half a dozen B&B owners. As I wandered over, the spiky-haired woman I'd seen before peeled away and went across to the food. Josie reminded me of their names – her husband, Mike, then Kim, Jason and Katie – and pointed to Shona, laughing that they couldn't pull her away from her food.

"I hear Grant didn't manage to find his dog," she said.

I pulled a face. "No, but not for lack of trying."

She looked sympathetically at my bruised cheek, which a fresh layer of foundation had failed to mask. "I heard."

Dan chinked his glass with a teaspoon, interrupting us. But his efforts were drowned out by others, who called for silence or made loud shushing noises. He stood by the drapes, waiting for the noise to fade, then gave a cord a tug. The drapes fell, to a round of applause and whistles. Someone – Keith? – snapped off the overhead lights and turned on the spotlights that lit up the ornate bookshelves. In the children's section lights twinkled like stars, while the buildings in the window display became a lamp-lit dusk scene behind which the real-life orange and purple sunset flared.

"I declare The Rover's Return bookshop well and truly open." Dan chuckled. "From Monday, because I'm not working any more tonight. Help yourself to drinks and what's left of the food. Enjoy!"

I went over to chat to him but, when a familiar car drew up outside, I swerved towards the street. Meg staggered out of the car, still wearing her grass skirt and frilly top. She reached inside and lifted Ruby out. I'd never seen the little dog before, but I recognised her from the posters. I gasped. We'd given up hope of finding her, but here she was, looking pristine – nothing like the poor dogs at the puppy farm.

Grant eased himself out of the car, wincing. "That was a long journey. All the way to High Wycombe and back."

Wearing a huge grin, Dan came out. Meg placed Ruby

in Grant's arms. As I stroked her soft fur, she lapped me with her little tongue.

"This has made my night," Dan said.

I could smell a faint aroma of perfume. Not Grant or Meg. Frowning, I said, "Have you bathed her?"

Meg rolled her eyes. "That was Sylvie's mum – you know, Stan's wife, Sylvie. She had her all dolled up like a ridiculous princess. She stank of perfume. We had to drive back with the windows open."

At least it was perfume and not the awful stench from the puppy farm, I thought, but I kept it to myself. Instead I said, "How did she end up with her?"

Grant rocked Ruby like a baby. "Sylvie's mum's always wanted a Pomeranian. So Sylvie decided to get her mine, even though she had a breeding bitch at the puppy farm—"

"She wouldn't have got one for her mum from that awful place where they kept the others. Not with all the health issues they'd face from interbreeding and everything." Meg made coochie-cooing noises as she tickled Ruby's chin. "Nasty Sylvie wanted only the best for her mum, and that meant stealing lickle Wooby. Luckily, the policy-weesy found you. But now Sylvie-wilvie and nasty Stanie are in big trouble and they'll be put away for a wery, wery long time."

"Do you want me to order a pram?" I teased.

"Pram? Do I look pregnant?" Meg stroked her stomach and tugged at the hem of her grass skirt. "I know we had to stop for a McDonald's on the way back, but I didn't think I looked that bad."

"I meant for the dog." But I didn't bother explaining further. I'd never been great at making jokes. "So Stan and Sylvie are going to be charged."

Grant nodded. "With animal cruelty and theft among other things. Not just Ruby, but they'd stolen other bitches for the puppy farm. The police have caught the other crooks involved with it too. I hope they throw away the key. If I had my way…" He clenched his fist, leaving me under no illusion what he'd do.

Becki and Keith joined us, fussing over Ruby and Grant, so I shifted backwards, bumping into Dan. He didn't move but gazed down at me, smiling. Instinctively, I went to step away, then decided to stay. It felt flirtatious being so close to him, but right. I longed for him to reach for my hand, to pull me into his arms, but Grant broke the spell by giving a walrus yawn.

"I'm going to take her home."

When Meg made a move to leave, he said, "You stay. I need an early night."

She hesitated, then smiled. "Of course. I'll see you tomorrow." Then she looked past us to Dan's shop front. Her mouth fell open. "I-It's…" She spun around to Grant. "Did you know it wasn't a pet shop?"

"What?" He frowned. "I knew it was something to do with travel. I had no idea why you kept on about a pet shop, but every time I went to say anything you told me to shut up, said you didn't want to talk about Dan's sodding business."

Meg opened her mouth as if to retort, then clamped it shut, apparently thinking better of it. I guessed Grant's use of 'sodding' had been taken straight from the horse's mouth.

As Grant drove away, Meg pulled at her skirt. "I'd better get changed."

I put my arm around her shoulders, drawing her towards the shop. "Borrow one of my tops, or something from my wardrobe. Amber's in the lounge with Roo."

A wall of warmth hit us as we walked through the back of Dan's shop, sidling and squeezing between laughing groups. I pointed to the back door, telling her to go through to the courtyard where she'd find my door open. She reappeared ten minutes later, poured into one of my fancy cocktail dresses that I hadn't worn since I'd moved to Torringham. Keith gave her a low whistle and a mock wink but Meg ignored him, wriggling and hitching the strap of the dress into place.

"It's a bit tight, but it'll do."

Someone caught her eye and she went off to chat. When she returned, she tapped Dan on the shoulder. "Look, I know I didn't want to hear about your place, but you could have said something. It's incredible. I could do with a few bits like this around my arts and crafts section. Who did all the carvings and painting?"

"My friend."

Meg guffawed. "Of course. Mates' rates!"

Dan frowned. "No, I paid the full amount."

"Why, if he was a friend?"

Dan spoke kindly. "*Because* he's a mate. If I make him work for free or little money, he'd be losing out. What sort of friend would that make me?"

Meg grimaced. "Point taken, but I still want Jenn to give me discounted rates on dog food for Amber."

I chuckled. I didn't mind. She did more than enough for me in return. A warm glow enveloped me, no doubt due to the fizz I'd been drinking, and I gave her a cuddle. "I love you too."

She disentangled herself from my grip and took a swig of her drink. "Give me five minutes to catch up and I'll love you just as much."

Dan left to socialise with other people, leaving me feeling strangely bereft. At various points during the next hour, I spotted him with his phone as he strolled between the partygoers. When he returned, he held it out in front of us. Becki and I stood smiling, waiting for the flash. Beside us, Meg – who'd emptied several glasses by then – posed with her hand behind her head, looking out from beneath her eyelashes with a trout pout (although no doubt she believed she looked more like Marilyn Monroe) before turning to the other side, putting her hand on her hip, breathing in so her boobs stuck out, and beaming.

"Choose the best pic," she called as Dan grinned and moved on.

By midnight, a few stragglers remained. Meg had fetched Amber. The dog bounced around her owner's unsteady feet. When she stumbled into Keith, he chuckled and told Becki that they'd better help her back. Their departure gave the last of the party-goers the impetus to leave. With a sigh of relief, Dan called goodbye and bolted the door behind them.

Smiling, he came over to me. "Meg is funny. I've got a brilliant video to blackmail her with in future."

Confused, I gazed at him. Then I twigged and chuckled. "That was a video you took of us? Not a photo?"

"Yep."

I burst out laughing. He'd sized Meg up and now it seemed my lovely friend had met her match.

Dan reached out to caress my cheek. A thrill ran through me. The shop's twinkling lights reflected in his deep brown eyes. I'd craved this moment all night. For longer. We stood gazing at each other until he leaned forward to me. His lips touched mine, and I allowed myself to sink into them.

To think I'd worried that Dan would destroy my future. Now it was more secure than ever. My finances, my shop, Roo – and now this. Dan enfolded me in his arms and pressed his body against mine. Who knew where this night would lead? But I knew one thing. We'd have a lot of fun finding out.

Mishaps and Mayhem

at the little shop on Beach Street

As explained in the introduction to this book, all the characters and businesses are fictional. The traders in Brixham are hardworking and dedicated, working together to serve their customers and create a better environment. Many businesses have gone through a challenging period recently, and they will value your custom. If you do visit Brixham, please take time to support our small traders.

I chose to set this book in a pet shop after seeing the hilarious antics of the dogs living with my friends and family. Most of these dogs are older, rescued pets – but one is a puppy who, like a toddler, has brought joy and chaos in equal measures to his household.

Torringham is loosely based on Brixham, a seaside town in South Devon famed for its fishing industry. If you do visit Brixham you will find some of the scenery familiar, including the beautiful harbour bowl. When I wrote about Pixie Cove, I pictured wonderful Fishcombe Cove, and you may recognise parts of Penfold Cove if you take the coastal path to Elberry Cove. Brixham is a wonderful town and Devon is a gorgeous place to visit.

Other books by Sharley Scott

A Little Birdie Told Me…

Maddie Meadows Series:

The Two Lives of Maddie Meadows

The Gift of a Rose

**The Devon Seaside Guesthouse series
(set in the fictional town of Torringham):**

Bedlam & Breakfast at a
Devon seaside guesthouse

B&Bers Behaving Madly at a
Devon seaside guesthouse

Printed in Great Britain
by Amazon